THE
GUILTY
ONE

SOPHIE LITTLEFIELD is a rising
star in the US, where she has been
nominated for the Edgar, Barry and
Macavity awards, and has won the
Anthony Award. *The Guilty One*
is her second UK novel, following
2014's *The Moon Pool*.

Also by Sophie Littlefield

The Moon Pool

THE GUILTY ONE

SOPHIE LITTLEFIELD

HEAD ZEUS

First published in the USA in 2015 by Gallery Books,
a division of Simon & Schuster, Inc.

First published in the UK in 2015 by Head of Zeus Ltd
This paperback edition first published in 2016 by Head of Zeus Ltd

9 7 5 3 1 2 4 6 8

A catalogue record for this book is available from the British Library.

Paperback ISBN 9781781856901
Ebook ISBN 9781781856871

Printed in the UK by Clays Ltd, St Ives Plc

Head of Zeus Ltd
Clerkenwell House
45-47 Clerkenwell Green
London EC1R 0HT

WWW.HEADOFZEUS.COM

For all the people,
In all the rooms,
With their mistakes and their scars,
Who showed me the way to go on.

HOW WAS SHE SUPPOSED to choose among these treasures? A photo in a tarnished frame. A ceramic dish made by small hands, thickly glazed, signed with a wobbly C. A silver teaspoon with a design of roses, one of a set her sister now owned but never used. Maris picked up each object and set it down again on the cold, smooth expanse of marble in the master bathroom of the house she was leaving today.

"Mar?"

The voice startled her—it didn't belong here. Hadn't in a while. In two weeks and five days, in fact: he left on a Tuesday, which she remembered because he didn't even take the bins to the curb one last time. As though, having made up his mind, he was excused and exempt from every responsibility of the life that once connected them. As she dragged the bins back up the driveway that evening, she'd imagined their marriage as a wicker basket, the strands now broken and sprung, the bottom about to give way. But unlike Jeff, she had expected to shatter. *Wouldn't you?* she'd thought despairingly, watching the quiet street through the bedroom window, as her neighbors came home from their jobs, their errands, their exercise classes and children's playdates. *Wouldn't you have broken too?*

"I just needed a few things from the garage," Jeff said sheepishly, looking not at Maris but at the newel post. She stood at the bottom of the stairs. He stood half in and half out the front door, letting in the heat. She thought about the air conditioner: she must remember to turn it off when she left.

"What things?"

"Just—you know. My clubs, the barbecue tools." He scowled. "I didn't know you were home. I already loaded up the car."

A lie, and one into which he put very little effort. Her car was in the garage too; he couldn't have missed it. Besides, where was she supposed to have gone? She had haunted this house like a wraith for a year now; it was careless of him to pretend otherwise. But that was as good a word as any for what Jeff had become. *Careless.* He didn't care. He couldn't care less. About her, about the life she thought they would cling to together, about—and surely it wasn't true, she shouldn't even allow herself to think it—about Calla.

"I'm going to Alana's," she said abruptly, too tired to correct him.

"You mean—to stay?"

She shrugged. How to answer that? The future lay ahead of her, unknowable, unimaginable. If there was another option—like, for instance, just disappearing, winking into nonexistence like a light turned off—she might very well take it. "For now, anyway."

"Does that mean we can move ahead on the house?"

All traces of guilt were gone from his voice now. Anger surged inside Maris—cold, sharp, more real than anything she had felt in a long time. Her phone buzzed; she took it out of her pocket, barely glancing at the screen. "I have to take this," she snapped.

Jeff held up his hands, conciliatory, aware—maybe—that he'd pushed her too far. He backed out the door, mouthed "see you later," and scuttled toward his car like a kid on his way to recess. Maris shoved the door unnecessarily hard and it slammed shut.

It was a 925 number, not one she recognized. Ordinarily she'd let it go to voice mail—the truth was she let nearly all her calls go to voice mail, even Alana's—but the afterburn of anger at Jeff propelled her to answer.

"Hello?"

"Maris." A voice she never thought she would have to hear again. "It's Ron. Ron Isherwood."

"You." Her voice came out like dried leaves. Pain like she hadn't known since the early days, searing and slicing. "How can you—what do you—"

"I just want to say . . ."

There was a rushing sound, which Maris thought was her own mind ripping from its moorings—finally, finally, splintering apart. She was only surprised that it had taken so long.

But she recognized a pattern to the sounds coming through the phone: the tap of a horn, the rush of passing cars. Ron Isherwood was calling her from the side of a road. But there was something more in the sound of tires on asphalt, a metallic whisper that didn't fit.

"I'm hanging up," she whispered. Through the glass side

panels flanking the front door, she saw Jeff's car drive away, wavering like a mirage through the textured glass.

"No, wait." Ron Isherwood cleared his throat. "I—I'm . . . this is the last thing I need to say. I wanted to tell you I'm sorry. How very sorry I am. This—this is for you." He was crying now, the way men cry, choking off every syllable, the words melting together.

"Ron, don't. Stop." Maris's voice came back, and along with comprehension came rage. Her vocabulary of emotions diminished to shades of fury and sorrow. How dare he—how could he do this to her? When she'd finally, maybe, almost become numb enough to take a few tottering steps, to leave this place. Escaping to Alana's was cowardly, but hadn't she earned a measure of cowardice?

But even that was too much to ask, apparently. She knew what Ron was doing—he was throwing it all back on her, in the guise of a gift. His life, as recompense. Because *he* couldn't endure any longer. *He* was breaking under the weight of it, and so he would make her complicit.

But that was her lot, a mother's lot. Had been, since that murky night eighteen years ago in the thin-walled little apartment in San Ramon she and Jeff had lived in after they married, when Calla was conceived in a jerking fit of cheap-wine fervor. She took a deep breath, closed her eyes, put her hand on the hall table for support. "Where are you?" she demanded, in the steady, no-nonsense voice of the mother she had once been.

"I'm"—indistinct snuffling, sobbing—"The bridge. I'm on the bridge. I wanted . . . whatever you want me to do, Maris. I'm ready. If it helps, if it could—"

4

"Stay there."

Maris opened her eyes and found herself staring at her own reflection in the mirror hung over the hall table. She looked grim, exhausted, awful—but she was still standing. You don't spend all your working hours with suburban privileged teens, urban dead-end kids, your *own* child—because yes, damn it, Maris had raised that child from birth through all the usual struggles into a pretty amazing young woman, *she* had done that while Jeff flew business class and played golf and struggled to uproot himself from his own family— you don't do all of those things without building up a reserve for moments like this. Moments when the weak ones fail, the battered ones give up, the broken ones cry out for someone to take their hand.

"Do *not* do anything. I mean it, Ron." Maris squeezed the phone harder and gathered her strength. *"Please."*

A long pause, the cars going past, the moments of this life, hers and his, twined together in links forged in misery, splattered with the blood of all that had ever been precious. "I just wanted to give you something," he finally said, his voice thin and breaking, just before he hung up.

two

HE SAW THE PATROL car pull over and knew he was too late. God, he'd fucked this up royally. He shouldn't have called her; he should have let the act speak for him, let it say everything that everyone needed to hear. Or a letter. A letter would have worked; he could have mailed it before driving into the city, dropped it into the mailbox out in front of the Noah's Bagels on his way from the office to his car. Maris would have gotten it Wednesday, Thursday at the latest, she could have read it in private, decided on her own if she was going to just throw it away or . . . or if it might have helped her, just a little.

Two cops got out of the car. One was a woman, young with a pretty, smooth face. The other one was faster, though, walking purposefully with his hand on his belt. Reaching for what, his radio? Taser? Some small corner of Ron's mind wondered what the protocols were for this, even as he chastised himself for not thinking it all through, for wrecking what was supposed to be his last act.

He looked down, the wind rippling the fabric of his pants near his ankles. It really was windy out here, something they mentioned in the tourist information. Ron had googled "Golden Gate Bridge" last night, which was kind of pathetic. He and Deb had been meaning to walk the bridge for how many years? Since Karl was a Boy Scout, at least, because they'd almost done it then, a family event organized by the scoutmaster, but then Karl had gotten strep. So Ron had to look it up: "Park in the southeast parking lot . . . be prepared as it's usually windy and cold." That had prompted what was perhaps the most surreal moment of the last twenty-four hours: going to the coat closet for his windbreaker, despite the fact that it was ninety-four degrees outside and the air conditioner was running full blast, and hiding the jacket in his car so Deb wouldn't see it and wonder what it was doing there. As Ron stuffed the jacket under the driver's seat, he realized he was making provisions for his own comfort in what were to be the final moments of his life, a thought so absurd it made his head spin.

But now he was glad he had the jacket to protect against the cold wind. The zipper pull snapped up and hit him in the chin. It hurt. Other cars were slowing; soon there would be a traffic jam. He wondered if someone had called the cops or if they'd just happened on him . . . it seemed like he'd read that they patrolled the bridge regularly. Looking for jumpers. Looking for guys like him.

"Hey, how are you?" The male cop shielded his eyes from the sun with his hand and gave Ron a friendly grin. He was good-looking. Fortyish, chiseled features, big jaw, all of that. His partner was also attractive, and they smiled at him like they were all old friends.

This was embarrassing. Ron wondered if there was any way to pull off acting like he'd just been stopping to think, that he'd never . . . but no. Not when he was standing on the wrong side of the orange metal wall like this, holding on to the cold steel cables. He'd chosen this spot because there was a space that was mostly hidden from traffic, a support behind which he'd managed to clamber over the wall, and then a drop of a few feet to the ledge he was now standing on, so it would be pretty hard to see him unless you knew what you were looking for. The only risky part was the climb over, and while Ron had waited until there was a break in the traffic and managed it pretty nimbly, someone must have spotted him.

Such a stupid mistake. What he should have done . . . if he had to call Maris, if he couldn't have put his thoughts into a letter—which was probably the case: Ron had the hardest time putting anything in writing, his mind just didn't work that way—he could have called her while he was walking out on the bridge, had his say, and *then* scrambled over and gotten the job done.

Of course, doing it this way—it was like he wanted someone to stop him. Wasn't that the conventional wisdom? He had built in the risk factor on purpose, hoping to be seen, to be talked out of it. And that's just what Maris had done. Had he seen that coming? Did he have some deep vein of gutlessness he wasn't even aware of?

Sure, he'd fantasized about doing something like this for a while now. Had let himself consider various means and methods before finally choosing the bridge, mostly because the problem of the body's discovery would be taken care of: there was no way Deb would be the one to find him if he jumped, and a very real possibility that his body would never be recovered. She could choose to memorialize him or not. She could let her life close over his absence much like the freezing cold water would close over him, and get on with things.

A selfless attitude for a man bent on dying—if he'd been sincere. But he wasn't. Ron *was* gutless. He was only here because he just didn't have it in him to go another round with Deb over their son's innocence or guilt. The terrible day a month and a half ago when the verdict was read—it had savaged Ron, but it had also brought him a strange measure of comfort. Because it was finally over. Because they wouldn't have to walk into that courtroom again. He could go back to work and lose himself in his job for a few hours a day. Finally, the atmosphere inside his home would be free of the weight of Deb's frantic, desperate hope.

Such an existence was far from perfect. It would never be good again. But Ron had finally been beginning to think they had leveled off, found their new normal. That they could endure. And then fucking Arthur Mehta had driven his ridiculous Mercedes roadster—with a woman who was not his wife in the passenger seat—into the median strip along North Main two nights ago, causing his tire to blow out and attracting the attention of a cop. This being Mehta's third DUI (Ron cursed himself for not taking that into consideration when they hired him to defend Karl), the media vultures were all over it, and Deb had worked herself into a frenzy yesterday as the images played over and over on the news. *Grounds for an appeal*, she'd bleated to him, the skin under her eyes gray with exhaustion, her fingers moving restlessly on the hem of her sweater. *Gross misconduct.* And all Ron could think, as he pretended to listen and agreed that they should move quickly while Mehta's arrest was still in the news, was: I can't do this again.

God, this was hard, trying to marshal all the directions his brain wanted to go. Especially with the two officers staring at him expectantly. And the flashers on their car . . . did they have to put on the damn flashers? Probably a traffic safety issue, but this was just going to draw even more attention. *Shit*.

"Hey." His voice was swallowed up by the wind. He was still holding the phone, so he stuffed it back into his pocket, coughed, and tried again. "Hey."

"It's a hell of a view, isn't it?" The male cop was grinning. Esteban—the little rectangular name tag on his shirt read Esteban. Ron had to squint against the sun to make out the female officer's name on her tag: Officer Dane looked considerably less comfortable with this whole exercise than her partner. She could stand to take a few pages out of Ron's favorite book, which—though no one knew this but Deb, who had found the paperback in a used bookstore in the early, flat-broke days of their marriage—was titled *Sell, Sell, Sell: Top Secrets of an Irresistible Pitch*. Ron had studied that book like the Bible, and it, more than all the career coaches and strategy seminars and corporate retreats in the decades since combined, was the secret to his success. A few years back, before he sold the silicon panel manufacturing business he'd built from the ground up—more to amuse himself than anything—he'd gone looking for the book, but it was long out of print.

So here Ron was, probably the greatest success story ever to profit from that forgotten decades-old business tome, crouching on the outer ledge of the Golden Gate Bridge, mere seconds from death. It seemed a shame that F. R. MacAuliff (Ron would never forget the author's name, or his grinning round face above a too-tight shirt and shiny wide tie in the photo on the dust jacket) had never known the effect he had had on his protégé. MacAuliff was probably dead now. Ron looked down at the water far below—murky and choppy today, suitable for despair—and then back at his would-be rescuers. Esteban and Dane—like actors on a seventies cop show, with just the right amount of appealing yet nonthreatening multiculturalism—and a girl with nice tits!

MacAuliff, Esteban, Dane. The 1970s—was fate trying to tell him something? The thoughts in Ron's head were starting to feel a little crowded. He'd been born in the sixties, but it was the seventies that had shaped him. His father had never laid a hand on him until he was eight years old. Magnus Isherwood's rage hadn't reached its peak until Ron was a teen, but Ron's memories of that decade were marked by his father's snarling fury, the fierce grabs that threatened to pull Ron's arm from its socket, the humiliation of being taken down by a kick to the back of the knees. His father's laughter as Ron gasped for breath after a gut punch. "Knocked the wind out of you?" he would jeer, as though even that was a sign of Ron's weakness.

And it was Magnus's voice that whispered in his head now, cackling, cocksure. *You couldn't even get this right, could you, boy? How hard could it be—all you had to do was jump!*

"You like sports? You following the Giants?" Esteban said now. Dane was edging closer, to the left. "Man, I could stand to get out of the wind, how about you?"

Ron swallowed. His hand was cramping around the steel cable. Some orange paint was flaking from the steel plate at

11

his feet. Underneath, the metal was tinged with rust. Ron rubbed the toe of his shoe on it and a flake came free and fluttered lazily down toward the water. The sight made his stomach flip, and he turned away from the water, gripping the cable ever tighter as he considered his would-be rescuers.

"It's a good day," Esteban said, suddenly serious. "I mean, every day's got its challenges, right? And also, its good moments? I'd love to talk about that. Want to come up here and talk? We can go somewhere and take our time."

"You don't have to make this decision right now," Dane finally piped up. She sounded even younger than she looked. "It's a big decision. How about if we talk about it from up here?"

Ron wanted to respond, but he was having trouble putting the words together. Somehow, he'd gotten stuck in that lost era. It wasn't just his father's face . . . it was Karl's too. Karl's face twisted with rage the last time Ron had seen him. The hatred written there. And somehow, Ron knew he was responsible. It was entirely reasonable for Karl to hate him for what he'd passed along in the blood, because, after all, Karl was the one who'd paid.

"I always got away with it," he managed to choke out, his teeth chattering. Was he cold? He *was* cold. Freezing, in fact.

The officers exchanged a glance. For half a second he saw Esteban's expression slip, and then the friendly grin was back in place. "Well, I don't know about that, but what I *do* know is that the future's wide open, my friend. It only seems like you can't—"

"You always got away with what?" Dane interrupted. She closed the gap, shuffling to the edge and resting her forearms

12

on the metal wall, her hands only a couple of feet from Ron. He glanced down and thought about pushing off with his feet, hurtling away so fast she wouldn't even have time to reach for him.

Behind her, Esteban muttered something, and Ron figured Dane had departed from their script. But she had his attention.

"If you come up here, I'll listen," she said, speaking low and earnestly. To him alone. "You can tell me what you got away with. Take as long as you like."

And the thing was, Ron believed she wanted to help. For some reason—maybe it was the cheap diamond-chip gold cross on a thin chain around her neck, maybe it was the gap between her front teeth, or the way she was pretending it was just the two of them, when clearly Esteban was running the show—he trusted her. Not for later, when there were bound to be all kinds of reports and paperwork and maybe even mandatory evaluations, but in this moment, right now, he trusted her.

"It's okay," he said. "I don't really need to, you know. I mean, I know what I am."

"And what's that?"

Her eyes were brown, with a tiny scar through one eyebrow that left a furrow of white skin. She had a thin line of royal blue eyeliner above each eye that looked like it took forever to draw on. Deb's skin had once been every bit as perfect as this young police officer's.

There was nothing stopping him from telling her what he was: a monster, receptacle of his father's rage, a coiled punishment waiting to be unleashed. Maybe not so potent anymore. It had been years since it broke free.

But that was only because he'd passed it on. The rage had found another vessel.

He looked directly into Dane's eyes.

"We should never have had him," he said, his voice clear even above the whipping winds.

"All right." Dane nodded. "All right. Now give me your hand."

And he did.

three

OUTBOUND TRAFFIC SNARLED BY three o'clock, but coming from the other direction, Maris was able to make good time. She kept her hand on her phone as she raced through the city, thinking she should call Alana, call Jeff, call someone, but unwilling to take the time or the risk to dial. That would be some kind of punishment for her hubris, wouldn't it, if she looked at her phone and got into an accident and therefore didn't reach the bridge in time. Her dead body laid out in twisted metal and broken glass while Ron's corpse caught on some sunken flotsam halfway out to the bay. A Greek tragedy of an ending.

She'd expected ambulances, backups, bystanders out of their cars with their hands over their eyes blocking the sun. Instead there was nothing; nothing but the usual summer weekday traffic, the jockeying at the toll lanes and metering lights. She drove in the slow lane, glancing left and right, seeing nothing but the breathtaking views. On the other side she had to exit and crawl through the jam before she could get back on. And then the same thing, driving the other direction: only a few tourists walking along, enjoying the view.

At the other end she pulled over, into the tiny parking lot next to the gift shop and cafe. A bicycle cop was just strapping his helmet on while his partner tossed a paper cup into the trash.

She had to shout to be heard. "My friend—he said he was going to jump."

The cop, a dusky-skinned man with a thick beard, shook his head and frowned. The traffic noise was deafening. She tried again, jabbing a finger past the gift shop at the traffic moving slowly onto the bridge.

"I am afraid my friend might try to jump off!"

This time the cop understood. He nodded and ushered her around the corner of the building, which was sheltered from the wind and quieter. Maris followed him there, keeping her eyes on the badge pinned to his windbreaker, the holster on his belt.

"Your friend, he's a man? Adult man?"

"Yes—"

"He didn't jump. He came here during the earlier shift, they waited with him until his wife—" The man stopped and looked at her carefully. Maris was conscious of her stricken expression, her lack of makeup and lank, greasy hair. "Until a woman came to pick him up. You know who this might be?"

Relief flooded Maris. "No one jumped today?" she said.

"No. There was just this one man who went over the edge midspan, but he talked to the officers and came back."

"And they let him go home?" With Deb. Of course Deb would come immediately. She was a good wife, one who stayed by her man no matter what.

"Yes. I can have the officers call you if you want—"

"No. No. Thank you, I don't need to, I just needed to know that—that he's, that he's all right."

Already Maris was backing away. She knew her thanks were inadequate, that she had misrepresented herself. She hurried back into the noise and wind, practically ran for her car. When she started the engine, she was trembling. She drove slowly, carefully, the way one drives after being stopped for speeding.

The air in the car was chilly and stale; she'd driven all the way here with the air-conditioning on high. The weather today was Maris's least favorite kind, hot and windless, the sky a hazy steel blue. Back in Kansas, where Maris had lived with her mother and sister until high school, such a sky would lord itself over August wheat until lightning ripped through, announcing splattering storms. But here in California, there was no lightning, no storms, just endless talk of drought and ruin, the hills burned brown and fields left unplanted. Inside the house where Maris retreated, there had been nothing but the hum of the air conditioner, the clink of ice shifting in the freezer. Jeff's departure had galvanized her to ask Alana if she could come stay, but Maris hadn't been sure she would be able to pull it off, actually putting her things in the car. Actually driving away.

She might have chickened out about going to Alana's, chosen to stay numb, to simply give up and die in the house rather than venturing out into the world again. And then Ron had called, and what he threatened to do had ripped her from her self-imposed exile. And maybe she ought to thank him for that. Except—how dare he?

Maris gripped the steering wheel hard, claustrophobic in the slow-moving traffic through the Presidio. How could he have possibly thought that his life could be worth anything to her? Even if he could die a thousand times, it would never make up for Calla, for the fact that his son had killed her daughter. Maybe she should have told him to go ahead and jump—if only as punishment for his audacity, his selfishness. No, his self-*indulgence*. Because wasn't that really what his call was all about? *Poor me,* she imagined him thinking, drawing out the exquisite luxury of self-pity. A truly repentant man would have simply jumped—he wouldn't have given himself a lifeline in the guise of that damn phone call.

Do it, she should have said. *Jump!* And then she could have gone to his funeral and savored Deb's loss, her pain. Not that the loss of a husband could ever compare to the loss of a child. But it would have been something.

A horn honked, then another. A cacophony of them as traffic struggled around a truck stalled on an exit ramp. Ridiculous, to attempt this at this time of day, with no way to get around the city crush and the Bay Bridge approach, the rush-hour commuters all heading out. There, at least, was one advantage of being homebound by grief: no traffic.

As she edged the car forward in the snarl before the tunnel, merging with the traffic from Berkeley, her phone rang. Maris glanced at the screen: her sister. She deliberated for a moment before answering, but she couldn't put Alana off all night.

"Hey."

"Hi, Mar." Caution in her voice, the gentling that was so unnatural for Alana. "I was just checking in to see if you got on the road when you thought you would."

"Oh, Alana, listen." For a moment Maris considered telling her what happened—Ron's call, the sounds of cars rushing

18

by, the cop in the black windbreaker. The sense of relief followed by rage. "I don't—I think I'll just wait and come in the morning. It's taking me a little longer than I thought to figure out what to pack."

"Just throw some things in a bag! We can drive back on Saturday and get more, if you want. I'll help."

Maris was exhausted just thinking about her sister going through her dresser, choosing what to take and what to leave behind. "Yes, I just—I know, Alana. I'm grateful. Really. But at this point I'll have to wait until after six to miss the worst of the traffic and I wouldn't get down there until seven thirty, at least."

"Oh, Mar." Alana's exhale was audible even over the phone. "You sure? I hate to think of you there by yourself. Besides, I picked up some wine. A nice one, a pinot gris. We can sit outside after it cools off."

"I'm sure." Maris relaxed fractionally; her sister had relented. "We can figure all of this out tomorrow. I just want to take a shower and go to bed early."

But at nine o'clock, when she climbed into the bed she'd shared with Jeff, she still hadn't showered. Not today, and she wasn't sure if she'd had one yesterday, either. That would have to change now. Alana couldn't see her like this, with her hair greasy and stringy, her nails ragged and bitten. She had to make her sister think she was managing, if just barely.

Starting tomorrow, she would get back into a strict grooming regimen. Exercise too—she'd pack her sneakers and gym clothes and use her sister's treadmill every day. She'd make an appointment with a hairdresser, get her roots done, a manicure.

It wasn't like Maris expected sleep to come easily. She'd accepted the middle-of-the-night wakefulness, the long march of empty hours toward dawn, as part of her penance. But tonight she couldn't seem to slow her thoughts at all, even after she'd gone through all the breathing exercises Nina had taught her.

Would sleep have come more easily if he had jumped?

Would Maris have felt something—anything—when the news cameras turned their inexhaustibly greedy lenses on Ron's funeral, panning over the mourners as they had a year ago when nearly a thousand people came to Calla's service? Would Maris feel better when, some future day, she passed Deb Isherwood on the street and saw the familiar ravages of loss in her eyes?

four

DEB WAS CRYING. RON knew she was trying not to, trying so hard he could practically feel the effort she was making, the way her teeth ground together and her fingers gripped the steering wheel tightly.

She'd held it together while talking to the cops. Ron had stood slightly off to the side, chastened, as though he had been caught pulling the fire alarm in middle school and his mother had come to pick him up. Already the enormity of what he had almost done had dissipated, the decision he had reached a distant and hazy memory. It seemed almost silly, a misunderstanding, and yet there was his wife in her sleeveless blouse, her white sandals with her red-painted toenails peeking out, looking fresh and pretty and appropriately concerned, twisting a lock of her blond hair around her finger.

They held hands as they walked back to the car, after finally convincing the officers that Ron didn't need to go to the hospital for an emergency evaluation. Deb had said, "I'll drive," and Ron had almost argued, out of habit—Deb was a slow and cautious driver, and he got impatient in the passenger seat—before closing his mouth tightly. This was only the first of the concessions he would undoubtedly have to make, now that he had done this thing, and he felt his mood changing to grim penitence.

What made the most sense would be for each of them to drive their own cars home, but he knew that wasn't going to happen. Deb had nodded along with the promises he'd made to the cops: not to be alone, to let someone else pick up his car, to make an appointment immediately with a mental health professional.

Still, Ron knew he wasn't crazy. And he wasn't ever going to kill himself, he saw that now. Which hadn't made him wrong, exactly; he'd needed to go to the brink to see where he stood, what he was willing to trade. He still didn't have much worth living for, Deb notwithstanding, and he still had a debt he couldn't possibly repay, a net negative balance on this earth.

But he'd dutifully consulted Maris, and Maris had turned him down, and that was that. They were members of a very select group now, the two of them. Maybe it was unforgivable of him to put himself in the same category as her—her child was dead and his was not, but Karl's life had been altered so completely that it felt like he had lost his son. The person sitting in Panamint Correctional Institution for Men, two and a half hours away, was not Karl, not as he had been, at any rate. (Which didn't excuse Ron from going to see him, he knew that. He had other reasons, other excuses.)

But he and Maris both woke up each day to experience the horror of loss all over again. In some way, it was always new, it was always shocking. Deb suffered too, of course, but she had her belief—fantastical and pitiable though it was—in Karl's innocence. That belief was her first thought in the

22

morning and her last at night, and it seemed to give her what she needed to sustain her each day. And she had all the rituals of homemaking, the comfort of which had been incomprehensible to Ron even before last year: finding her life's meaning through him, their son, their home; counting her own value in how meticulously she took care of all of them.

Deb's devotion to him had never flagged, and she drew strength from their marriage. Ron wished he could do the same—if there was some elixir he could take that would render him as dependent on Deb as she was on him, he would do it. Just so he wouldn't have to be so *alone*. But it wasn't possible. He loved Deb now as much as ever, perhaps more, but he didn't *need* her. He faced all the terrible moments alone and knew that it wasn't in him to do different.

Not that it mattered in the end. The guilty verdict was inevitable, that was obvious after jury selection, the first time Karl was led into the courtroom and the jury got a look at him. Karl had engineered his own sentence with his behavior, his impenetrable mien, his palpable indifference, the hint of scorn that attended every gesture and sigh and proclamation of innocence.

Maris and Ron had never spoken, all those long hours in the county courthouse. They settled wordlessly into a pattern, the Vacantis and Isherwoods, of staggering their arrivals and departures: the Vacantis coming early so they could have their seats close to the front, and him and Deb coming as late as possible, glad—though they never discussed it—when they could squeeze in somewhere at the last minute so they didn't have to endure any more attention than necessary. It was reversed at the end of the day when Deb insisted that they

23

try to catch Karl's attention, offer a word of encouragement, gestures that were rarely returned or even acknowledged.

But Ron stole glances at Maris whenever he could. He knew her back by heart, the way her highlighted hair curved under itself an inch or two past her collarbones. Her shoulder blades, sharp and angular under her clothes. Her soft-looking sweaters in dull colors like gray and steel blue.

At least she must know by now he wasn't dead, so any responsibility she had (arguably, none) to ensure he didn't kill himself was over. He was still the parent of her daughter's killer. Maybe she'd like to kill him herself.

The thing was, he had something new to apologize to her for. Causing her more pain, reminding her of his very existence by threatening to snuff it out—he didn't have the right. Hell, he'd apologize to her for existing, if he could figure out the words.

"We could call Azalea Pearce," Deb said in a brittle approximation of cheer as they drove through the hills toward the eastern suburbs of San Francisco. "Just for ideas."

"Deb, sweetheart," Ron said. He was impressed by his own calm. "I don't think that's a good idea."

"She's a therapist. She could give us names, she probably knows just the right person—"

"Let's not bring anyone from the neighborhood into this, though, okay? I'm not saying anything about Azalea, I think she's great, but still."

People would talk. Azalea would tell Ernie, and he'd let it slip to someone. Never on purpose. The last year had taught them that: people really didn't mean to squander the confidences they received. It just happened—human nature.

"Well. Then let's call Sam." Deb's voice quivered a bit, on the brink of tears, but Ron could tell she wasn't going to give up.

"I'd . . . really rather not."

"I know that, Ron, I do. But I think . . . I mean, and he's a professional, he knows."

This shorthand they used, it had been a blessing at first, letting them skip over the most painful discussions, getting through them at a higher rpm. "What happened" was a place-holder for that horrible week last June. "Him" was what they called Karl; both of them avoided saying his name, though they'd never talked about it. "Panamint" was their shorthand for the state prison in Panamint County, on a bleak stretch of farm road 150 miles east of Linden Creek in the Central Valley. And for Calla and Maris and Jeff they had no short-hand at all, because they never, ever spoke of them unless absolutely necessary, which was why Ron couldn't even begin to tell Deb why he'd been on the bridge today.

He didn't need to, anyway. He was nearly positive that his wife thought she understood why he'd gone to the bridge. Deb believed she knew everything that mattered about her husband, inside and out, for all of the twenty years that they had been married. He wasn't going to let her find out now that she was wrong. He wasn't going to take that away from her. Let her think that he just couldn't go on, couldn't con-tinue to face the people at the office, the familiar faces they ran into in the grocery, church, the neighborhood. Let her think, even, that it was his shame over the one failure she couldn't forgive him for.

She was right to blame him, even to despise him. But Ron couldn't bring himself to tell her that she had the wrong reason. It wasn't his inability to forgive his son that had caused him to toy with the idea of killing himself, but his dread of reliving the awful unfolding of events again, the slow and inevitable march to sentencing. The hopes that, despite his best efforts to quash them, clamored in his head until he began to believe that things could be different, that they could be all right again.

"Hey," he said now as she lost her battle with her tears. He hated seeing her cry. Or rather, he hated seeing her cry like this. Deb cried all the time, over sad movies and Hallmark cards and when he sent her flowers and when she read Facebook updates about people losing their parents or going into treatment for cancer. But this was different. This was Deb breaking on the inside, and she'd already been breaking for far too long.

She held up her hand. "No, it's all right, I'm fine," she said, and forced her mouth into a smile. "I mean, this might finally get you to take a few days off and stay home with me."

Ron laughed—he actually forced out a fake laugh, but he meant it as a gift. "Sweetheart, I'm not sure that's something most people would consider a benefit . . ."

"Most people aren't us," she said, her voice just a little lighter. Ron had the power to do that—her moods hinged on his, even after everything. Which made him all that much more of a bastard.

When they finally reached the entrance to Cresta Hills, he hit the clicker and waited for the gate to swing open, waving at the guard in his little shack. A month into the trial, they'd put their house on the market and received multiple offers within a week. He had no idea how many of those offers had

26

something to do with their notoriety, and he forced himself to pretend not to care. They'd bought a new, slightly smaller house in Cresta Hills, the only gated community around where anyone couldn't just walk in through a pedestrian gate. The gate might provide only the illusion of security, but after months of battling the media and the protesters and the merely curious, Ron was willing to pay for that illusion.

Their house was on a premium lot on a cul-de-sac. Deb pulled into the garage, put the door down behind them, and turned off the engine. For a moment they just sat in the dim light of the car. Ron reached for Deb's hand, and squeezed it.

"I'm so sorry," he said haltingly, the apology he couldn't begin in the daylight. "I hate myself for putting you through that."

"Don't ever do it again," she said in a strangled voice he'd never heard before. She turned her face to his and he saw the tears shining on her cheeks. But when she spoke again, she bared her teeth. "Don't you *dare* quit on me. I can't go through that now. I *can't*."

"Baby, I swear to you, it'll never happen again." He reached for her, meaning to pull her into his arms the way he had a thousand times before, to tuck her small blond head under his chin.

But she resisted him. Her shoulders were stiff, her arms pressed close to her body. "Ron," she said, her voice hard, "now that Arthur's discredited, we have a chance. A real chance. It's not going to be easy, but I've already talked to Kami, and she's coming up with a list of attorneys. We have to act fast, while it's still in the news, and I need you to *promise* me you'll do everything you can. For Karl. And for me."

Ron froze, his hand inches from her, his body turned toward her. "It's not that easy," he whispered.

"I mean it." Her mouth began to wobble, and then the tremor seemed to take over her whole body. "Ron. I'll never forgive you if you don't."

With that she opened her door and got out of the car. She went into the house, letting the door close behind her. A moment later the car light went out, and Ron was left sitting in darkness.

five

THE NEXT DAY WAS a Tuesday, the most ordinary of days. The inertia of the night before had dissipated when Maris got up. The packing that had seemed so daunting took no more than a few minutes, the selection of what to take for a stay at her sister's place seeming perfectly obvious. Clothes, toiletries, a few books and journals. Maris swept the little collection of precious keepsakes she had been collecting into her dresser, nestling the objects among the out-of-season sweaters; she would get them next time she returned, when the future seemed a bit less hazy.

She was out the door by ten, having outwaited the morning commute, and in Oakland forty minutes later. She attended to her errand with brisk detachment. When she came out again into the heat of another ninety-degree July day, blinking in the sun, she was buoyed by a sense of accomplishment.

Until she got back to her car. Standing with her hand in her purse, searching for her keys, her brain tried to make sense of what she was seeing: the jagged hole in the rear window, the sidewalk littered with broken glass. It was pretty, the way the shards sparkled in the sun, and some part of Maris's mind was having trouble making sense of what she was seeing, processing how this changed her circumstances and what she would have to do about it, even as she marveled at the broken bits sparkling like the pavé diamonds in the anniversary band Jeff gave her on their tenth anniversary.

Shit. The jewelry. She had forgotten to pack her jewelry.

Maris bent down and picked up one of the tiny little pieces. Safety glass—wasn't that a lovely turn of phrase? It had so many other uses. Like coffee table tops. And sliding glass doors. People were always accidentally crashing through those, weren't they? Like Jeremy Guttenfelder after the junior class prom. Calla had gotten blood on her dress trying to help clean up.

Maris stood and put the bit of glass into her pocket. Her fingertips touched the little slip of paper, the claim check. She hadn't even needed it. The man in the shop remembered her. In her other hand she held the package he'd given her, surprisingly heavy and wrapped in white paper over bubble wrap. Well. She couldn't leave the package in the car now, could she! A manic little laugh burst from Maris's lips. She peered in the backseat. Of course it was gone, all of it. The large suitcase, the Vera Bradley duffel, the two large Crate & Barrel bags. Ha. Good luck with that.

People who broke into cars in Oakland were likely just looking for things to sell for drug money, for their next high. For a *chunky*, for a *dirty*, Jeff would have said. He was embarrassingly proud of the lingo he'd picked up from his crime shows: *burners, hoppers, carrying weight.* He'd say these things ironically, self-deprecatingly—God, he was good at that fake self-deprecation. You don't live with someone for more than two decades without knowing what lay beneath the fragile glib exterior. And still, all that time, he never seemed to accept that she heard things too, she knew things. And the things she knew were actually true.

Once the depth of his disinterest in her life became clear, Maris didn't bother to tell Jeff that the kids didn't really talk like that, not even the ones in East Oakland. Before Calla's death, Maris volunteered once a week for a literacy program at Morgandale Elementary School, working with a fourth-grader in one of Oakland's worst neighborhoods. But maybe Jeff was right to be skeptical. Here in front of her was evidence that do-gooders like her made no difference at all—her possessions sold off for, what, a single afternoon's relief? Her clothes, toiletries, books, her journal, what kind of money could they possibly bring? A size-twelve wardrobe—expensive, yes, but out of date. Not one thing purchased in the last year. And what would a junkie do with a jar of Estée Lauder face cream?

At least Maris's laptop was in her purse. She'd go across the street and get some coffee and file a report. She knew damn well that cops didn't actually come for things like this anymore, not in Oakland. You just went online and filled out a form and the system assigned you a number, and then at least you had something to show the insurance guy.

The package in her hand was uncomfortably heavy. Maris hitched it up under her arm and crossed the street, not bothering to walk back to the crosswalk on the corner.

The diner was staffed by an Asian couple. The woman stood at the register, sorting through a pile of receipts. The man was scraping the grill. There was one other customer in the shop, a mumbling, shuffling black man with a coat whose sleeves came well past his wrists. A coat, in this heat.

31

Maris stepped wide around him but still she could smell him.

"I'd like a large coffee," Maris said. And then, because she might have to sit there for a while, she scanned the menu for something else to order to justify taking up table space. "And a bacon and egg sandwich."

"White or wheat?" the woman asked.

"Wheat."

The man got to work without looking up, setting down his spatula with a clang and reaching for the package of bread on a shelf above the grill. What a life this must be, working with your husband from early in the morning until closing time at night. This heat, these smells, the grease hanging in the air, and every day, only each other.

"I'll bring." The woman handed Maris her change and gestured at the table.

There was only one, a Formica round top on uneven legs. The chairs were the white plastic outdoor type you could buy for fifteen dollars at Home Depot. The table had been wiped, but there was still a greasy smear. Maris rubbed at it with a napkin before she set her laptop down.

She should call Alana. Let her know she was delayed again. God. Dread unspooled in Maris's gut. Alana had made it plain that she'd cleared her evenings this week, that she'd try to take off early in the afternoons. That the guest room was "move-in ready." At the thought of what lay ahead, the ease with which Maris had been navigating the day guttered like a candle in the breeze and she shut her eyes and forced herself to take a series of deep breaths. Just the thought of that place—Alana's condo building with its designated landmark plaque, its turret room and coy little arched windows . . . the way Alana's heels clicked briskly on the refurbished floors. That was Alana: always so brisk.

The woman set Maris's sandwich down. It arrived on a paper plate stained with butter, wrapped in waxed paper and cut in half.

"You work?" the woman pointed to Maris's laptop.

"No," Maris said, embarrassed. "I mean, yes. I have to . . ."

She didn't finish the sentence and the woman made a small tsk'ing sound and went back behind the counter with her husband. The shambling man was gone, leaving behind a sense of industry as they all three went about their tasks. Maybe that was what the woman meant, that Maris *should* work, as if at this hour of the day it was the only reasonable thing to do. Actually, Maris would agree with that. It was a little after eleven. Once, when she had a job, this had been her most productive time of the day. Even this last year, as her leave dragged on and on and everyone tacitly seemed to conclude that she was never going back, morning was when Maris worked the hardest, even if it was just ripping weeds from the cracks between pavers or scrubbing the dust from the baseboards.

She unwrapped the sandwich. Suddenly, she was ravenous. This was the sort of food no one ate anymore: plain square slices of pale soft bread, an egg shiny with butter, the bacon limp and folded back on itself. It was delicious. Maris ate the first half, starting with the triangle corners, and then after wiping her fingers on the paper napkin, she ate the rest.

She got up to refill her cup from the pot on the counter.

"Refill fifty cent."

"Oh." Maris dug her wallet from her purse, embarrassed, and then realized she hadn't tipped when she paid. She laid down a dollar, then two more. The woman stared at the bills with what might have been contempt.

Maris took her cup and sat back down. She should open the laptop. She should get the report over with. She would search "Oakland police report theft." Or burglary? What was the difference? Maris sighed, staring out the window across the street. Her car, a three-year-old Acura with less than forty thousand miles on it, was wedged between a purplish Ford Taurus and an old blue Corolla.

The shop where she'd had Alana's fittings replated was around the corner, a long cramped space with a glass counter right out of the 1950s and a proprietor to match, an old bent man with white close-cropped hair and a narrow tie. "Only place in the Bay Area still does the triple plating," he'd said, like an accusation, when she brought the fittings in. Silver services and brass doorknobs, babies' cups and old-fashioned hand mirrors lined the shelves, looking as though they'd been awaiting pickup for years. "Been here since 1972," the man said gloomily when he ran her credit card.

Maris wondered what the neighborhood had been like when he opened his shop. The houses were large and once must have been nice. Take the one across the street. Blue plastic sheeting was nailed over parts of the roof, and the window sashes were peeling and rotting in some places, but the eaves were ornately trimmed and the porch rail sat on turned spindles. Leaded-glass windows in a diamond pattern framed either side of the front door.

While she was watching, the door opened and a young

man flew out, barely pausing to slam the door shut. He had a backpack slung over one arm, a plaid short-sleeved shirt whose tails flapped over his shorts. Black socks, the kind Maris's father had worn, and white converse sneakers. He jogged across the street without bothering to look for traffic and headed for the diner, pushing open the door with a shove of his shoulder.

"I'll have a pancake sandwich?" Only then did Maris realize that it was a woman, not a man. A girl, really, her fine light brown hair cut short with longer bangs falling in her eyes, and white teeth that were a little too large for her face.

The man at the grill started pouring batter from a metal pitcher without acknowledging her. The girl put a bill down on the counter and helped herself to a coffee cup. After filling it she looked at Maris and frowned. Maris opened the laptop self-consciously and pretended to study the screen.

"Hey, do you mind if I sit here with you?" the girl said, and without waiting for an answer, slid out one of the white plastic chairs with her foot.

"I—no, of course not."

Maris glanced up, giving the girl a closer look. She had a silver bar in her ear that entered near the top and pierced the shell-like middle before emerging near the lobe. A tattoo peeked out from her shirt, but it was impossible to tell what it was—all Maris could make out was a curving barbed tendril. She dug into her backpack and took out a book, dog-eared and marked in half a dozen places with Post-its.

The book was *East of Eden*. Calla had read it junior year. It was still sitting on the shelf in her room back in Linden Creek.

A sound came out of Maris, a blunted wail.

"Hey," the girl said, looking up in alarm. "Hey."

Maris waved her hand, dabbing at her eyes with her crumpled napkin. Usually she could cover up these dangerous slips, which generally came when she was in CVS or driving past the library, small moments in unremarkable days. She had perfected a cough and swipe of the eyes that masked the upwelling of agony.

But today was different. Today was an ending and it was supposed to be a beginning, but Maris suddenly knew that there was no new beginning for her, that she could not go to Santa Luisa to her sister's home that smelled of toast and Balenciaga Florabotanica. There was this moment, this girl and her book, sitting much too close, and Maris heaved, the sandwich suddenly roiling in her stomach. "I'm so sorry," she mumbled. "I think I'm going to be sick."

"Hey!" The girl shouted, jumping up from her chair. "The lady's sick! Give me the key!"

The woman behind the counter looked up from stocking a display of energy bars. Her mouth tightened and she looked directly at Maris, judging, assessing. She reached under the counter and slammed a large metal serving spoon on the counter. A key hung off the end.

"Come on," the girl said. "It'll be faster to go around."

six

MARIS JOGGED TO KEEP up. Down the cracked sidewalk, into an alley that ran between a vacuum repair shop and a shuttered restaurant. The asphalt was crumpled and strewn with litter. The skeleton of a bicycle was chained to the side of a building, its tires long gone.

Around back, a lean-to shed was tacked onto the rear of the building. There was a smell of garbage, obscenely ripe—Maris couldn't hold it in. The sodden mass of food surged up through her throat, gagging her, making her eyes water. She bent double over a narrow patch of weeds along the edge of the building and let it come, wave after wave, trying to stifle the worst of the noise.

"Shit," the girl said softly. "Shit, well, you might as well get it all out."

After a while the convulsive heaves stopped. Maris spat, then wiped her mouth on her sleeve. Glancing at the girl, she saw a splatter near the hem of her shorts.

"Oh my God," Maris said. "I am so sorry." She thought of the tissues in her purse, then suddenly realized she'd left it in the diner. "My purse, I—"

"Here."

37

It was slung over the girl's arm. Maris hadn't even seen her pick it up. A fleeting thought: *Now the girl takes off with it, and I'll have nothing,* but the thought evaporated—after all, the girl had come back here with her, in the stinking alley, to help. Also, Maris knew where she lived.

"My laptop?"

"In here." The girl patted the purse. "Listen, you want to come clean up at my place? This bathroom's kind of . . . I don't think you'll want to go in there."

Maris looked at the flat steel door standing slightly ajar. The smell from it was worse than the stench of her own vomit; the word Bathroom was unevenly written in Sharpie, the last few letters squeezed to the edge. But, to accept more help from a stranger . . . and in a bad part of Oakland, where walking into someone's house could mean walking into anything. Wasn't there a good chance that this would lead to something stupid, some con she couldn't see coming?

The girl had a sweet voice, rather high-pitched and vaguely inflected with a midwestern flatness. If you heard only that voice you'd never believe she was capable of malevolence. It was jarring, though, in contrast with her appearance: the bar in her ear, those bangs above the nearly shaved scalp. A scab on her neck.

"I should probably just go."

The girl made a tut sound. "Seriously? I have to change, anyway."

That's what did it—after all, Maris had been the one to soil her clothes. To *hurl* on them, Calla would have said. She couldn't walk away now.

"I . . . would very much appreciate that," she said humbly.

38

"Let's go this way, don't need that bitch watching. All she does all day is stare out that window."

"But what about the key?"

The girl yanked the bathroom door open a few inches and tossed the key into the sink, where it clattered against the porcelain.

"Should I try to . . ." Maris gestured at the ground.

"Clean up? You kidding? She'll never know that was you." The girl gave her a flash of a grin. "You don't look like the type. You know, not to make it to the shitter."

Maris blushed. Even now, after everything, there were corners of her that refused to be worn down, little bits of her old carapace that still clung when the rest had been sloughed off by grief and horror. *Shitter*: that was a word that she had never spoken and that she hadn't heard in years. A coarse word that had no place even in the percussive, obscenity-laced torrent that issued from the Morgandale kids (*Mrs. Vacanti, I need to go to the* baff-*room*).

She followed the girl around the end of the block, approaching the house from the other direction. The temperature seemed to have risen even in the short time they'd been outside. A thin trickle of sweat rolled down the small of Maris's back. She hadn't dressed for the weather, thinking she'd be at Alana's condo by now. Alana kept the air-conditioning on all summer, ostensibly because of her allergies; the windows were never open. Another reason that Maris dreaded going there. To be sealed up in that place . . .

The girl led her up the stairs to the porch, opened the door. Inside was a dim foyer, carpeted stairs going up, a cheap door on the right that she opened with another key. Maris followed her into a large, sunny room, every corner stuffed with bright-colored furniture and pillows and throws, fabric panels hanging from the ceiling, curtains pulled all the way open. In the center of the room, up against the bay window, was a bed, neatly made and covered with a patchwork quilt. Along the opposite wall were a tiny stove, a huge old refrigerator, a single cabinet that wasn't even fastened to the wall, and a pair of cheap bookcases that held dishes and cups and food in addition to piles of papers and textbooks.

"Bathroom's through there," the girl said. "You go first, I'll change."

Maris went through the arched opening. Once, it must have led to a formal dining room, but it had been walled off, a bathroom wedged in the space between. Inside, the tub enclosure was coated with soap scum. There was a dusty layer of grime on everything, worst on the floor, where used Q-tips cluttered the corners along with clots of hair and dust. Maris washed her hands at the sink, then cupped water in her hands and rinsed her mouth, over and over.

She ought to pee now, because who knew when she'd get another chance, but the toilet was filthy. The ring in the bowl was at least a half inch wide. After a moment's deliberation, Maris sat anyway. She couldn't summon the energy to be appalled.

While she sat, she looked around the bathroom, inspecting the few items lining the windowsill and sink. There were no cosmetics. *Poor thing,* Maris thought before she could stop herself. Just because the girl had more of a . . . the word *butch* was what came to mind, but surely that wasn't the proper word, the respectful word—sort of look didn't mean she couldn't do a little more with herself. After all, even boys wore makeup now. On the tub ledge was a cloudy bar of soap embedded with bits of something. Drugstore shampoo—two-in-one, no need for conditioner. Razors, tampons, deodorant. Secret brand—made for a woman, wasn't that how the old ads used to go?

Maris washed her hands a second time and came out into the main room.

"I feel worlds better," she lied. The truth was she felt neither better nor worse. Since leaving the house this morning, driving out of their neighborhood and through town and onto the highway on-ramp, she'd had the strange sense that her emotions had been sucked out of her by the heat, laid waste along with the parched earth and withered brown hillsides, victims of the relentless drought. The heat scoured and the dust coated what was left. The drought had officially lasted over a year; it dated almost exactly to Calla's death, something she and Jeff had never spoken of, though surely he must have thought about it too.

The moment in the diner, when the girl took the book from her backpack—that had been an aberration, because Maris was mostly beyond feeling these days. Even when she had seen her car window in bits on the ground, even when she was bent over that patch of weeds, it felt as though it was happening to someone else—or more precisely, that it had happened to her in the past and she was reliving it from the distance of time.

The girl was washing her hands at a tiny sink bolted to the wall near the refrigerator. Above it was a drawing of a car next to a building, done in impossibly bright colors: purple shadows and orange bricks. She dried her hands on a towel and twirled. "Good as new," she said. She'd changed into plaid madras shorts, the sort old men wear for golf.

"You never told me your name," Maris said.

"Pet. Short for Petra." The girl smiled. "I'm like half Czech. Try having that name in middle school."

Maris was about to say that she understood—other than the character on *Frasier*, she'd never met another Maris.

The thing about her name, though. Maris Vacanti. It was distinctive—it was recognizable. She had a trick, one she'd started using shortly before the trial started. What made it possible: she had never formally changed her name. For the first three years she and Jeff were married, she still went by Ms. Parker at school. Later, after Calla was born and Maris cut her hours and eventually quit teaching altogether, she meant to get around to changing it. Their mail came addressed to Mr. and Mrs. Vacanti; bills and magazine subscriptions and Calla's school directory listed her married name. Even her family eventually starting using Vacanti, and still she never submitted the paperwork, and when she renewed her driver's license and did the taxes every year there was some small . . . satisfaction? Was that what she had felt, holding this small part of herself back, seeing the name Parker on the forms?

Had some part of her always known about Jeff, about what was dormant in him even then?

"Maris Parker," she said firmly, banishing the thought. She held out her hand, and the girl took it, squeezed rather than shook.

"Maris?" The girl said. "Do people ever call you Mary?"

"Sometimes," Maris said, and then—for no reason at all, it just popped into her head—she said "Actually, my friends call me Mary."

"Okay. Mary. So, I have to ask, what the fuck are you doing in this neighborhood?"

Maris laughed the fake little laugh that she used to buy herself time. Framing how she wanted to say things—not that she had ever been the type for conversational chatter; she'd always preferred to speak precisely. But these days, there was always the equation, how much to hold back, how much to reveal. "That's a long story. Am I keeping you from something? Work?"

"Nah." Pet fluttered a hand. "I don't have to be at work until four. I'm just killing time until then. I ought to be studying, but I was going to go to CVS—but, you know, I can do that whenever. Do you need . . . ?"

She let the sentence trail off. Maris looked down: was it that obvious on her, the damage, the aimlessness, her need for escape despite having nowhere to go other than Alana's? Jeff had tried to talk her out of leaving like this. So had Nina, for that matter. At the time Maris had felt defiant. Now she just felt ridiculous.

"I—I could stand to rest in one place for a while. I have some things I need to figure out."

"Well, you're welcome to stay here. I'll probably just draw."

Maris looked at the colorful drawings tacked around the room. "These are yours?"

Pet's smile faltered. She stared at the floor. "Some of them. Most of them."

"Pet . . . they're really good. Really impressive. Do you, I mean is your work—"

"I'm a bartender." A quick, ironic glance. "Total cliché, right? Except I'm not, like, really trying to make it as an artist or anything. I'm not good enough, and, I mean, don't feel like you have to say I am. But, yeah, for now I bartend at night and I'm getting my associate's degree over at Merritt. Maybe I'll try to get into Cal after. Or something."

She shrugged toward the corner of the room, and Maris saw what she had missed at first—a desk made out of a plywood top set on sawhorses. It was the least cluttered part of the room. Hanging on the wall above it were metal shelves holding clear plastic bins full of crayons, pencils, markers. Large sheets of blank paper were clipped by clothespins on wires suspended from the ceiling.

"So anyway I could like make . . . well, I was going to say tea, but I don't think I have any. Diet Coke? And you can totally take the chair or you can sit on the bed, whatever."

Pet picked up a stack of books from a TV tray table standing next to a worn red upholstered wing chair. She moved them to the floor along the wall. The TV tray was decorated with a hunting scene: a buck standing on a hill above a lake, antlers wider than its shoulders.

"I really can't tell you how much I appreciate this, Pet." Maris felt her voice catch in her throat. The girl was too trusting, by far.

"It's no big deal."

"Maybe I could . . . could I take you to lunch?"

"If you feel like it, I guess. But don't worry about it. Look, I'm going to put my headphones on, but just yell if you need something, okay? The internet's SloLow. S-L-O-L-O-W. Password is blue taco 1. All one word, capital B." She shrugged. "Don't ask me why, my landlord picked it."

She put her headphones on and her hand hovered over a bin full of crayons only for a second before she picked out a bright red stub and made a bold stroke on the paper.

Maris thought she could lose herself in watching the drawing take shape. She was suddenly exhausted. It might be nice to sit here in the enveloping chair that smelled like dusty sachets and watch this odd girl draw. But she had things to do. Which was, on reflection, a sort of novel feeling. For months, for the entire past year, she had felt that her life was sweeping her out to sea, that she was powerless against the tide of it, her only task to keep her head above water as she was carried along. At some point, there had been a fork in the river—on one side, the gentle, benevolent stream she had expected her life to take: Calla off to San Diego in the fall, leaving Maris more time to concentrate on her night classes, maybe take a trip with Jeff for their anniversary. Their twenty-second—not a milestone, but still an accomplishment. Instead, she had been swept to the other fork, to waters more turbulent than she ever could have expected: raging rapids, treacherous rocks and falls. Was the change in course all due to a caprice of fate? Inattention? Some crime Maris had never been aware she'd committed, or an accumulation of small sins?

She'd certainly had time to wonder. (Nina had acknowledged that self-blame was common, but cautioned against it. One of the many times Maris thought balefully that she ought to take the $125 an hour and just burn it, as Nina's counsel often seemed almost insultingly obvious. Still,

45

she had been highly recommended.) You get your detective assigned to you, you hire your lawyers, your coworkers and friends organize themselves into platoons of support. Food arrives. Your lawn is mowed. It begins to seem like the purpose of all that expended energy is to keep you in a childlike state, with no responsibilities and no agenda, nothing but the waiting and the thinking and the endless replaying. "Relax," they say. "We'll let you know when there's news." "We'll deal with the media." "We've covered your shifts." "I took care of the bills." "I had the cleaners put the flannel sheets on the bed." All your decisions, made for you. Your hand held. Your needs anticipated. Your mail censored, your "Thinking of You" cards opened before being tucked back into their pastel envelopes.

But no more.

Maris got the laptop from her purse, settled it on her lap, feeling the warmth of the little machine against her thighs. She had chosen this. She had chosen to leave, to act, to change. A shiver—fear, anticipation, rebellion—traced up her spine as she settled her fingers on the keys. Leaving, that was one thing—going to stay with Alana, getting out of the house, all of that was just reacting. But the minute she made this detour to Oakland, she'd tripped a lever that set something else in motion. Something she hadn't even named yet.

Life was funny that way, how you could mold your path to a truth even before you knew it to be true. If you were brave. If bravery was the word for it. People sabotaged themselves all the time, when they weren't ready to face things. But sometimes they also created circumstances that forced the changes they weren't ready to make deliberately.

46

The brass fittings—it was true that Alana had wanted to restore the window handles and hinges from her condo in a historic building in downtown Santa Luisa, the sort of exquisite detail that had become her odd passion. Maris had researched a place that could do the work; she had thought it would be a novel and meaningful gift to mark her moving in with Alana, however temporarily. All of that was true. But Maris had still chosen this errand that took her out of the smooth arc of her getaway, picking up the fittings on the very day of her departure, when she could have waited until another time, or done it in advance. Had she gone directly from Linden Creek to Santa Luisa this morning, she would already be standing in Alana's light-filled kitchen, sipping a glass of lemon seltzer. Instead, Maris had come to this neighborhood, this pocked patch of ruin bounded by freeways and abandoned schools and barbed-wire fencing, and while she hadn't broken her own car window or stolen her own belongings, she might as well have.

The thought was oddly thrilling.

As Maris searched *Oakland police report robbery*, she realized that she had left the package in the diner. But she could no longer imagine giving her sister a set of six brass door cranks and hinges as a gift anyway. Let someone else have them. She scanned the screen, raising an eyebrow at the "homicide tip line" ("tips may be made anonymously") before clicking "citizen police report" and being rewarded with paragraph after paragraph of text. She read it twice, registering only a few details ("report theft of dog" seemed oddly quaint), but her mind was already far ahead.

If she reported the robbery, she would have to give all the

details—the true ones, who she really was. Surely the police would know the name. Or was that a naïve assumption? That police here would care at all about things that happened out in the suburbs? Still, it wasn't worth taking a chance. She would never get her things back. Their total value—well, it wasn't much, was it? Besides, she had money, a little over twelve thousand dollars in the account she had opened last week, in her name only, the proceeds from the sale of Jeff's stock that had just vested. She had to make it last until she and Jeff worked out the rest, but for now it was plenty, especially since Alana wasn't going to charge her rent, at least until they made some long-term decisions. She'd buy clothes, toiletries. She'd figure it out.

She opened a Yelp window and searched "auto glass." There were dozens of options, one of them promising on-site service within three hours. Three and a half stars, that would do. She dug her phone from her purse, ignoring a text from Alana ("On your way? ETA?"). It took a call to her insurance company, but in moments she had an appointment an hour from now.

The phone buzzed a new text. She glanced down, impatient with her sister, wishing she hadn't promised Alana she'd be there for dinner. Alana would make a thing of it, takeout from that Italian grocery she liked, a bottle of wine that would be expensive enough to make the occasion seem celebratory. Alana meant well, but today was not a celebration. How could it be?

But the text was not from Alana.

At Alana's yet? You still haven't given me an answer about the 10th.

The tenth . . . that was less than two weeks away. Christ. Maris stabbed the phone savagely and dropped it into her purse. How Jeff could ask that of her . . . how he could ask anything of her . . . how could people actually look at that man and call him strong, right in front of her face?

Her thighs were sweaty under the thin cotton, heated by the laptop. She closed it and put it back into her purse. Her hands were trembling. She couldn't call Jeff, couldn't stand to hear his voice, not now. She couldn't see Alana, couldn't abide her orchids and slivered almonds and Eileen Fisher linen shifts, her curtain of smooth silvery hair. Her eternal kindness. Maris couldn't deal with one more second of stillness, of forced rest, of the calm and numbness that seemed to be the atmosphere of this strange world that she now lived in.

"Pet," she said, her voice a hoarse whisper. She cleared her throat and tried again, louder. "Pet."

The girl set down her crayon—the drawing taking shape featured a lot of red and orange, with accents of lime and cornflower blue—and smiled at Maris, tugging her earbuds out. "You get ahold of who you needed to?"

"Oh—yes. I found someone to fix the car this afternoon, in an hour. That was lucky."

"That's awesome. You can totally hang out here while they're working on it."

Maris waited for the convulsive shrinking away that was her reaction to kindness these days, an almost instinctive reaction to the pain, but it didn't happen. Her breath eased in and out, her pulse stayed even. She could stay here, for a while. Here felt strangely safe. Anonymous. "Thank you. Listen. I was wondering. I might . . . need to find a hotel, for a few days. Near here. Do you know of somewhere? Not fancy, just clean and, you know, safe."

Pet blinked, frowning. "You mean, while they work on your car? For just a window?"

"Oh no, the car will be done today. It's just that . . . well, I need a few days to, um . . ." *Collect myself. Think. Tie up loose ends.* Nothing that came to mind sounded right.

To not lose my shit. It popped into her head unexpectedly, the voice of Calla's friends. Not Calla—who was proper in a way that chagrined Maris, who wondered if she had inadvertently passed down her own vein of prissiness—but her girlfriends, who were unfettered and ebullient and crude. And this girl, this odd half-Czech girl who could be beautiful but clearly didn't want to—it seemed like something she might say.

"It's just," she tried again, wiping her sweat-dampened hands on her pants. "I'm kind of moving from one life to another. Oh, that sounds so new agey, I'm sorry. I'm getting divorced, and I don't want to live in the town I used to live in anymore, and I'm not exactly sure where I want to go next."

"Wow," Pet said. "That's a lot to handle. Where were you living?"

"Linden Creek. For almost twenty years."

"Oh . . . nice," Pet said. "I mean, I've never been there. But it's nice, right?"

Maris wondered what the girl knew of Linden Creek: third highest per capita income in the Bay Area; overpriced restaurants; manicured parks and neighborhoods full of cookie-cutter mansions. Voted Republican, rare in Northern California.

50

"Yes, very nice. But I need a change."

"But not here." Pet laughed. "I mean, there's nice parts of Oakland. There's all these new condos downtown."

"Maybe." Maris didn't bother to explain that she actually knew her way around at least one truly bad part of Oakland. By comparison, this area was just medium-bad, but unfamiliar. "I mean, that's a ways off. I need to figure out what I want to do first." She waved a hand. "A job . . . if I want to move near family, all of that. I just need a few days to get my shit together."

She snuck the word *shit* in there at the end, breathless, bold. It felt both reckless and tantalizing.

Pet nodded, biting her lip thoughtfully. "There's this big Hyatt down by Chinatown—"

"Not a Hyatt," Maris said quickly. "I need something inexpensive." Which was true, but that wasn't the real reason. She wanted somewhere that she would be ignored. No concierges, no uniformed desk clerks and bellboys. "There were some motels on Telegraph when I came off the highway? You know . . . look like they were built in the seventies?"

Pet raised her eyebrows. "I know the ones you mean. Look . . . they're not like totally safe. A lot of prostitutes. There's been some crime. There was a murder . . . couple years back?"

"Oh," Maris said, embarrassed. She had thought maybe people stayed in them because they were close to the hospital. She'd imagined old people with suitcases, visiting even older relatives, returning to their rooms at night to watch cable TV and wait for the flip of the coin, recovery or death. But yes. Prostitutes, that was much more likely.

"And they're not even all that cheap, like you'd think. I mean, like sixty bucks a night? For that?"

It took Maris a second to realize that she meant the rooms, not the prostitutes. "Well, is there somewhere else, I don't know, even if it's a little more expensive? An old hotel downtown or something?"

"Not really. I mean, other than the hourly ones. It's not like tourists come here." Pet laughed shortly. "Listen, I do have an idea, though. There's an apartment behind this one. Norris—my landlord—he's just fixing a few things before he rents it out again. Guy moved out last week. Maybe you could rent it for a few days?"

"I don't need a whole apartment," Maris said, and then thought—*a whole apartment*. Hers, not Alana's. A place where she could be alone. A place where no one would find her, even if it was just for a short time.

"I mean, it's not fancy at all. And it doesn't have good light like this." Pet swept her arm, indicating the light that spilled luxuriantly across the scarred wood floors, the riot of fabrics on the furniture, the drawings on the walls. "And the guy who was in there—it's probably pretty disgusting."

"I don't care about that." Maris could feel her mind grasping at this chance, this possibility. It would be even more anonymous than a motel, a place no one would think to look for her. "You know . . . it just might work. And I could pay cash up front."

Pet gave a little half smile and picked her phone up from her worktable. Her thumbs flew across the screen, that impossible pace that Calla too had perfected. All of the kids, while she and Jeff had to struggle for every character. "I'm texting

Norris now. He's usually pretty good at getting back. Maybe he can meet you here after work or something."

"Thanks," Maris said once Pet was finished texting. She stood up and shouldered her purse, feeling suddenly oddly formal again. "I suppose I'd better wait for the glass guys out front. Thank you so much for helping me out today. This wasn't . . . planned."

Pet shrugged, yawning. "Hey, in this life, nothing ever is, right?"

seven

PET CAME OUT ONTO the porch as Maris was paying. She was signing the form on the clipboard, watching the glass repair guy out of the corner of her eye to see if he'd reacted to her name, thinking that if she was going to continue this ruse of using her maiden name she would have to get a new credit card.

Pet watched, with her arms folded, as Maris slipped the guy a twenty-dollar bill from her purse. He'd taken only twenty minutes to replace the window. It seemed as though the job should take longer, but he worked quickly and confidently, humming to himself. Maris supposed they did a great business in Oakland. Near the school, cars were broken into sometimes in the brief interlude it took parents to pick up their children. That was the main reason the principal had offered her a space in the teachers' parking lot, a perk she accepted guiltily. He didn't offer it to the student volunteers from the St. Mary's teaching program, who drove old, dented hand-me-down cars.

Her Acura looked good as new again, with its glass replaced. The lease would soon be coming due, but Maris had treated it well and put so few miles on it. Another thing Maris would have to decide: buy this familiar car, or maybe get some little cheap import, easy on gas, another token of trading the old life for the new. But that was not a decision for today.

"They rip you off," Pet observed. "Well, not you, but the insurance company. Whatever the company will pay, plus your deductible, that's what they bill."

That wasn't really a rip-off, Maris thought. Just the way business was done. She'd paid her hundred dollars and she didn't care what other money exchanged hands beyond that. Already she was cherishing this new sealing off of herself, this anonymity.

"Norris called. He's on his way." Pet smiled hopefully. "You're still interested, right?"

"Yes." Maris tried to inject a note of cheer into her voice, but the afternoon was catching up with her, stealing the bravado she'd felt earlier. The sun beat down, unrelenting even as it slid low in the sky. There was no relief in the shade. Her scalp felt greasy, her body stale.

"Good, 'cause I hate to see who else he's going to drag in here. Two renters ago? The guy was a registered sex offender. He *said* all it was was a public indecency thing, he was peeing out back of a bar. But I looked him up and he did something with a kid under fourteen."

"You *asked* him?" Maris was both impressed and troubled by the thought. She would have feared that the question alone would provoke such a person. But then again, she realized the image that came to her mind was the shambling man from the diner. Not all sex offenders looked like what they were. Why should they? Murderers didn't look like what they were, either.

"Yeah." Pet grinned, cocked a hip. She was tough, or trying to be. "I told Norris too—Norris didn't want any trouble, got rid of him."

"How?" Maris knew about tenants' rights issues from the news. It wasn't as bad in Oakland as in the city, but it was still enough to quash the passing interest she and Jeff once had in investing in real estate—luckily, as it turned out, since the crash came almost right after. As it was, it took years for their own house—the one she had driven away from this morning—not to be underwater on the mortgage. "Isn't it almost impossible to evict someone without all kinds of paperwork?"

"Oh, I imagine Norris *warned* him," Pet said. There was complicity in her grin: the kind of warning, then, that fell outside the bounds of paperwork and regulations. What was Maris considering getting into? "Speaking of whom."

A black SUV turned slowly into the drive that ran next to the house. Maris brushed a leaf from her blouse while she listened to the engine turn off, the door opening.

A man walked slowly back toward the front of the house, staring into his phone. Even as he rounded the steps he was staring at the little screen. He didn't look at Maris and Pet until he was a few feet away.

"Hey, Norris, this is Mary," Pet said.

Maris held out her hand. "So nice to meet you."

He grunted and gave her hand a limp, reluctant shake, the kind a man gives a woman when he doesn't expect her to shake hands at all.

Norris was tall, his posture stiff, his skin both freckled and brown. His hair was short, his cheekbones and chin strong and jutting, his mouth set in an implacable frown. He wore a short-sleeved dress shirt buttoned almost to the top, his undershirt visible through the striped fabric, a plastic pocket protector in the breast pocket. The brass plating was wearing off the buckle of his belt, revealing dull metal underneath.

"You interested in renting the apartment short term," he said, looking not into her eyes but somewhere around her chin.

"Yes, I am." Maris was conscious of a straightening of her spine, the meticulous speech that she so disliked in herself, but that was almost unavoidable when she was nervous.

"Just how long we talking?"

"Well, for several days." She made a snap decision. "Two weeks."

He thought for a moment, twisting his mouth. "Most people like to move on the weekend. I could get someone in here this weekend, likely. But two weeks, starting today, that puts us to a Tuesday."

"Okay, through the weekend, then," Maris said quickly. "Two weeks and, what would that be, three days."

Norris nodded slowly. "Place is a mess, though. That's the thing. I was going to clean it up tonight."

Behind him, Maris saw Pet roll her eyes. So Norris was trying to work her—that was okay. Now that she'd seen him speak, he didn't frighten her.

"I'll do the cleaning myself. I don't mind." And she didn't—she would have gone over every surface anyway, just to expunge any trace of another person's presence. She wanted to be the deepest kind of alone, with no one else's shadows around.

"Paint's pretty bad, though, is the thing," he said. "I'll be repainting it before the next tenant. You'd have to take it the way it is. And the floors, they're pretty scratched up. Wood, you know. No carpet."

"I don't mind," Maris repeated. A wood floor could be scrubbed; carpet couldn't. Carpets held on to stains, especially the worst kind. Vomit, urine, blood. In her days of presiding over a household with a baby, a child, dinner parties, and craft projects, she'd cleaned any number of things off the floors and furniture. It was a matter of pride to Maris that she didn't leave the worst stains for the house-cleaners to deal with, at least not without making a token effort first.

This was what had appeared, in her path. If Maris believed in God, she might have thought he'd given her a gift, directing her toward this apartment. Or at least a consolation prize, she who needed consolation so badly.

"Seventeen days—that'll be eight hundred. Up front, cash. And another five hundred security deposit. Also cash."

"Hey," Pet objected.

"That's fine," Maris said crisply. A cash payment could save her from having to pass a credit check, a raft of paper-work that would probably include her social security number, driver's license, other things with her name on them.

Thirteen hundred dollars, if he kept the deposit, was still less than she would pay for a motel.

"It's fully furnished," Norris said. Now it was his turn to sound uncertain. "Linens too. Plates and cups, silverware, all that."

"Can I see it?"

He grunted in affirmation, glaring at Pet until she shrugged and backed off. In her doorway she turned. "Good luck. I have to head to work. It's the Coal Mine, on MacArthur. Come by if you can. If you want to. I'll be there till closing."

She closed her door. If the apartment didn't work out, this would all be over, this fragile stack of hopeful maybes. Maris wouldn't be going to any bar then, to visit this strange new acquaintance. Probably she would give up and drive down to Alana's.

Alana. Oh no. As Maris followed Norris down the driveway, squeezing past his SUV, she stole a glance at her phone: three texts from Alana, but without her reading glasses she couldn't read them. She stuffed the phone back into her purse: it would have to wait.

The back door had a hand-lettered sign, a piece of wood sanded and painted, nice: 126B 1/2, in an old-fashioned type, gold on red.

"Upstairs, that's me, 126A. Front apartment, Pet's, that's 126B."

She saw Norris stiffen just as the smell reached her nose: garbage, rot, chemicals. He put a hand on the doorjamb and spoke testily over his shoulder. "I told you I hadn't had a chance to clean."

Maris took a breath, squared her shoulders, and nodded. If it was too awful, she would just leave. She hadn't given him any money yet. Still, she was curious now, she needed to see.

Norris flicked a switch. The overhead fixture had a flickering bulb, lighting the main room weakly. It was both kitchen and living room, a big square space lined with pine cabinets on two walls, avocado green appliances, shredded curtains with an old-fashioned vegetable print blurred by dust. This was the house's original kitchen, and Maris guessed it hadn't been touched since the building was converted. In the sink were dishes—coffee cups and aluminum pots and a scratched nonstick pan with what looked like scrambled eggs crusted on it, patches of what might have been spaghetti sauce on the counter. A trash can with no lid, clouded by flies, the blackened skins of a banana resting on wadded plastic and crushed paper plates. Something coated the floor under her feet, both gritty and sticky.

A small shape dashed by along the wall. Maris expelled her breath, and was glad she didn't shriek. Back home, a mouse would have had her running for Jeff.

Norris kicked something out of the way, a wrapper or trash bag. "If I'd had tonight," he snapped, as if it was her fault.

"Let me see the rest."

"Now hang on." Norris paused again, barring her way through the passage to the rest of the apartment with his body. "Upstairs I have a new mattress and box spring, never used. I was going to set it up for the next tenant. You help me get it down the stairs . . ."

Maris nodded once, noncommittally. Maybe. But she had to see the rest. Just how bad had it gotten, for the one who came before her?

Norris snapped another light switch and let her pass. A tiny room led off the kitchen, barely wide enough for the single bed and old painted wood nightstand. A small square window over the head of the bed was strung with tangled metal blinds. The linens had been pulled most of the way off the bed, revealing a stained pink mattress, sagging toward the center.

Maris knew that most mattresses, at the end of their useful lives, were stained. Even those belonging to the most meticulous. Her mother's, before she died . . . the one Jeff had when they were dating. But the stains on this one were too large, too dark. She blinked and turned away, focusing her gaze on the wall. *Plaster and lath,* she made herself think, a purposeful distraction. *In surprisingly good shape.* Her gaze traveled down: scratched, dark-stained wood floors, a few dust bunnies, nothing terrible there. Finally, she forced herself to look at the bed again. The comforter was covered in pastel swirls, a pattern from the eighties, synthetic and pilled. An edge had unraveled, the batting leaking. A sour odor rose from the sheets.

"There's somewhere to dispose of the old?" Maris asked, her voice formal and unnatural.

"I'll call someone. Whatever you put out on the curb, I can have it picked up in the morning."

"All of that goes too." She pointed at the mound of linens, the pillow coming out of its case, as stained as the mattress.

"Yeah, I know," Norris sighed, as though they had already agreed. "I have an extra fan, probably fit that window."

"What was this, anyway?" Maris asked. "The laundry room? Pantry?"

"Yeah."

It wasn't an answer, but she didn't press. All that was left was the bathroom. She went in first, expecting a filthier version of Pet's, but when she turned on the light, she got the first nice surprise of the day.

It was dirty, of course. Along the baseboards, the floor was covered in a brown film embedded with dust fibers; a mildewed plastic shower curtain hung from only half its rings, the rest torn. The toilet seat was pink faux-marble. But the bathroom was large, the old tub was in good shape, framed in an arched opening. There was beautiful octagonal black-and-white tile on the floor; the walls were accented with a row of pink tiles on point, the grout fairly clean. The overhead fixture was milk glass and the medicine cabinet's mirror was etched in a wheat pattern. Built-in shelves held only a razor, a flattened tube of Crest, an empty bottle of Advil on its side—there was room for everything Maris had ever kept in their bathroom at home.

"All right," she said briskly. "I'll take it. If it's okay with you, I'd like to get the mattress taken care of now."

Norris returned moments later with a box of black plastic lawn and leaf bags. "You can have these," he said, handing the box to her like a gift. "Trash pickup's not until Monday, but whatever you can put out tonight, my guy will haul it off."

Maris was glad Norris didn't offer to help her clean. She didn't want help. She stuffed the comforter into a bag while he pulled off the sheets, trying not to think about her hands touching the fabric. A cloud of dust lifted into the air. Maris imagined the tiny motes, the furred mounds under the bed— dead skin, whiskers, pubic hairs, who knew what else—and fought off a faint wave of nausea. She picked up the pillow by a corner and dropped it into the bag, then tied the top tightly. A double knot.

Norris stood with his own lumpy, half-filled bag in hand. He had lost momentum. "I'll take this end," Maris said, finding the plastic handles along the mattress.

They made several trips, working in the awkwardly polite way of people who don't know each other well. With your own husband, you anticipate his moves—some people fold sheets together multiple times, some want the other person to meet them, an origami dance. "To your left a little," Maris said.

"I think we'll have to turn it sideways," Norris replied.

After the third trip, the trash bags sat on top of the mattress and box spring on the sidewalk. In the front of the house, a single light burned through Pet's windows. She'd closed the curtains before she left for work, so Maris saw only the haloed glow through the bright fabric.

Norris opened the front door with a key. They went up the stairs to the left of Pet's door. Another key, a neat shiny brass lock. Inside wasn't what Maris expected. The furniture was tidy, simple, almost Danish-looking. The floors were refinished, and there was an Oriental rug that looked, if not valuable, at least hand-knotted of real wool. A hutch held row after row of fussy cut crystal and teacups hanging from little hooks.

"Down here." Norris was back to being gruff. They passed a small, tidy kitchen, two closed doors. At the back of the apartment, the second bedroom, as spare as a convent. Two twin beds, the mattresses still in their plastic. The headboards would look at home in a little girl's room, curved and painted cream with pink rose bouquets. There was nothing else in the room except an entire wall of neatly sealed and labeled moving boxes.

Mom Dining Room.

Mom Pictures.

Mom Papers 2001–2003.

Like that.

Another two trips down the stairs. Maris insisted they lean the mattress and box spring against the kitchen wall where the sofa was. On closer inspection they looked like they'd been purchased long ago, the labels yellowing, the plastic cracking. At least the plastic would protect them from the filthy floor until she could get the little bedroom cleaned. "I'll be able to get them onto the bed myself," she said, needing Norris to leave so she could be alone, and he didn't argue.

"There's some cleaning supplies in the garage, if you want to use them," he said. "Just remember to put them back when you're done." He wrote down the code to the padlock on a pizza flyer that he found on the counter, using a pen from a drawer.

"Just one thing," he said, on his way out the door. "Seeing as this is just short term, anything you buy for this place, I can't reimburse you."

And then Maris was alone, the kitchen finally cooling off as the sun slid down across the bay.

eight

RON HAUNTED THE HALLS of the office as people left for the day. The company had been renamed after he sold it, and half the current staff had been hired since, but his presence still had the power to intimidate. It was Karl too, of course; he had been forced to accept that no one ever looked at him anymore without the knowledge of what his son had done in their eyes. Instead of making him a pariah, though, it seemed to have had the opposite effect: people were deferential, even awed.

Ron alone knew how little he actually did anymore. That was a result not so much of any intention on his part but of the shell game of responsibility in the upper reaches of the company, especially since they had acquired two smaller competitors in the last eighteen months. After the arrest and during the trial, Ron had been excused from many responsibilities and given credit for work others had done. But even after he'd made it clear that he was back full time, people treated him gingerly and made allowances he never asked for.

Sometimes he was grateful for this extended recess. It allowed him to participate in the rituals of the workplace and, more important, keep him out of the house while what he was really doing was . . . *processing*, he supposed, to borrow a term from the airy-fairy folks in human resources, people he'd personally put in place because he knew the supporting statistics even if he'd never personally felt the need for such coddling and hand-holding. His involvement in the various team-building and workplace enhancement exercises was genial, even avuncular, popping in occasionally but always slipping away before he could be called upon to share, to feel, to emote.

So he walked the halls, tapped at his keyboard, dropped in on meetings, kept his door open for consultation. A part of him was present—was even, occasionally, the nimble strategist he used to be. And the rest: a gentle, quiet, whirr; a damping down, a wall carefully maintained.

At six fifteen on Tuesday, the only people left in the office were a small team working together in the conference room. Ron waved to them as he left, his stomach already tightening with the prospect of going home. He stopped on the way for a bag of shockingly expensive peaches and a bunch of delphiniums. These gifts for his wife were a regular habit, and well compensated, but today they were also a defense, a bribe.

When he walked in the door, Deb took the packages from him with barely a comment, clearly distracted. "You said you were going to be late," she said, and he remembered that when they talked before lunch, he'd mentioned he might get a beer with Frank—but Frank had to be at his kid's band concert.

"Sorry," he said, bending for a kiss on the cheek which she did not return.

"It's just that Kami's here."

Now he heard the soft cough from the living room, registered that the car in front of the house didn't belong to a stranger. "Oh," he said carefully.

"We were almost done—"

"You know what, I need to make a call anyway. I'll do it upstairs."

He went up without waiting for her to answer. There was no call; they both knew that. Ron's relationship with Kami had started well enough, in the early days when he'd still been able to make himself imagine a version of events where it was all just a terrible misunderstanding, where Karl had been in the wrong place at the wrong time, confused with the other, the *real* killer. Back then, he'd drunk down her zeal, her practiced rhetoric, as greedily as Deb. Now, though, he couldn't look at her without wondering what sort of woman would do this sort of poorly paid, hopeless work on purpose.

The Youth Innocence Project was connected with Cal State Dylon Beach, and nearly all of the youth they were trying to exonerate were black, poor, and had been questionably represented by state-appointed defenders. Moreover, their staff consisted mostly of law faculty and interns. Kami was the exception: a program coordinator, a glorified office manager who had taken a personal interest in Karl and offered her help outside the official scope of the program but with their hazy, tacit approval. Or so she had claimed, and so Deb had chosen to believe.

Soon after Karl's arrest, Ron had begun to understand the hopelessness of the cause. Despite Karl's insistence (and on this he had never wavered; Ron had to give him credit for that) that there had been another man there that night, a stranger, someone that a neighbor named Gloria Kirsch (seventy-eight years old, hard of hearing, self-reported insomniac) had reportedly seen peering into windows around the neighborhood and had even called the police about the prior week, the evidence against Karl had been too damning. He and Calla had left the party together, after multiple people reported seeing them argue and Karl pushing or shoving Calla. Two of Calla's best friends swore that she had said she was "afraid of" Karl in the days leading up to her death, and one said that when she broke up with him, he'd threatened her. And most damning of all, Karl's car—the eight-year-old Explorer that Deb and Ron had bought when he passed his driver's test—had traces of mud in the wheel wells that matched the makeup of the soil at Byron Ranch.

The more impassioned Deb's insistence on Karl's innocence, the more convinced Ron became that he was guilty. The divide seemed a natural if tragic one; it was a mother's job to defend her offspring, just as it was a father's job to provide expectations and consequences. In this, Deb could be said to have succeeded where Ron failed, and it was perhaps this knowledge that led him to support his wife without agreeing with her.

But even so, he couldn't tolerate Kami, with her shapeless hand-dyed clothes and her head wraps (ridiculous, on a middle-aged white woman) and her maddening habit of holding on to his hand too long and staring into his eyes as though she were trying to bore holes into them with her gaze.

For twenty minutes, Ron sat on the love seat in the master bedroom, attempting to watch an episode of *Ice Road Truckers*. When he heard the front door close, he shut off the television and steeled himself. A few moments later Deb appeared, her cheeks flushed, smiling tentatively.

"Ron. It's—" She gestured, taking in the whole room. "It's amazing, really. With what's happened to Arthur, and

68

I mean, I wouldn't wish it on him, he's not a bad man, but now we can start over. With everything we've learned. Kami says—"

"We're not appealing."

She looked as though he'd slapped her, her smile quivering out like a snuffed candle. After a moment she came and sat on the love seat, as far from him as possible, leaving several inches between their thighs. "You know it's not our decision, if it comes to that."

"It is if we're paying for it." He knew what she was saying, a threat she'd circled before but never presented head-on: Karl, at almost twenty, was a legal adult, entitled to make his own decisions.

"I have my own money."

Ron raised an eyebrow, surprised—even if it was an argument that didn't even bear considering. The paltry inheritance Deb had received when her mother died a few years back wasn't even enough to warrant a review with the accountant. Still, it wasn't like her to come back at him like that.

"But it isn't *about* money," Deb said, recovering. "It's about *our son* sitting in jail when he didn't do this thing. When he should be getting on with his life, putting all this behind him."

"Deb." Ron raised his hand, let it drop weakly. Once, only once, he had told her exactly what he thought, that while it might have been the result of a moment of unchecked emotion, even an accident, he believed his son had taken his former girlfriend's life on a warm June night the prior year. Deb had been so devastated by what she considered to be a betrayal that she barely spoke to him for a week and a half. Since then, this gulf between them went unnamed and unspoken.

"It won't cost anything to at least *talk* to them," she said, the doggedness returning to her expression, the manic brightness to her eyes making Ron uneasy. It occurred to him that maternal protectiveness might, in the end, prove a stronger impulse than marital loyalty. "Kami has two lawyers in mind. They're both interested, according to her. The opportunity is a good one for them, they might be willing to—"

"A good opportunity?" Ron interrupted, recovering. "You know what that means, Deb. It's just publicity for them. You seriously want to go through that all over again? Reporters at the door all hours of the day? Chasing you around the Safeway parking lot?"

"But we're in a gated community now, we've got—"

"I *know* we're in a gated goddamn community," Ron said, biting off each word. "I was the one who sold our home and took a huge goddamn loss on it, frankly, just so I could come home at night and not worry who was following me. But you think Vashi's going to be able to stop them at the gatehouse this time, if things get stirred up again? Or Pearl? You think they're any match for Calida Beale and her goddamn tank driver?"

Tears welled in Deb's eyes; Calida Beale was a Channel 2 reporter who'd brought a crew to the house the day before the verdict was read: one of the "cameramen" broke through the police barricades and somehow got away before he could be identified and charged. Channel 2 had run the footage of Deb with her arms over her face, trying to get to the car, her purse falling to the ground.

"Vashi can . . . Pearl isn't . . ." Deb's voice petered out as she struggled to compose herself. Ron felt bad: Deb had worked hard to cultivate a good relationship with the security guards who staffed the entrance to Cresta Hills, but even she had to know that the sixty-something, arthritic Vashi, and Pearl, with her long acrylic nails and mountainous hips, had little power to protect them.

"Deb," Ron said gently, after several moments had ticked by. He put his arm around her and pulled her close, her head nestled against his shoulder. She didn't resist. They were still good, he thought, for a couple that had been through what they had been through. They soldiered on, in spite of everything. He had to be grateful for that. "Look. I'm sorry if I overreacted. I just don't want to see you hurt again. *All* of us . . . hurt again."

She went stiff, then pushed him away. "*Hurt*." She practically spat the word.

Ron backpedaled madly in his mind. This, also, was new, this minefield of his wife's emotions. But before he could trace the latest trigger, she yanked a tissue from the box on the coffee table and wiped it savagely under her eyes.

"You weren't thinking about *hurting* me when you went out on the bridge," she said hoarsely. "You made that decision all by yourself, didn't you? Didn't think about how it would affect me. About how I would feel. So maybe I get to make some decisions without you too." She gave up on the tissue and wiped her eyes with the heels of her hands, smearing her makeup.

"Oh, Jesus, Deb, I never—honey. Honey, please." His voice broke, surprising him, and Deb looked up at him and sighed.

"Forget it. It's over. But what I'm doing, it's for *Karl*. Don't you see that I can never quit, not if it's for him? Whatever I need to do, I'll do. And I need you, Ron, I do. I don't need you to agree with me, I'm not asking you that. Just . . . don't try to stop me. Okay? I tried to keep you from having to deal with Kami, I know you don't like her. I didn't expect you home until later. I'll . . . . you won't have to do anything, really. I'll arrange everything. But . . ."

What was he going to be asked to do? He steeled himself: in the barter system of their marriage, during their rare arguments, he would extend the first gesture of peace and she would collapse like a pretty parasol. But she was different now. Things had changed.

"It's Karl," she said briskly. She spoke quickly, as if she was trying to get out a speech she'd rehearsed. "It's the stress of being transferred to Panamint, the new environment, new rules, new everything. And, just, you know. But he's balking at this. He's not sure . . . I need you to talk to him. Get him on board."

"Wait, wait," Ron said. "You're saying Karl doesn't even *want* to appeal?"

Deb tightened her mouth, blinking. "It's not that—look, you haven't seen him in a long time—"

"I went with you when he was transferred—"

"But other than that. Which, I'm not blaming you. But you haven't talked to him. Haven't seen . . . he's not himself."

Of course he's not himself, Ron wanted to yell, *he's a convicted murderer in state lockup*. It had been hard enough to see his son in Montair County Jail while he awaited sentencing, and it wasn't just the distance, either, though Panamint was nearly two hours away.

"But you want me to talk him into this? Isn't it kind of up to him, Deb? I mean, he's an adult and—"

"He's my *son*." She glared at him defiantly, not even bothering to pretend to be chastened by her mistake: *her* son, not *theirs*. Her chest rose and fell with her breathing. Maybe that's how she really saw it—that Karl was hers alone, that Ron had abdicated.

"All right," Ron finally said. Yes, he felt guilty for not visiting more often; yes, he'd needed a reason to do better. And he could go alone; Deb would have no way to police what he said to Karl.

"Good. I made you an appointment for tomorrow. Three o'clock."

"You . . ." Ron stared at his wife, at her chin thrust out, the challenge in her gaze. It was audacious, especially for Deb, who had until the past year deferred to him in most things. She had been that kind of wife: old-fashioned, pampered, soft and pretty. A homemaker, in the traditional sense. A helpmate. The wind, as Ron had joked at their twentieth-anniversary party, beneath his wings.

"I know you might have to move some things around at work," she continued, "but I was lucky to get the slot."

Ron nodded. She could afford to be conciliatory, now that she'd won. He could have refused, argued that he couldn't get away from work, forced her to move it to another day. But the online visit scheduling system was notoriously flaky and unforgiving. Deb had it down to a science, logging on the minute new blocks of time opened up to schedule her weekly visits. Getting a cancellation was never guaranteed.

Ron was no longer sure where the line was, marking the debts they owed each other. But it was clear that his wife was not going to give up. "All right."

"Thank you," Deb whispered, sounding exhausted by her victory. After a moment Ron reached for her, almost expecting to be rebuffed, but she sagged against him, letting him wrap his arms around her. He could smell her perfume and her faintly sour breath.

The prison sentence that Karl had received was only the start. Who knew what reparations lay ahead—for all of them?

The rest of the evening settled into brittle normalcy. Deb heated up some dinner for Ron; he ate it in the living room, watching Netflix, while Deb knitted. At eleven they went upstairs. Ron brushed his teeth and got ready for bed; when he came out of the bathroom, the bedroom was empty.

On a rare impulse (he ordinarily wasn't the sort of man to be overly concerned with how his wife occupied herself in her own time; he was a believer in practical distance in a marriage), he walked quietly down the hall to the bedroom Deb had converted to her "office." Here, she had a desk, fabric-covered bulletin boards, her sewing machine, bins of wrapping paper, and boxes of Karl's school papers. Shelves containing mementos and bins of craft supplies. A little television and a chaise where she sometimes liked to lie while she talked on the phone to her sisters.

She'd left the door open, and she was sitting, as Ron had known she would be, at the desk, haloed in the light of a porcelain lamp. In front of her was the carved wooden box that her great-grandfather had made and brought with him from Finland. Her hand rested on the top. There was a key; Ron had seen it once, a tarnished, pretty little brass one on a faded silk ribbon. Ron didn't know where Deb kept the key, and he didn't see it now. The box was closed, her hands folded on top, her head bowed.

Everyone was entitled to their secrets, Ron thought, turning back down the hallway toward their bedroom. Lord knew that he had his own. He'd wondered, of course, about the box, especially in the months after Karl was gone when she first got into the habit of taking it down from its place on the shelf in the evenings.

But tonight, for the first time, he began to wonder if there was something in the box that he ought to see. Some secret clue to his son, his wife; something he could use to spin the fragile strands that held them all together.

nine

MARIS DELETED HER FIRST attempt at a reply to Alana. There had been a fourth text while they were moving the bedding—Srsly beginning to worry CALL ME—but how could she explain what had happened? It would seem to Alana that Maris had made a decision, but it didn't feel that way to her at all. Sitting on this rickety metal kitchen chair, after she had wiped its brown vinyl seat and back with a wadded sheet of newspaper dampened under the kitchen faucet, she felt as though she had arrived here on a raft swept along a river by a current. The river hadn't been especially frightening; it wasn't the stuff of cartoons—rushing rapids and jagged rocks and deadly waterfalls. The last few days had been more like the Mississippi River after a spring flood: dull, lugubrious, devoid of beauty, studded with potential hazards whose threat was impossible to discern until you were upon them.

And she, to carry the clunky metaphor to its conclusion as she sat sweating under the flickering light fixture in the stinking kitchen, was the near-drowned dog that got in over its head, fought hard just to stay afloat, and was now lying exhausted on a muddy bank, more dead than not. And this was all she could come up with:

> So sorry I didn't text earlier. Decided to stay w a friend
> tonight.
> Long story. Will call u tomorrow.

She powered the phone all the way off. Her charger had been in her luggage. She would have to buy a new one tomorrow so she could call Alana.

So much to do tomorrow. If she could just sleep for now . . . if she spread newspapers on the floor, then put the box spring on top of the newspapers. Slept in her clothes. She was certainly tired enough, exhaustion slamming her moments after Norris left.

Except what if whatever was on the floor seeped through? And how could she sleep with the smell, the still-hot air, the taste in her mouth that she had no toothbrush to scrub away?

And Norris had someone picking up the trash in the morning. If she missed this chance, she would have to live with the mess until Monday. Even if she bagged all the trash, she wouldn't be able to leave it out in case animals got into it. It would have to sit in these two rooms, ballast that would keep the space tainted.

"I can do this," Maris said out loud. As mantras went, it wasn't much of one. That was what happened when you lost a child, though: you didn't have enough of yourself left to come up with much. You were all crushed shards and severed bits, and when Nina told you *just a phrase, it can be anything at all, it can be as simple as "I can do this,"* your broken brain echoed back like you were only a toddler yourself.

I can do this had gotten her through the days with all of their terrible milestones. It had been a barely adequate trick, and Maris had put in a barely adequate performance, but she was here, wasn't she, she was still breathing, and besides, the next few days didn't require her to be anything more than barely adequate.

She took the key that Norris had given her and worked it onto her keychain, next to her house keys and car keys and the key to Alana's condo. The keychain was an enameled-pink metal daisy that Calla had given her for Mother's Day a month before her death. It had come from the Coach store and Calla had paid for it with her babysitting money. The enamel was wearing off at the edges. Maris let herself out, a bright spotlight on the back porch coming on automatically, triggered by a motion sensor.

It had cooled off considerably outside. She headed for her car, parked half a block away. It was crazy to walk around this neighborhood by herself after dark. It was asking for trouble. At least she should hold her keys between her knuckles, the way she'd seen on *Oprah,* ready to slash, to aim for the eyes. But Maris left her keys in her purse and her purse over her shoulder. No one was going to come after her, not here, not now. She didn't have that kind of luck. Whatever bitter fate had cursed her wanted her alive.

Safe in her car, she passed the shuttered diner where she'd first met Pet. In apartment windows she saw figures moving, the blue glare of televisions. She found the Walgreens that she remembered from this morning—had it only been this morning? It shared an intersection with a Carl's Junior and a mortuary. Cars drove by her, speeding through yellow lights in the intersection. As Maris waited for the light to change, a woman pushed a stroller in front of her and talked into her phone, staring at Maris as she passed. The baby was wide awake, waving its tiny fists.

Inside the Walgreens, the air-conditioning hit Maris along with a cool, chemical smell. She picked up a blue basket and filled it with Windex, Comet, bleach, green Scotch-Brite pads, a roll of paper towels, and two packages of cheap thin rags before going back to the front of the store and exchanging the basket for a cart. She added a plastic bucket, a broom and dustpan, a two-pack of rubber gloves, another package of rags, and a small box fan. A twelve-pack of bottled water, feeling a twinge of guilt because she hadn't packed her stainless water bottle, though it would have just gotten stolen anyway. A box of Fiber One bars, toilet paper, a toothbrush and toothpaste, hair elastics, shampoo and soap and a bottle of Jergens moisturizer, which had been her mother's brand.

At the register, a *People* magazine, a pack of gum. If the clerk thought either Maris or her purchases were noteworthy, she gave no clue. Maris signed the charge on the little device and headed back to her car.

Two men were standing behind it, talking in low voices. They looked like they were in their twenties. Maybe younger. They were black. Despite the heat, they wore jeans, not shorts. Silver flashed in their mouths.

Maris had worked with boys who looked just like these, but that was not what gave her the courage to push her cart within inches of their legs and look directly in their faces.

"Excuse me, I need to get in my trunk," she said. She was ready to shove them out of the way if necessary. She just didn't care.

But they stepped away.

Her energy returned when she tore open the package of gloves. She pressed them to her nose and inhaled the latex scent, crowding out the odors of rot and filth. That had been almost three hours ago.

With her hair in a ponytail and her pants rolled up, Maris had swept the tiny bedroom, then cleaned the walls first with a rag, wiping off cobwebs and loose flakes of paint, then again with more rags dipped into hot water mixed with Comet. She dabbed at the corners of the room with a rag hooked on the broom handle. She changed the water in the bucket before washing the bed frame and finally the floors. The rags she used on the floor were gray with dirt when she was done.

Maris thought about quitting for the night once she got the mattress and box spring in place, the fan balanced in the window, and moved her purse onto the bedroom floor. This one room was clean enough now, and the fan blew cool air scented with jasmine into the room. But her clothes were damp with sweat and she wasn't tired anymore.

She filled three bulging trash bags just with the garbage strewn around the kitchen, the abandoned toiletries in the bathroom, the contents of the refrigerator and the food left in the cabinets, mostly open boxes of cereal and cans of chili. She threw away the curtains from the kitchen window, the torn shower curtain and all the grimy rings, two dead plants in their pots, a brand-new package of men's V-neck undershirts she found in the dresser that served as an end table next to the sofa in the kitchen. She ran steaming hot water in the sink and added bleach along with the dish soap, and soaked the dishes while she went through the drawers and threw out everything rusted or bent or broken. She tore a glove on something sharp in the junk drawer while she was shaking its contents into the trash, and had to put on the second pair. She washed the counters and spread out clean rags to serve as a dish drainer, then washed the dishes and stacked them in a teetering pile.

She managed to sweep the kitchen and the bathroom before her aching muscles and back finally throbbed dully with exhaustion. There were now nine trash bags on the curb, and the smell of garbage was very faint, overlaid with bleach. The apartment was still far from perfect, but she could start with the kitchen and bathroom floors tomorrow. There was satisfaction to be had in the thick gray dirt transferring to the rags, the streaks of clean floor showing through as she worked.

In the bedroom, she stripped off her pants and shirt and shoes in the dark. As she folded the clothes, something fell from the pocket of her pants and skittered across the floor. Maris got down on her hands and knees and felt under the bed, coming up with the tiny square of glass that she'd picked up from the street so many hours ago.

She held it in her hand, turning it this way and that, seeing it sparkle under the overhead light fixture. She set it gently on the windowsill that she had carefully cleaned, next to the borrowed fan.

Her body was slick with sweat, her own odor in her nostrils. She left her hair in its ponytail and lay down on the mattress in her bra and underwear. Through the top of the window, above the fan, she could see the back of the neighbor's house, where a light still burned in an upstairs window.

A night owl, an insomniac, or just someone who needed a lamp left on for company? Maris had been all three in her life. She closed her eyes. *Babygirl, my babygirl,* she whispered. The fan whispered back, scenting the room with jasmine. It almost felt like comfort.

ten

THE SOUND OF KNOCKING penetrated her featureless dream and Maris came up gasping for air, the way she had so many times before. Her stomach churned and she pushed off the sheets, ready to run and check the locks on the doors, the drapes pulled tight at the windows, keeping them out, all of them with their endless questions and false sympathy and simpering greasy solicitations, the reporters and sensation peddlers anxious to flay her open and expose her beating heart and seeping lifeblood.

She blinked, once, twice. This room. This place. This faint smell of bleach and rot, her own stink rising from her body. The knocking came again, not loud but insistent.

Maris pulled on yesterday's clothes. The pants were creased and ringed with dirt, the shirt wrinkled and reeking. She shoved her feet into her sandals and walked to the door stepping on the leather backs, seeing on the linoleum floor the smeared places she'd tried to clean last night.

Pet stood outside, holding a brown paper Safeway bag in one hand and a small white paper sack in the other. "Hey, you survived your first night," she said. "I saw your car out front. I figured either you took the room or someone stole your purse and they'd find your body in Lake Merritt. Joke," she added, almost apologetically.

Maris was acutely aware of how she must look and smell. "I would invite you in . . ." she tried.

"No, no, I have to run, I've got class. I just thought you might want to borrow some clothes for today. And hey, I'm working again tonight, the place next door has a chicken wing special on Wednesdays, they're good. It's $8.99 for wings and fries and all that pickled shit they serve with it. I'll buy you a beer if you come."

Why is she being so nice? the voice in Maris's head demanded. Distrust had become her resting state, another toxic pebble rattling along with her grief and anger.

But she couldn't bear to wear these wretched clothes another second. "Thank you," she said, accepting the bags.

"That's a bagel," Pet said, handing her the white bag. "Place a few blocks from here. They're supposedly 'Brooklyn style,' whatever that means." A mirthful giggle bubbled from her. "Brooklyn by way of Oakland. I read somewhere they're saying Oakland's going to be the next Brooklyn. Hipsters and baby strollers and shit. Anyway. Hope to see you if you get a chance."

"I really do appreciate this," Maris said. "I'm going to do laundry and pick up some things today, and then I can return this to you."

Pet waved. "It's just old stuff." She peered around Maris unself-consciously. "You got a lot done last night. I saw the bags on the curb. It must have been pretty bad, right? That guy." She shook her head, whistling.

"I think there's still a long way to go."

"Well, you're only here for a couple of weeks, don't go too crazy. It's not like Norris is going to cut you a break on rent for it."

A couple of weeks. It echoed in her head, stirring up anxiety for the future that Maris couldn't deal with right now.

"It's not like I have anything better to do," she said, forcing a smile that felt like someone else's.

The Oakland Target wasn't like the one in Linden Creek. The checkout clerk asked if Maris had brought her own bags and she felt guilty saying no. The plastic bag ban hadn't reached Linden Creek yet—the affluent were slower to adopt the measures that gave Northern California its reputation for environmental fervor.

In Pet's denim shorts—Maris checked the label, suspecting they were men's shorts, awkwardly long and much washed—and faded T-shirt with the logo of a cereal brand that Pet couldn't possibly be old enough to remember, Maris felt shabby. She'd washed her sandals under the sink and the leather was unpleasantly damp against her skin. Her hair had air dried into a frizzy mass, but at least it was clean, and she'd scrubbed her skin until it was pink and raw, cleaning under her fingernails with the sharp corner of the toothpaste tube. In the mirror she looked like her mother's friends back in Kansas: plain, graying, middle-aged professors and attorneys who claimed not to care a bit about their appearance.

Four hundred and eighteen dollars later, Maris had purchased two pairs of shorts, two sleeveless shirts, a six-pack of underwear, and a bra. A full set of bedding, the comforter and sheets and bed skirt all in one bag. Lightbulbs and a pillow and towel and hand towel and two washcloths and a shower curtain. On a whim, a romance novel with a pretty embossed cover—the book that had been stolen from the car was a dense, dull book-club pick that she hadn't been able to get through. And all the toiletries and basic makeup to get her through until she figured out her next move. Makeup was a hell of a lot cheaper here than at Nordstrom, a fact Maris knew but hadn't thought about for a while. It had been such a pleasure to take Calla to the makeup counter at fourteen and help her pick out her first mascara, her first blush. Now Maris had a plastic sack full of Cover Girl just like she'd bought with her own money over thirty years ago because her mother was too busy and didn't believe in makeup anyway.

She bought a coffee at the Starbucks counter wedged in the corner of the Target, and pushed her cart to a table along the wall where there was an outlet. Peeling off the packaging of the phone charger she'd bought, she plugged it in and then wiped off the table with a paper napkin. The phone buzzed a series of sounds as it powered up, the emails and texts arriving in pings and chimes as Maris sipped. She closed her eyes and focused on the rich black coffee, imagining the caffeine entering her bloodstream, cutting through her torpor like the harsh Comet dissolving the sticky grime on the floor last night. She could do this—she was already twenty-four hours into the abrupt U-turn she had made of her life, and she was still breathing, still moving forward—she'd even, possibly, made a new friend. Although she had been passive in that—Pet had been dropped from the sky, a gift. Still. It was a reversal worth noting—for the last year, most of Maris's relationships had shrunk and withered until she was left only with the ones who had no choice.

Like Alana. Maris took another sip and then picked up the phone. The dense string of texts made her heart sink, especially when she saw that most of them were from Jeff, not Alana.

Call me.

Please give me a call when you get a chance.

This is really important.

Why did he care? As far as Maris knew, he'd been back to the house only the one time, two days ago, to pick up the things he'd forgotten in his haste to move out. And before that, he had been as absent as her—more so, even, because he'd been honing his secret-keeping skills for so much longer.

Jeff knew—she had made sure he knew—how much she loathed him. How much she blamed him. And he hadn't fought back, he wasn't the type. He was a retreater, an abdicator. A coward.

This is really important or I wouldn't bother you.

At one time, such a text would have meant one thing only to Maris: *Calla, oh my God, something has happened to Calla.* That was gone, and nothing else mattered. But it wasn't wise to ignore Jeff for too long. He had a vindictive side few saw, a petty vengefulness he unleashed in private. Probably his text had to do with the stock sale, and yes, she should have asked him first. After all, she'd DocuSigned his name, since she still knew his passwords at the brokerage. Sloppy, really; if it had been her, she would have cleaned up better after herself. But then again, Maris had never shattered anyone's life before. She was always the one being blindsided.

She called him back. As she waited for him to answer, she wondered idly if what she'd done was illegal. Probably.

87

Even though they were still married, at least legally. It had amused her, this year when she did their taxes by herself for the first time, to discover that there was something called an Innocent Spouse Relief form. Jeff had never been innocent. So maybe the last twenty years of their returns were all built on lies, like their life. But now she was committing sins of her own, and the stock sale was only a minor one. So all the lines were blurred.

Jeff picked up. "Maris. Jesus. I've been trying to get you."

"It hasn't even been a day," Maris said, her voice chilly.

"You didn't go to Alana's. She has no idea where you are."

So Jeff had talked to her sister. It figured. The old resentment, all of her family circling around Jeff whenever the two of them were having issues, stirred inside her. Even now.

"I'm staying with a friend," she said. "It's just for a few days."

"A friend *where*?" It wasn't just exasperation in his voice, but that other thing too, that supercilious condescension. As if she had no friends, no one who would be willing to take her in. Jeff had always been proud of his own long-standing friendships, his connection to people going back as far as elementary school. Once a friend of Jeff's, forever a friend.

The irony of *that* thought made her expel a bitter laugh. "A friend you don't know," she said.

"Look. Mar. We need to talk."

"We *are* talking." She could afford this petulance, this immaturity now. He didn't own her anymore. The upper hand had cost her, God, had it cost her, but now she might as well use it. "Is there something in particular you need to tell me?"

"Well, you might be interested in knowing that they're appealing."

Stuck on his mincing annoyance, it took Maris a second to catch up, and then she absorbed what he was saying. "The Isherwoods?" she asked faintly.

"Their new attorney called. His office. As a courtesy."

"Oh, God . . ."

"It's not definite," Jeff said, relenting, now that he'd regained the upper hand. "I don't know if you've been paying any attention to the news, but Arthur Mehta got picked up on a DUI with some skag in the car. Gives credibility to an appeal if they go for incompetent defense."

Maris said nothing, the possibility taking shape in her mind like a gaping black maw, ready to swallow the small progress she'd made. An appeal meant the case being back in the public eye, Calla's memory brutalized all over again.

"Anyway. That's not what I called about. Look, let me get straight to it. You cashed in the Pfizer stock."

"Yes." She drew a shaky breath, recovering. She would think about the implications later. Without *him*. "I did. I needed some cash. We can sort it out when we meet with the mediator. Take it out of my half."

Jeff swore, a muttered epithet that surprised Maris. He didn't approve of cursing, said it was the sign of a lazy mind— Jeff, who'd had Maris proof his papers in grad school, whose malapropisms she'd long since become inured to.

"I'm sorry, I know I should have checked with you first. But you haven't exactly been very present lately."

"Look, Maris, I need you to transfer half of it back to me. You obviously have an account I don't know about, which, I

89

mean, that's a whole other subject. But just put half of it back, okay? Today would be good."

"Today would be *good*?" Maris felt her anger rising in her chest. "Why, you have a big date tonight? Need to buy a corsage?"

"That isn't—"

"If you haven't noticed, I've been dealing with a lot myself. I didn't just leave our house yesterday, the house I thought we'd live in forever, the house where I was going to have *Thanksgiving* with my *grandchildren*. My car got broken into yesterday. They took everything. I had to file a police report. I'm in a Target buying drugstore *body* lotion."

There was a silence. "I'm sorry," Jeff finally said, his voice tight. "We both have a lot on our plates. We both have a lot to deal with right now."

"Just take it out of one of the other accounts," Maris said, suddenly weary of the whole conversation, her anger dissipated, replaced by the old familiar numbness. The coffee roiled in her stomach. She needed to eat something; she'd only been able to manage half the bagel Pet brought her. "Keep track, we'll settle it up later."

"Maris." A pause. "There *are* no other accounts."

"What do you mean? Just use the BancWest one."

"Haven't you been looking at the statements? There was about two hundred dollars in there after we paid Kurtzman's last bill. I closed it."

"Don't," she said, bitter and knee-jerk.

"For Christ's sake, Mar, it's time to get over that. What am I supposed to say—okay, our *lawyer's* bill. I paid our *lawyer's* last bill and that was the end of the BancWest money."

"*Your* lawyer," she said, an automatic snipe, her trigger so fine-tuned after all of it. Besides, she wasn't the only one who had set up limits, names and words she couldn't bear to think, much less say. Like how they just called it "the BancWest account," for instance. For seventeen years it had been "Calla's college account."

"What matters is, it's gone."

"How can it be gone?"

There had been over $130,000 in it, enough for Calla to go anywhere, to go to Berkeley twice. They had hoped she might use the extra for grad school. Or, someday, a house. They had been proud of starting early, of building it over time, the way you were supposed to.

Once, they had been the couple that did everything the way you were supposed to. At least, Maris had been. All the while, Jeff had been someone else.

"I'm not going to explain this to you now," Jeff said tightly. That smugness, that arrogance. "It's not rocket science; Kurtzman's bills are in a folder in the filing cabinet."

"Well, then, sell some Vanguard. Or the Kauffman."

"Maris, are you even paying attention here? We haven't had those since 2010. Remember?"

Did she? That had been a tough year. Jeff's second layoff, the one that lasted nearly eleven months, had given them a big enough scare for Maris to take the branch manager job when they offered it to her, for the benefits. She knew they'd dipped into savings, but Jeff had always taken care of that kind of thing. Maris had been a teacher—Jeff had the MBA.

"Well, what are you telling me? We have no savings?" Her voice sounded prissy to her.

91

"Yes. That is exactly what I am saying. I've been trying to tell you that for months. I tried to tell you last Tuesday, you might remember."

Tuesday, when he'd wanted to have dinner, a gesture so flat and wrong she hadn't even returned his call. What could they have to talk about?

"You didn't—"

"Christ, Mar, I told you we can't afford two households right now. I've been trying for months to tell you we have to think about selling, not starting up some whole new life and leaving the house standing empty."

"But you've been saying we should sell the house for years. Before everything. And you were the one who moved out first!"

"You. Don't. Have. A. *Job*." The impatience in Jeff's voice set Maris's teeth on edge. "There's no way I can meet with Realtors and have showings and all of that right now. I'm working sixty hours a week, I'm—"

"And yet you somehow still find time to golf," Maris said coldly. Of all the things he'd taken on Monday, the golf clubs rankled most, for some reason.

"Maris!" he shouted, and Maris jumped, knocking the table and almost tipping over her coffee. Jeff never shouted, never raised his voice. "We are *out* of fucking *money*! I need you to put that money back or the mortgage isn't going to clear. The savings are *gone*. The BancWest is *gone*. We need to sell the house and we need to sell it now." She could hear him, breathing hard, over the phone. She was too shocked to respond.

When he spoke again, his voice was calmer. Steely. "I don't

92

make enough to meet our monthly expenses, not until I get a bonus in the fall anyway, and that's not guaranteed. You need to go back to work. We might need to borrow off the 401k until the house sells. I think if we pay it back this calendar year we won't take a tax hit. I'll look into it."

"Jeff . . ."

"I'm not kidding, Mar, it's time for you to snap out of your little fantasy world where everyone just waits for you to *feel* like facing reality, and pull your own weight like the rest of us."

"Oh, like *you* faced reality? Like you finally decided to take away the only thing we had left?"

"*We* didn't have anything," he said, deadly quiet. "There hasn't been a we in forever."

"I'll never forgive you." Something she had thought a thousand times, but never said aloud; she wished her voice didn't wobble.

"You know what, I don't even care anymore. Bottom line, you need to get a job. And figure out a way to unload the house. But before you do either of those things, you need to put the money back."

"You, you—*fuck* yourself." The words had a taste to them, bitter like a crushed pill.

"Nice, Maris." Now he just sounded weary. "But just so you know I'm serious, I emptied the checking account. And I'm not sending you a dime until you start acting like an adult here. If we need to meet with a mediator, a Realtor, whatever, we have to do it—we have to get all of this done. I mean, you don't like it, I guess you could sue me for support, but the thing is, you're the one who already broke the law."

So he did know about the password thing. Maris squeezed her eyes shut.

"Jeff." A whisper. "How can you be like this? How can you act like it never happened?"

The phone beeped twice. He'd hung up on her. Somehow, that was more shocking than everything else. Maris had never hung up on anyone in her entire life. You just didn't do that. Didn't squander people that way.

But she wasn't innocent, either. She wasn't sure how, but if she'd done her job, none of this would have happened. If she'd been a good enough mother. A good enough wife. If she'd been able to hold on to the only things that mattered.

She sank to the table, cradling her head in her arms. Around her, she could hear voices and the sounds of commerce, of people shopping for their ordinary lives in this most ordinary of stores, stopping, perhaps, for a Starbucks as a reward, a treat before heading back out into the hard work of living. All of it ordinary, generic, unremarkable. Maris once had so much more than that.

eleven

THE DRIVE TO PANAMINT was just shy of two hours in no traffic, endless droning miles through the Central Valley, nondescript fields of strawberries and corn and tomatoes broken up by the occasional orchard. Ron passed small towns populated with abandoned shacks and edged with rinds of fast-food joints, considered stopping for a coffee, a sandwich, but the thought of it was too depressing. The only other time he'd come, six weeks ago when Karl was first transferred, he and Deb had stopped at an Arby's. She'd gone to the bathroom, and while Ron waited for her, sipping at his sweating root beer in its clammy plastic cup, he'd had to endure watching the sun-burnished farmhands in their greasy caps, their sagging jeans, waiting patiently in line to order—and know that every one of them had more honor than his son. Karl—given every opportunity—had thrown it all away, while every one of these indistinguishable, hardscrabble men had suffered greater hardships and somehow found a way to make a life.

When he was within thirty miles of the prison, Ron narrowly missed being sideswiped by a truck loaded with tomatoes. The momentary adrenaline rush turned the tide of his thoughts, and afterward he sank into a resigned melancholy. What was the point of being angry at Karl? He was too young to understand that he had robbed his parents of their serenity, that they would never be whole again. Ron slowed, watching the truck jounce ahead, putting distance between them.

During the trial, Ron had read an article about the breakup violence phenomenon among young adults. He couldn't talk about it with Deb, who would brook no suggestion of Karl's guilt, but the article stayed with him: it suggested that an adolescent's still-developing frontal lobe would not have been equipped to overpower the impulse that led him—perhaps even without being aware of his own actions—to commit violence.

And if that was true, maybe he could find a way to forgive his son for taking Calla's life.

But how was he supposed to forgive him for dumping her body after? For denying it ever happened?

Maris had called the morning after Jade Rowland's graduation party, frantic with worry, to say that Calla had never made it home. Ron listened to Deb's half of the conversation, increasingly aware that something was very wrong. Later that day, a Sunday, Jeff had come by. Karl had seemed shaken. The three of them had stood in the living room, Jeff struggling to maintain his composure. They'd all shaken hands. By then Ron was privately wondering if Calla had gotten caught up in the new hybrid drug thing; there had been a piece on KTVU about kids in Berkeley living under overpasses begging for money to stay high. The shit they were using was so much worse, so much scarier nowadays; even Ron's brief flirtation with LSD seemed tame by comparison. He'd watched Jeff drive away with pity as well as a strong sense of gratitude that Karl, as far as he knew, didn't even use weed.

And he was pretty sure he'd know. Karl wasn't the kind of kid to leave them guessing as to where he was or what he was doing. Since breaking up with Calla, he'd been staying closer to home, it was true, but even when he was out it was usually with guys from soccer or kids he'd known since middle school. Families the Isherwoods knew well enough not to worry about.

Monday morning he'd managed to forget about the whole thing while he sat in on a series of calls in advance of what was going to be a better-than-expected quarterly earnings report. When he felt his phone vibrate, he checked it discreetly under the table. Seeing that it was Deb, he stepped out of the room. Deb rarely called him at work, and his hand was gripping the phone tightly, anticipating the worst, when he said hello.

"They found her," she said, her voice wobbling. "Can you please come home?"

Her body had been found at Byron Ranch.

Deb met him at the door and hugged him tightly. "Jemma called, she's staying with Maris until her sister gets there. Jeff's with them."

"Did you talk to either of them?"

"No, no. Jemma says Maris is hysterical."

Maris, Ron thought, hit with an onslaught of memories. When it was just Jeff, that was one thing. But now he couldn't keep it abstract any longer. He gave himself directions with one part of his mind even as he tried to process what Deb was saying with another. *Move your hands over her back, the way she likes. Brush the hair back where it's stuck to her skin with her tears. Don't let her see your eyes.*

He knew he couldn't trust himself right now. Deb knew him too well. She'd always been able to tell when he was lying, when he was trying to keep a secret from her, even if it was only a surprise party. And right now, if she looked at him, she would see.

"What are we going to tell Karl?" Deb said, her voice muffled from her face being pressed against his shirt. She was holding him so tightly he could feel her nails digging into the skin of his back. When he got home he'd found her sitting on the edge of the wing chair in the living room, the one no one ever sat in because it was so uncomfortable, her hands gripping each other tightly. She had one sneaker on. Eventually she'd told him that she got the call while she was dressing for yoga; the other shoe was still on the floor of their bedroom. She didn't remember coming down the stairs.

What were they going to tell Karl, indeed?

"They have people—people trained for things like this," he managed. "By the end of the day they'll have counselors lined up. They probably won't make an announcement at school until tomorrow if they can keep it out of the news—"

"It's too late for that!" Deb pulled back and looked at him. Ron automatically froze, trying to keep his expression neutral. "The news is already reporting they found a body. A girl. You know how they are; they'll come out and say who it is the minute they get confirmation. Besides, it's probably all over the school already. Think about how many people the Vacantis called last night, looking for her!"

"No, no, you're right, that's not what I meant. I just meant, after we talk to him, tomorrow, if he needs some help, to process things, they'll have professionals available."

He didn't really know if this was true, except that he'd seen it on the news. Sandy Hook, Newtown, there were always "counselors on hand."

"But, Ron. Karl and she were so close. It's not like it's just some kid at school. He's going to take this hard."

Look at her, Ron thought. It hasn't even occurred to her, not for a fraction of a second. That people might suspect Karl would have done something.

He hated himself for thinking it. Of course he knew his son wasn't capable of something like this—of taking a *life*, my God, Calla's life. But there would be questions and there would be suspicions, and the natural place, at least one of the first places they were going to look would be, hey, was there anyone in Calla's life that she was having problems with? People who didn't like her, people she'd argued with?

Jeff, sitting at the Isherwoods' kitchen table the day before, looking into Karl's face so earnestly, desperate for answers, for clues, for anything that could help him find his daughter. And what had brought Jeff here, of all the homes in all of Linden Creek?

The thrum of fear twisted tighter. He gently disentangled Deb from his arms. "All right," he said, "all right, let's think this through. Should we go pick him up?"

"From school?"

Ron went to the cabinet next to the sink and got a glass. Filled it from the tap and drank, focusing on keeping his hand steady. Buying a few seconds to think. "I don't know, maybe. Do you think that's what other parents are doing?"

"Well—they're not in elementary school," Deb said, hugging herself. "I mean, I would guess the thing they want most in a tragedy like this is each other. *Oh*. God."

"What, honey?" Her eyes had filled and her hand went to her mouth, and Ron set down the glass and went back to her. She leaned on him, her thin shoulders shaking.

"It's just I was thinking of all the times she sat here—right here, in our house. That poor girl."

"I know, I know," Ron murmured. He pulled a chair around and helped her sit so that his knees were touching hers, holding her hands in his, rubbing them.

"She was . . . she was just so *good*. You know?"

Ron nodded. Calla had been a sweet girl, the sort, frankly, who wouldn't have caught his eye when he was eighteen . . . but not all that different from the woman he ended up marrying. But when you looked at them, these Gale Academy girls with their long shiny hair and shimmering makeup, weren't they all innocent? Weren't they all guileless and fragile, at least to their parents?

All over town, now, as women saw it on the news and called their husbands, as kids texted on phones hidden under their desks, parents were thinking the same things. One of ours. And all of them thanking God that the sacrificed child wasn't their own.

Ron was grateful too—of course. Imagining something happening to Karl—he almost couldn't bear it, couldn't allow the thought to fully form in his mind. Even now, with Karl moving away from them these last few years, growing up and becoming distant, he was the heart that beat inside Ron, he was the hard kernel of meaning in his days. Life without his son wouldn't be life. And when he thought of Jeff and Maris, confronted with this loss that would decimate them in ways they couldn't even imagine now, his heart filled with grief for them.

But his grief was tinged with unease.

"Deb," he said, willing his voice to be even, "I think I will pick him up after all."

At the school, Ron took his place in the carpool line, wishing for greater invisibility. He had driven the old Explorer they'd bought a few years back and kept around for skiing in the winter and towing the boat in the summer. Deb and he occasionally talked about how ridiculous it was for a family of three to own three cars, but what could you do? The registration on the old Explorer was cheaper than renting would be, and the guy they'd bought the house from had been something of a car nut and had built a six-car garage out back, so room wasn't an issue.

He'd pulled on a baseball cap and pushed the seat back, trying to stay out of visual range of other drivers. Mostly, it was only the parents of freshmen who came to pick up their kids; older kids either drove themselves or rode with friends, or were too embarrassed to be picked up and found other ways home. Karl himself had only lasted halfway through freshman year before managing to arrange to be picked up by a sophomore who lived a couple of blocks away. And then the next year, Deb and Ron had bought him the Explorer. Used, of course, and they'd consoled themselves that it wasn't exactly the sort of car that would inspire recklessness and showing off: they weren't dumb enough to buy him a sports car, anything that would elevate his status among his peers.

They didn't spoil him, in other words. Hadn't even paid for a parking spot for him so he could drive to school. Ron had kind of a thing about that, abhorrence for the sense of entitlement you saw in some kids, especially at a school like Gale. The Pickard boy, for instance, who had wrecked his Camaro a month after his sixteenth birthday and was rewarded with another, a model a year newer—and had responded by getting suspended for breaking into the snack shack and vandalizing the refrigerators with a few other equally repugnant kids. Karl would never do something like that. But the same firm discipline and solid moral foundation that Ron and Deb had tried to instill in him—in Ron's case, with punitive measures and withholding that other parents probably would have found draconian—there were times that he wondered if he'd taken the right path. Sure, he had a kid other parents admired, one who could be counted on to be respectful. But Karl had also become silent, reserved, keeping things to himself. Had Ron quashed something in his son, something that, in himself, had managed to survive his own father's heavy-handed discipline?

The car in front of Ron inched forward, and he followed suit. Three eighteen—school had gotten out eight minutes ago, and the line had barely moved. Some of these parents must have been here half an hour early; as it was, Ron was all the way back by the chain-link fence surrounding the parking lot, only now rounding the corner with a view into the back of the school.

Ah, there it was. Evidence that this was not an ordinary day, that news had reached the kids. Deb said no name had been released yet by the media, but they had to know. Over there, by the shade structure, a cluster of girls were hugging each other and crying. There was Blake, the school's head of security, talking with two other men, both wearing ties—detectives, maybe. He pressed further back in his seat.

Perspiration popped out along Ron's forehead, even with the air-conditioning on full blast. It wasn't as effective as it once was; he probably needed to have it serviced, next time he took the Explorer in for an oil change.

The cars inched forward.

There was Karl. Coming out of the exit, talking to some girl Ron didn't recognize—short, thickset, wearing glasses. They stood, talking, on the steps for a few minutes. Karl didn't look up. He didn't look upset, did he? Or was that some sort of numbness on his face, the stunned feeling he must have, receiving the news? Hell, half these kids looked like they were in shock—all of them in little groups, no loners today.

Ron rolled the windows down and shut off the A/C—it wasn't working anyway—and tried to hear what people were saying.

"—Said they were going to have it on Channel 2 at six—"

"—Just saw her at the softball dinner—"

"—Can't believe they didn't make an announcement—"

"—Said animals got to the body—"

Someone knocked on the passenger window, making Ron jump. He peered over, saw Adrian Hern. His mouth was twisted in a tense grimace—he fought to relax it. Not a smile, of course. Adrian herself looked like she was trying not to cry. No, she *was* crying, her mascara smudged, her nose running.

"Ron. Oh, God, did you guys hear? Is Deb all right? Is she at home? I tried to call her."

103

"Adrian," Ron said. "We're—I mean—it's awful. It's terrible. I can't believe it."

"You're picking up Karl," she said, her fingers curling over the edge of the window glass. Ron thought that if he pushed the button, her fingers would be squeezed painfully. The correct thing would be to roll the window down, but he just couldn't bear the idea of conversation right now. This was how women processed things—Deb had tried to explain that to him a hundred times—but he wasn't a woman and he shouldn't be here, in their territory, in their milieu. "That's probably a good idea. Poor kid. Oh, they were so close, the two of them."

Ron was caught off guard, unsure what to say. Everyone had known that Karl and Calla were dating—Gale wasn't a big school, barely 150 kids in the senior class, and they had been well liked. Good kids.

"Look, I should go get back in the car," Adrian said, taking her hands off the glass. "Tell Deb to call me. I'm just so sorry."

So he'd escaped. Relief washed through him. The cars moved ahead, a couple of them moving into the U-turn as the parking lot cleared out. Already most of the kids' cars were gone, only those staying for after-school activities remaining.

Karl spotted him and gave a wave, his face somber. He said something to the girl he was talking to, who went back inside the school. Karl jogged to the car, his backpack bouncing over his shoulder, and got in.

"Dad. Oh my God. Did you hear about Calla?"

Ron wanted to reach for him, to hug him, but it was impossible; he had to maneuver out of the lane and into the U-turn.

He patted his son's shoulder briefly and examined his face, taking in as much as he could before he had to turn his attention to the road.

"Mom talked to Mrs. Lipsky. We don't know much. Only that they found her. That they found . . . Calla."

For a moment Karl was motionless, his expression almost wooden. Ron took the long way, past the school, right on Olive, a narrow street most people avoided because two cars couldn't easily pass.

Karl made a sound, half sob, half grunt. "Dad . . ."

Ron pulled the car over, turned the keys. Took Karl into his arms, awkwardly, the console between them. Karl was already sobbing. After a long while, he wiped his face on his sleeve and pulled away.

"They told us in fifth period. But people were talking all day. You know? Ever since second period, someone said they found a body out by Byron Ranch. A girl. There were all these rumors. I mean . . . I was in English, I wanted to leave, to find out if it was true, but Mr. Duarte said anyone who got up, he would consider it a missed quiz, he would . . . and I was going to anyway, but girls were crying, like, everyone was crying."

Ron patted his back like he did so long ago, when Karl had been a restless toddler, one given to fits of inconsolable sobbing. The only thing that could quiet him, all that time ago, was to be held, bounced, rocked, walked . . . for hours, sometimes.

Too many times, Ron handed Karl off to Deb. Too many times, he woke her up with a few words of apology—"big meeting tomorrow," "got to catch that flight," whatever excuse was convenient, and Deb wouldn't complain, she'd take the baby and get up from their bed, go downstairs so the sound wouldn't travel.

But once in a while Ron held him, and rocked him, and patted him. Like this.

"Someone said she'd been attacked. Her body." Ron could feel Karl swallow, wrestling with himself, trying to get the sobbing under control. "That she was almost . . . her arms, they were like, *eaten*. I can't. I can't."

After a while the crying slowed and then stopped, Ron making the hushing sounds he remembered. Funny how it came back to you, like nearly two decades hadn't passed. Someday, he'd have grandchildren, and he'd have another chance—God willing, he'd be granted another chance—to do this right.

"Son," he said, his own voice hoarse. "No one knows what happened yet. These things, before there's official word, things tend to get out of control. I wouldn't think, I wouldn't believe the things you hear. I mean . . . I think it's safe to say it was her. That much is true."

So what did the rest really matter, then? Calla, whatever she meant or didn't mean to Karl, was dead. Maybe he was taking the wrong tack here.

But even as he grappled for the words, the right ones, the ones that would help his son make some sense of this, another emotion shaded everything: relief. Because Karl was devastated. He was shaken to the core.

And that meant he must be innocent.

twelve

DESPITE TAKING HIS TIME, despite keeping his speed down after the close call with the tomato truck, Ron was still twenty minutes early. He stared out at the rows of cars in the prison parking lot. Surely these weren't all visitors. Ron didn't remember all these cars being there last time. Certainly they didn't have to park all the way in the far corner of the lot like today.

He tried to ignore the familiar nudge of guilt. No one made Deb come every week. That was her choice. Still, he didn't like the idea of her making the trek, in her pressed skirt and purse clutched tight, across the parking lot in heat like this.

At least his parking spot was in the partial shade of a spindly young tree, and for the first five minutes after his arrival, he tried to figure out if the angle of the sun meant that the car would grow more or less shaded as the afternoon wore on. The temperature had registered ninety-five degrees on his car's thermometer, and he had the door open and both windows rolled down, but still his shirt was soaked under the arms and sweat trailed down into his eyes. Dozens of people already lined the steps leading to the entrance, waiting to go in; what kind of conversation could you possibly have in such a line? Especially Ron: *yeah, I'm that kid's dad, the one you've heard about, the one who's worse than yours.*

By unspoken pact, Deb never shared the homely details of her visits: who she talked to while she waited and where she parked, for instance. But Ron could see now that there was a whole other world here that she had experienced without him.

The last time Ron had seen his son, he hadn't realized that he would have so much trouble returning. Ron thought he had it in him to set aside the complex tangle of emotions that had taken permanent residence inside him. But he'd learned just how weak he was, hadn't he? Though the offer he'd made on the bridge had felt brave at the time (perhaps, even, if he was honest with himself, heroic), he now understood it was the opposite. That the duality he hated so much in his father—that of the bully/coward—was present in him as well.

And not just in him: it proved a vigorous legacy, undiluted over generations. While Karl was still in county jail, awaiting sentencing, it had been possible for him to pretend that it was all temporary. That like the inmates on parole violations and drug charges, he was just passing time while waiting to be arraigned. But once Karl had been moved to Panamint, he had seemed to both finally accept his fate and give up. He had been familiar yet somehow barely recognizable in the pale yellow, shapeless clothes the inmates wore, his swollen face so assiduously blank, his hair shorn and his posture slumped. Ron had weathered that first visit in a robotic haze, letting Deb carry the conversation, his glance skittering away whenever Karl looked his way. "See you soon, son," Ron had said when they left (unlike at the jail, no touching was allowed here, not even at the end of the visit, so he'd stood with his arms hanging uselessly at his sides), and then he'd never returned, because how could he stand to see the fear in his son's eyes?

Ron checked his watch, again. A few minutes after the hour. The line moved steadily, all but the last few visitors inside the building. Ron got out of the car and walked slowly through the lot. In his pocket, change jingled. He had brought nothing for Karl. Deb brought things to share with him, clippings from magazines and photos she printed out on a little printer she'd bought for that purpose. She deposited money in his commissary account. Within the narrow parameters of what could be brought and given, she did it all.

Ron took his place at the back of the line. No one would try to talk to him now; everyone was focused on the person they had come to see, anticipating. Ron wondered how many of the others were here out of a sense of duty, and how many truly wanted to be here. What if it was your wife? How would he feel, visiting Deb here? But of course that example was ridiculous, because Deb would never do anything that would land her here. And even if she did, no one would ever suspect her, no jury would ever convict her.

Ron felt the familiar dizziness from the senseless cycling of his thoughts. Could he say that Karl had ever *seemed* innocent, the way Deb did? The way, to Ron's best guess, he himself did? It was an accident of fate that there was something about Ron that invited trust. It was part of what he'd once jokingly called the Isherwood Plan for World Domination, one of the skills he'd talked to Karl about when he thought he was grooming him for a career like his own, an asset he could transfer like the firm handshake and the unwavering eye contact.

But Ron had done little to deserve the respect he commanded without even trying. As an altar boy at Divine Savior in Sacramento forty years ago, Ron had pushed his luck any number of times. He lied in confession, he convinced the other boys to drink the communion wine; but the trick—of not blinking, of neither smiling nor frowning, the sincerity that Ron could produce on command—this was not something he could teach the others.

Take this place, for instance. When Ron reached the registration counter, he waited for the guard to look at him more sharply after he said his name. But no. The guard was indifferent, incurious. Ron went where he was told, sat in a row with the others. The prisoners came out one at a time. So many of them were smiling, so many of them looked like they'd longed for this moment, been buoyed by their anticipation.

But look, there was Karl.

Deb had told him that Karl had put on even more weight, but Ron wasn't prepared for his son's appearance. It wasn't just a five- or ten-pound weight gain, a little softness under his jaw or around his waist: Karl had easily put on twenty pounds, and he looked slack and puffy, his skin grayish and dull. (*Lardo!*—Magnus's voice echoed in Ron's mind, though that was the nickname reserved for poor Keith, the least athletic of the Isherwood boys.) Karl's eyes, roaming the faces of those waiting, found Ron, and stopped. But there was no joy, no lightening of his expression. Karl's hand went to a spot on his face and scratched. Acne, or a scab. Ron felt the urge to turn away—to leave. This was a mistake—he wished he hadn't come, but what would people think of him if he walked out now? Until this moment, he had believed he could justify his decision not to visit in the intervening

110

months: it was just too hard; he needed time to heal before he could prepare himself to renew his relationship with Karl. Deb must have recognized the fear in him even then, but she had accepted every excuse he offered her; she didn't judge, or at least if she did, she kept it to herself. "When you're ready," she said when Ron had first announced that he wasn't returning—and she'd said it again as recently as last week, perhaps with a little less conviction.

"What are you doing here?" Karl slumped into the plastic chair, his arms clattering onto the table that separated them like logs dumped from a bucket. Up close, Ron could see that it was actually a rash that his son had been picking at, red and angry-looking, along his hairline on one side of his face.

"I came to see you," Ron said.

"Well, no shit, obviously. I just wondered why. Why today, of all of the time I've been here. Is today special? Because it doesn't really feel any different to me."

If Karl chose his words to wound Ron, he succeeded. Well, that was a revelation, right there. You ask yourself, after your son has been ripped from your home and accused of something unconscionable, if you can ever be hurt any more profoundly; you come to believe that the protective scrim has been worn clean away, that the light burning inside you, exposed to the elements, has sputtered out.

But it isn't so. You can still hurt. It never leaves.

Ron breathed with care. In, out; in, out. He let the seconds tick by while he formulated what to say. His mouth tasted bad, despite the gum he had been chewing on the drive down.

"Karl," he finally said, trying to hold his son's gaze and settling for staring at his mouth, which was compressed and

111

angry. "I tried to kill myself the other day. I went to the bridge. The Golden Gate. I stood on the little platform on the side and looked down at the water. I really believed I would do it too. Well, I'm sitting here with you so obviously, I didn't. But what's important, what I really want you to understand . . ."

At this point, the thread of the narrative became lost. What was it that he had hoped to communicate, to offer his son? Some message about love, about sacrifice, about what Ron had been willing to do. Except that he hadn't been willing to do much at all: he'd tried to pay a debt in worthless tokens.

". . . is that I believed I was about to jump," Ron finished lamely, a lie that would have to stand in for the much more complicated truth. "And the last thing I did was I called Mrs. Vacanti."

But the name didn't sit right. Karl was no longer a boy—despite his doughy softness, which had the effect of making him seem younger. He was incarcerated with men and so, in Ron's mind, he should be treated like a man, and as such he wouldn't call other adults "Mr." or "Mrs." as a child would.

"I called *Maris*," Ron corrected himself, his voice firming. "I wanted her to know. I was trying to even it up, see, for what you did. Trying to pay for what you did."

"Is that why you're here?" Karl asked, in a voice so bored and devoid of emotion that Ron, startled, looked him in his glazed and indifferent eyes. "You drove all the way out here to try to make me feel *guilty*?"

This wasn't going the way Ron had planned. Not that he had a plan . . . but he had a need. He'd envisioned speaking urgently, in a voice low enough that only Karl would hear, in the din of the visiting room; finding some common thread to which they both could hold fast; but now Ron understood that what he'd expected and hoped for was to devastate his son, to crush him with his words, with the sacrifice he'd almost made. In here, Ron couldn't strike Karl, shake him, or even tower over him; he had never had the opportunity to express what was inside him, all the fury and disappointment in his son.

That was what he needed, the feeling of his fist connecting with Karl's jaw, blood streaming from his nose. The shock of recognition in his body, the tingling urge to clench his fists, to throw Karl to the ground, to reduce him to snot and tears, a blubbering mass of regret and self-loathing. He wanted for Karl to feel everything Ron himself had felt so often at the mercy of his own father. That he was garbage. That he was a blight on the world.

"You *don't* feel guilty?" he challenged Karl. His voice had turned to a snarl; a roar barely contained. The rage doubled back on itself, intensifying. Ron had been denied any say in what happened, in what Karl had done not just to Calla but to him and Deb, to their family, to all of their futures. But look at him, puffed up and insolent, his mouth shining wetly, and what looked like gel stiffening in his hair. Was that what he used his commissary money on—hair products? While Calla's bones warmed under the summer earth after her first wretched winter alone in her grave?

"So you still don't believe me," Karl said, misery tingeing his voice, the first sign of emotion he'd shown during the visit. "It's still never occurred to you that I might be telling the truth, Dad? Not even once?"

113

Ron slammed his fist into the table before he could think. A guard stepped forward, Karl jerked back—finally a reaction!—in alarm. Ron's hand stung, the blow had jarred all his bones up and down his arm. "All right, all right," Ron muttered to the guard, holding up his hands in apology. "Sorry."

The guard glared at him, folding his arms over his chest. But Ron had heard the sound of his own voice, had felt the coiled, trembling excitement of rage, and he knew that in these moments he had become just like his father. Even when he backed down, when the guard stopped him, he aped his father's behavior when—it didn't happen often—for reasons known only to himself, Magnus had given Ron a reprieve, let him go without a whipping. *All right, all right,* he'd say. *Get lost, you piece of shit. Don't let me see your face around here.* And Ron would run away, his heart pounding, grateful every time to escape, even though he knew he could never really escape his father.

"Every day I try to find a reason to believe you," he said to Karl. "*Every* day."

"Why can't you?" Now, finally, Karl was looking him in the eye. "I get letters, you know. Like, at least five every week. People who believe me, that I didn't do it. Do you know there's a website?"

"Of course I do!" He would have shouted again, but he was mindful of the guard's watchful eye. "Your mother showed me. It's practically all she does—" He wanted to blame Karl for that too, for Deb's single-minded devotion to something that left no room for him.

"Well, *I* haven't seen it. We don't get Internet."

There was a quality to his petulance that reminded Ron of

114

when he'd been just a boy, eight or ten years old, called out for not doing his chores or sassing his mother. And it was this that softened him, deflating his momentary anger like a stuck balloon. He remembered why he was here and girded himself for it.

"Listen. Son. There's been a—"

"Don't change the subject." Karl's face had gone red and blotchy. His hands twitched on the table. "There are people in this world who believe me. Who don't think I'm a monster. But you've always . . . you've always acted like I was a piece of shit. Before this. When I was just a *kid*. Always."

Ron gaped. "I never . . ."

"Dads are supposed to . . ." Tears threatened, and Karl practically punched himself wiping them away. "You were supposed to be there for me. To think I was . . ."

He stared helplessly at Ron, and deep inside Ron understood, because hadn't he once looked at his own father the same way? Magnus was supposed to come to his games and cheer when he had a hit and brag to his friends, to put his report cards on the fridge and his drawings on his bulletin board at work, to call him his little buddy, to tell him he was—

The shame, as old as his very bones, billowed. *To tell him he was proud.* Ron would have never admitted, not then and not now, that it was the one thing he'd longed for more than anything—his father's approval. And now he saw his son losing the same battle with his own shame.

I did love you, he tried to say, *I was proud of you*, but his mouth wouldn't move and the words wouldn't come.

"Forget it," Karl muttered harshly. "Fucking forget it. What is it you want?"

And now, of course, the paralysis loosened and Ron managed. "Your mother asked me to come and talk to you. Because there's been a, maybe an opportunity. You know about Arthur Mehta."

Karl's eyes flickered uneasily. He looked away, took a couple of breaths, and when he spoke again his voice was steadier. "Yeah. Mom said he was arrested for drunk driving."

"Right. Yes. And now your mother and her, uh, some people who are interested in your defense are looking into an appeal. There are a couple of attorneys—"

"I don't want to appeal."

Karl bit off the words like shotgun rounds. He pushed himself back slightly from the table and sat straighter in the chair, folding his arms across his chest. Ron started to respond and Karl said it again, stonily: "I'm not appealing."

The arguments Ron had assembled fell away. For the first time, and he didn't know how the two things connected, he was unsure of his son—not just his guilt or innocence, but whether he had been reading him right at all, ever since Calla went missing. This conversation was pulling him in so many directions, with so many emotional traps and hazards, and he was struggling just to stay focused on why he was here at all.

"Can you," he said carefully, aiming for the detached tone he used in negotiating, as much to distract himself as to sway Karl. "Can you share with me what you're thinking? About the appeal?"

Karl looked up at him. "Dad," he said, and his voice cracked. "*Shit.*"

He seemed to shrink into himself, like someone anticipating a blow. Ron's defenses gave way and he longed to reach for his son, embrace him—but Karl had been the one living here, the one who'd learned the rules, lived them, and he stayed rigidly still as Ron reached for him and then dropped his hand. This rule, above all else—could they really expect people to sit here docilely, cramming truckloads of stored-up emotions into a few tortuous moments, and not touch? At the county jail, inmates were allowed two hugs, one on arriving and one at the end of the visit, and the guards were exacting and parsimonious about it: no covert gropes, no extra time, no kissing. And even so, Ron had come to crave the quick, glancing hugs that Karl endured and he delivered only reluctantly. Would he have tried harder, if he'd known what waited? That for the next seven years he could not touch his son?

"Shit," Karl mumbled again. He too seemed to have lost the anger that had gripped them both only moments earlier. "It's just that it's, you know, the appeal process could take so long, and I could be out in five years anyway. So just to gain, like, two years or whatever, if it even worked, and to have to go through all of that again." He glanced up at his father, almost shyly.

"Karl," Ron said. He didn't know what else to say. What he needed now was time—time to think about this, to examine it from every angle. Forget his own volatility—he couldn't keep up with the shifts in his son's mood. Because his son was talking like an adult; the boyishness Ron thought he'd perceived in Karl's face was deceptive. His puffiness looked dissipated, not youthful. His words came out sounding weary.

"I know Mom sent you here to convince me," Karl continued. "But it isn't going to work. I'm sorry, Dad, I don't mean

117

to be uncooperative, but I just can't do it. I can't go through with it."

"But if it could be overturned—" Now Ron was on the verge of doing the one thing he had forbidden himself from doing, ever: imagining what might have been—being tempted by the fiction that it still could be. To get the felony off Karl's record—Ron didn't even voice the idea out loud. It was too big. The simple things he'd given up hoping for his son, like voting and finding a job and richly unlikely things like going to college, even business school. Even having another girlfriend someday.

Sitting at their table for a holiday meal.

"Dad." Karl had regained himself, released the tight-coiled posture. He was shaking his head, rubbing a hand through his hair, mindless of the gel or whatever it was that he'd applied. His words sounded smooth if slightly rehearsed. "I know I don't have the right to ask you for anything. And I'm . . . I'm glad you came to see me. That's big, I know that. But please, can you just convince Mom? I don't *want* this. I just want to, you know, pass the time and maybe take some classes or something, figure out how to do something useful while I'm here."

Ron saw how it was going to be: he would return home without having accomplished what Deb had asked. He would disappoint her. But was he also disappointed? Had he changed his mind somehow in this confusing exchange?

"Look, I just, I mean, think about it, okay? Mom'll be here Sunday. I'll talk to her too. We'll just—"

He stopped; he'd been on the verge of saying that they'd *get through this together,* but how was that possible? They

118

weren't a family anymore, not really. When Karl got out in seven years—or even five, in five years he would be twenty-four years old—he would be a man, an adult; he would be a branch that grew far out from the tree.

The visit was soon over, the ache of watching his son walk from the room felt not just in his heart but in his arms that he could not put around his son, his boy. Still, despite every-thing, his *boy*. Ron made it barely ten miles from the prison entrance before he burst into great, heaving sobs. He couldn't stop, even after he pulled over to the side of the road and dug in the glove box for napkins with which to blow his nose. He cried until he had a headache, and then he sat for another ten minutes, simply staring through the windshield at the dried and dead fields.

What if? he thought, the idea inside him painfully taking shape. What if Deb was right? What if Karl really was inno-cent?

But how could that be? The witnesses—one after another, kids he recognized, others he didn't—called up to tell their damning stories. "He, like, pulled hard? On her arm?" Tentative, most of them, giving their statements in the form of questions, unwilling to look at Karl except for brief, fleet-ing glances. "She said she was, you know, afraid? Not of who he was, but of who he turned into? After the breakup?" Circumstantial, Arthur Mehta kept assuring them.

But later, when the mud from the SUV was identified and the expert witness from Stanford estimated the probability of the car having been at Byron Ranch as "so close to a hundred percent as to be statistically certain," even Arthur seemed less engaged. Less . . . committed, though Ron was certainly reading into his comments, his gestures and throat clearings. That was when he'd brought up the subject of manslaughter convictions and the best-scenario sentences each might carry, and Ron knew without a doubt that they were sunk.

Of course there were those whose belief in Karl's innocence never wavered—and not just Deb. The Fowlers, who had lived next door to the Isherwoods when their boys were in elementary school—Mindy Fowler called every few days. Karl's civics teacher, a coach he'd had before making the varsity team. Kami, once the Innocence Project took an interest. And all those strangers, with their website and their letters and their prayers, their teddy bears and balloons left at the curb.

Ron's head throbbed and his eyes felt swollen and itchy from crying. He stared at the key dangling from the ignition, willing himself to turn it, to pull the car into traffic and get on with it, get home to where Deb was surely waiting to hear how he had fared with Karl. The car's interior had quickly grown stifling, and sweat dampened his neck. At least he should roll down a window.

Instead he thought about Calla's band trip down to Orange County in the early spring before she died. Calla played flute, and the band had qualified for a state competition. Karl had been at odds that weekend, moping around the house, declining to join his friends for pizza after practice, deciding at the last minute to skip a party he'd planned to attend. Deb thought it was cute: "lovesick," she'd whispered as Karl made another sullen trip to the refrigerator to stare at its contents before making do with another 7-Up.

Deb also teased Ron about being sorry to be left out, a

reference to the prior fall when she had convinced him to serve as a parent chaperone on a senior class trip to Sacramento. In fact, it had been the trip on which the kids' romance had begun, which made it a sentimental milestone for Deb, who hadn't even been there. For Ron, memories of that trip were far more complicated, and Deb's teasing made him feel both irritable and guilty.

Maybe that was why he hadn't gone up to bed with Deb after the news. Instead, he'd stayed up, drinking beer and watching television, pointedly distracting himself. Around midnight he heard something thump on the floor overhead, where Karl's bedroom was located. Mildly concerned, he went up the stairs and down the hall and was surprised to hear Karl's voice raised in anger—then immediately lowered, quiet enough that Ron couldn't make out the words. Then nothing at all. Ron stood, indecisive, in the hallway; he knew he shouldn't be eavesdropping on his son, but Karl had become such a mystery to him, especially in recent months when he slipped quicksilver from their household every chance he got, to be with Calla.

Another barrage of words, indistinct but urgent. Then a single sharp exclamation followed by silence.

Ron waited, but there was nothing more. He was getting cold, his feet chilly on the hardwood floor. Just as he decided that Karl had gone to bed, however, there was an anguished sob and then a wall-echoing slam.

He rushed to Karl's room and tried the knob, but his son had locked the door. "Karl," he said, keeping his voice low, mindful of Deb sleeping on the other side of the house. "What's going on?"

After a long moment, the knob turned and Karl opened the door. He blocked the opening, not inviting his father in. Only the reading light clipped above his bed was turned on, but even so, Ron could see that his son's face was streaked with tears, his eyes red.

"It's nothing," he said woodenly.

"Come on—I heard—it's obviously not *nothing*." Ron scanned the room for evidence of what had happened.

His gaze fell on the wall between the nightstand and the desk. There was a reproduction poster from the Warriors' triumphant '75 season, when Karl hadn't even been born, affixed to the wall with some gummy stuff Deb had found that wouldn't mar the paint. The bottom of the poster was torn and crumpled. Behind it, the wallboard was dented, its painted skin broken.

"You hit the *wall*?" A stirring of dread moved inside him.

"I, look, only . . . Calla broke up with me."

Ron absorbed the news, trying to make sense of it through the cottony haze of five beers. He was caught off-guard—he'd assumed that Karl would be the one to end the romance. Even Deb agreed, though she'd refused to voice the reasons Ron assumed they both knew: Karl was athletic, good-looking, well liked by all kinds of kids and respected by teachers. Calla was . . . well, a little ordinary. A *band* girl, sweet, but without the edge that bound the most popular girls into cliques.

"Do you . . . do you want to talk about it?"

"No." The syllable bit off sharply. Karl moved the door slightly, narrowing the opening, cutting off his father's view of the damaged wall.

"But look, Karl, you can't—we have to—this isn't any way to handle things, right?"

Unable to come up with any more convincing platitudes, Ron withdrew from Karl's doorway after awkwardly assuring his son that Deb and he were there for him, to listen, to talk, to help in whatever way they could. He thought about adding a whole thing about how the end of a first love was always painful, that it would get easier soon, and every relationship had something to learn from, and Karl would look back on this and . . . but no, Karl didn't need that. Karl, with his brooding gaze and his quick intellect—it was astonishing sometimes, the speed at which he made connections—would see through such cheap solace.

As Ron padded to his bedroom and listened to the house settling back into silence, he reflected on how much smarter Karl was at eighteen than he had been.

And as he got back into bed, Deb murmuring softly in her sleep when he drew back the covers, he took a moment to be grateful that, unlike himself in adolescence, Karl had not done anything stupid.

thirteen

A LITTLE AFTER SEVEN that evening, light leached from the sky, thin merciful clouds gathering low and ushering in a breeze. Maris peeled off the gloves and dropped them in the trash, crossed her arms, and looked around the apartment. It was a different space from the one she'd walked into yesterday: The surfaces were scrubbed, everything that had belonged to the prior tenant had been thrown away, and it smelled of Method cucumber cleaner.

Had she done enough?

The question was too big to consider, so Maris dug her phone from her purse. Talking to Alana was another kind of challenge, but at least it would interrupt her trajectory of self-criticism. Choosing your anxiety: that was a tool she should tell Nina about, so she could pass it on to her other pathetic clients, these women in midlife with their disappointments and miseries. When you find yourself worrying about something you can't change, focus on something even worse.

Alana picked up midway through the first ring. "Oh my God! I thought you were never going to call!"

"I'm sorry, I know I should have called sooner. This was all just—I needed . . . I'm sorry."

"But where are you?"

Maris, leaning against the counter, squeezed the tiled edge with her free hand. She had practiced this lie while she washed the windows. "I'm staying at a house that belongs to a woman from yoga, someone I've known for years. She and her husband are out east for a few weeks. She needed a house sitter. So, you know, the timing worked."

There was a silence, just long enough for Maris to read Alana's hurt. "But we talked about it. How you shouldn't be alone."

Actually, Alana was the one who said she shouldn't be alone; Maris had merely agreed. Because it sounded reasonable, like something Nina, whom Maris had stopped seeing after the holidays, would say. But now, in her scoured burrow, *alone* felt like what she needed. Or not alone, exactly, but with people who didn't know her, who didn't know what had happened.

"I'm not alone," she said, surprising herself. "There's this girl—she's an art student, she's here too. In fact, I'm having dinner with her tonight."

"But I thought you said there wasn't anyone in the house."

"She rents the guest house." Maris shook her head, surprised at how easily the lies came; this was getting complicated, exactly what she wanted to avoid. "Anyway, it's just for a couple of weeks. I'm going to go for walks, journal, think about things."

"You were going to do all of that here." Maris could hear Alana's sigh. "Mar, look, I have the guest room all set up. I'm gone during the day, you'd have the place to yourself. I looked into getting you a guest pass at my gym. And in the evenings, you'd have company. I just—I just don't want you to have a setback."

Maris knew what she meant, the bad place she'd been before Jeff and Alana practically staged an intervention, finding Nina for her and forcing her out of the house to walk in the mornings, to eat a couple of meals a day. To be fair, if their roles were reversed (but how could they be? Imagining Alana as a mother, a wife, was like imagining the pope as a talk-show host) she would probably be saying all the same things.

But Maris wasn't going back to those semicomatose days, the lethargy and the light-headedness from not eating, the thinning skin and the hair falling out. And it wasn't that she was moving on, as she'd claimed to Nina and Jeff, passing through the stages of grief. At least, not the official ones that you were supposed to, the one that more cooperative clients apparently did. (And what kind of therapist specializes in grief, anyway? She must have her own issues, though Nina had been scrupulous in never speaking about her own life.) Maris was moving through her own stages, and while she doubted she would ever feel better, she knew the last year had changed her like lightning changes a tree or a landslide changes a hill, and she would never go backward, either.

She had to convince Alana, though, or her sister would come after her. That was Alana—relentlessly competent, just like their mother; a believer that for all problems there was a prescription.

"Listen, Alana. If I tell you something, you promise you won't come unglued?"

"What kind of a question is that?" Alana asked after a fraught moment.

"It's just . . . something happened on Monday. I didn't tell you then because I was afraid you'd . . . I don't know, that

126

you'd think I couldn't handle it. And the whole point is, I can. I *am* handling it."

"Oh," Alana said, and Maris could picture her sitting up straight, girding herself, holding on to the edge of her French walnut dining table. "Just tell me."

So she did: starting with Ron's call from the bridge and ending with the long drive home, coming back into her house and realizing that it held nothing for her anymore. In telling the story, Maris felt an unexpected unburdening, as though tissue-thin layers of painful habit were being peeled away, leaving the new growth of possibility exposed.

"And there's something else," she continued breathlessly, not giving Alana a chance to respond. Now that she was telling, she wanted to get it all out—everything but the hideout itself. She was Black Bart, confessing her last deeds before she went underground. "I talked to Jeff. It turns out that we have no money." It felt funny to say it, especially since she'd injected a little laugh, trying to make it sound like an amusing state of affairs. "I mean, I have plenty for now, but apparently Jeff isn't making enough to cover the expenses."

"Oh, Maris. I can't say I'm surprised," Alana said darkly. She was the CIO of a startup that had something to do with alternative energy; Maris had never known exactly what she did, but Alana and Jeff had always had a lot to talk about. "There was no way that position was going to pay him what he was worth."

"He was lucky to get it." A rogue urge to defend Jeff: this was the old dynamic, but it took Maris by surprise anyway. After all, he wasn't on her side anymore. "I mean, he's hoping they'll move him up once he's been there a year."

"So what are you doing? Selling stock?"

Maris took a deep breath, trying to decide how much to tell. Already, she'd built a more sizable lie than she had planned. "Yes, for now. But I may need to go back to work after all."

"They'd give you the director job?"

"No, they filled that a long time back. But I could pick up tutor hours tomorrow if I wanted to."

"Maris. Come on. This isn't a problem you can fix making fifteen dollars an hour."

"Just for now." No need to tell Alana that she'd rather die than go back to the Stern Center for Scholars, and see girls who'd played softball with Calla, boys who'd served in student government alongside her. Kids from the band, kids who would dutifully sit through the SAT test prep and apply to colleges and leave for the futures that Calla would never have. "I know I need to look for something else. Long term."

"I guess it won't make a difference if I point out that I have a ton of contacts? I could get you informational interviews, internal postings."

"I appreciate that. I really do. Maybe in a couple weeks. Alana, I hope you know . . ." But what, exactly, did she want Alana to know? Maris had doled out the truth in such a controlled stream: how she was handling things, what memories kept her awake at night, where she was when she found herself short of breath or on the verge of hysteria. Alana was the only person in the world who knew even a fraction of Maris's thoughts. But she didn't have it in her to give more. Not yet. ". . . I love you," she finally settled for.

"Mmm. Me too." Alana, like their mother, had never been

comfortable saying it out loud. "Listen. How about I come to you? Just for dinner, if that's what you want. I just hate for you to be alone right now."

Maris knew Alana wouldn't give up until she gave her something to hold on to. She couldn't tell her about the looming possibility of an appeal, or Alana would want to spring into action, and Maris wasn't sure yet what she could or would do if it came to pass. Everything had become so complicated. If only Ron had just gone ahead and jumped—or if only he and Deb could at least somehow simply vanish. "Maybe in a few days . . . how about I let you know?"

"I'd just feel so much better if I could see you. Please, Mar."

"Okay . . ." Maris thought fast. She couldn't let Alana come to Oakland. She wasn't ready for her to know that she was living there. It would require too much explanation. And Maris wasn't sure she could even explain it. She could meet Alana in Linden Creek, since that was where she was pretending to be house-sitting, except the thought of returning filled her with dread. She'd been gone only a couple of days and already it was unbearable to imagine running into people she knew, seeing the places that had been hers for so long. "Tell you what—how about if we meet in the city? Maybe we could go to the Slanted Door?"

The restaurant was a favorite of Alana's; and there was the Ferry Terminal to wander through, with its fancy shops, to keep the conversation from settling too long in difficult places.

"Are you sure?" Alana sounded doubtful.

"It's what I need—something to look forward to," Maris lied. "A chance to get a little dressed up. Maybe drink some wine."

"Well, it'll be my treat. I can do any time. We could meet this Saturday; I could see if I could get a reservation—"

"How about a week from Saturday?"

"All right," Alana said after a moment, in a tone that indicated it wasn't all right at all. "I'll do OpenTable and send you a confirmation."

Maris realized she hadn't been online since yesterday. She would have to remember. Running away only worked if she kept the illusion going, and there were people—not nearly as many as there used to be, heaven knew—who would wonder what happened to her and, eventually, reach out.

Maris ended the call. Thinking of the Slanted Door had reminded her that she was hungry. She'd had only a banana since this morning. Outside, night was deepening to purple.

She would have to make a grocery run. The refrigerator was clean—she'd even gone around the shelves with the scrub brush. But the thought of navigating the aisles was exhausting. There was the Subway . . . a Church's fried chicken. The diner across the street. Probably more choices over on Telegraph.

She grimaced, imagining the next two weeks brimming with fast-food take-out bags and soda cups, greasy egg sandwiches, and gallons of coffee. The sort of diet she followed in college, before she met Jeff and started trying to impress him with her domestic skills. Well, two weeks wouldn't kill her.

No matter what, she needed a shower before she ventured out. Maris ran water in the newly scrubbed bathtub and stripped off her clothes. She took her time in the cool shower, lathering her hair with the strawberry-smelling drugstore shampoo, shaving her legs. She toweled off, wishing she'd bought a hair dryer, but it was too hot and she'd end up sweaty again.

She dressed in one of her new shirts, a shell-pink sleeveless polo. White shorts. She needed a belt—something else to add to the list. It was amazing, the number of items one took for granted, just getting through the day.

Decision time: for the Church's drive-through, she wouldn't bother with makeup. Or if she ventured over to Telegraph to see what was available, maybe a little concealer and lipstick. It would be easy. She had her paperback, she could eat at the kitchen table; the light from the new bulbs was plenty bright.

She was ready to go ten minutes later, her hair drying into an unruly mass, when someone knocked on the door—a gentle tap on the frosted glass pane at the top, unlike Pet's enthusiastic pounding. She opened it to find Norris standing there.

"Hope I'm not intruding," he said quickly, before she could even say hello. "I just, I wanted to let you know, I stopped by at lunch today to fix that overhead light."

Maris glanced up at it—she hadn't even noticed that the flickering had stopped.

"I have a key, of course," Norris went on uncomfortably. "But I knocked first. I always do."

"Oh. Sure," Maris said, discomfited to know that someone could come walking in anytime, even if it was Norris, who seemed harmless. Awkward, maybe, and a little gruff, but harmless.

"And, I saw that you've done a lot already. I mean, wow!" He flashed a grin that was more of a grimace and tugged at his collar, staring at a spot over her shoulder, and Maris realized that he was actually shy.

131

"Would you like to come in?" she asked, pride at her handiwork mixing with relief. Shy, she could handle; she knew all about shyness, having battled it herself for much of her life.

Norris came inside and stood in the middle of the kitchen, hands on hips, looking around. Maris followed his gaze. She had stored her purchases in the dresser and bathroom shelves and kitchen cabinets; all that sat out on the scrubbed surfaces were the bottles of dish soap and hand lotion next to the kitchen sink, and the magazine and novel on the kitchen table. Her new dish towel hung neatly from the oven handle. The cheery new shower curtain was visible through the open bathroom door.

"Wow," he said again. "You really knocked yourself out. George said he filled up the entire back of his truck."

"George . . ."

"My friend, who hauled the trash away."

"Oh!" Maris's face was getting a little stiff from smiling. "Well, I definitely feel more at home here now."

"Yeah. Listen . . ." Norris scratched at his ear. "Pet says you're looking for work."

She did? Maris winced, wishing the girl had kept that to herself. "Well, I'm figuring out what I want to do next."

"Uh-huh, right. I was thinking, I mean, obviously you're an organized person. And hardworking. So, I have an opportunity, a few days' work, if you're interested."

Maris's guard went up, already casting about for a polite refusal, but Norris barreled ahead.

"Up in my spare room . . . you may have seen, the, uh. Well, my mother passed a couple years ago, and I haven't—I

132

mean, a lot of it's junk. Just worthless, really. I already took what I wanted. You know, what I could use."

Maris nodded, thinking of the cut-glass pieces in the china hutch. The sort of things a man might keep to remind himself of his mother.

"And there's a lot of paperwork in there; Mom was kind of a pack rat, I know there's things in there that are important, but I mean, she saved everything. *TV Guide*s from years ago, you know, that kind of thing." Norris seemed to relax fractionally. "Almost a hoarder is what she was. My sister and me, we threw out a lot of it when we were clearing out the place. But I had to pack some of it up and store it. Anyway. I could use . . ."

He got stuck, staring at the ceiling near the corner of the room, absently picking at a loose thread on one of his cuffs.

"You want someone to go through her things?" Maris guessed. "Sort out what's important from what isn't?"

"Yes, oh, yes," Norris said, expelling a breath he'd been holding. And Maris understood: the task was still raw for him.

"I'd be glad to," she said, before she'd even thought it through. "I'm not an accountant or anything—"

"You don't need to be. I thought you could just get all the financial documents together in one place and I can take them to my tax guy and have him go over them."

"All right," Maris agreed, imagining combing through the boxes stuffed with magazines, savings bonds, and old check registers. Her new landlord had complicated feelings about his mother's death, but then again, what adult child didn't? Maris's own mother had died almost six years ago, and it still caught her off-guard to remember that she was truly gone. But Nadine Parker had left her affairs so well ordered that there were no decisions to be made, and her few cherished possessions had slips of paper taped to them identifying who should receive each, just in case the detailed instructions in her will were somehow overlooked.

"I also thought . . . some of the stuff in those boxes, I think it might be valuable. I thought you might be able to, you know, figure it out. Maybe sell the stuff that can be sold, get rid of the rest." He screwed his face into a scowl and, addressing the floor, added, "It would be a weight off my mind to be clear of all that."

"Sure," Maris said. "What sort of things? If you don't mind my asking?"

"Well, she was a collector, she collected things, I know that." Norris shrugged. "Little, what do you call them . . . figurines, I guess you'd say. Coins, she had a lot of silver dimes and such. I don't know. Probably not worth much."

"Sure. Sure." Maris envisioned souvenir wineglasses and dusty church programs, and hoped Norris wouldn't be disappointed if it all turned out to be junk. "You know, this might be just what I need. Before I start job hunting for real."

"Well, all right then." Norris broke out into a real smile now. Why he'd chosen to trust her, a virtual stranger, she wasn't sure. Maybe Pet had put him up to it. "I work seven to four. I'm at the PG&E building over on Webster, is why I come home for lunch some days. But most days I don't, so you can work in peace. I don't guess it'll take you more than two, three days if you've got them. Take the weekend off, if it goes that long."

"I—I think I've got the time. I can start tomorrow. If you want me to."

"Let's make it day after tomorrow. Friday. That'll give me a chance to tidy up." Now that it was settled, relief seemed to have caught Norris in its tide and dragged him into a friendlier mood. "Tell you what—I'm just about to go catch a bite with George, he's the fellow who hauled all that trash away. What do you say, want to join us?"

"Oh," Maris said, taken aback. Despite her gratitude for this unexpected opportunity, dinner with her landlord and a garbage hauler seemed . . . inadvisable.

"It's at the bar," Norris added hastily, seeing her hesitation. "Where Pet works? George owns it. Nice place. I mean . . ."

"The trash guy? Owns the bar?"

"Yeah, well, he only does the hauling on the side now. He and I, we go way back, it's a long story. Anyway, we can get some wings—"

"$8.99 for wings and fries?" Maris interrupted.

"How'd you know?"

"I have my ways," Maris said, feeling better than she had in days. "I'll just grab my purse."

fourteen

RON WAS SITTING ON the bench behind the Whole Foods. He'd never seen anyone else sit on this bench in the eight years since they'd built the little upscale strip mall, but it had become his habit to walk down the landscaped path behind the shops to the bench occasionally when he wanted to think, to be alone. His phone rang, and he stared at the unfamiliar number for a moment before shoving it back into his pocket.

After the jail visit, he'd found himself driving to work, without really making a decision about it. He'd left word for his assistant that he had a doctor's appointment, leaving it open-ended; no one would have minded if he took the rest of the day off. But he wasn't ready to see Deb yet, wasn't ready for questions about how the visit had gone, what had been said and not said. Decided and not decided. And he definitely wasn't in the mood to discuss the appeal, or the psychiatrist she still thought he should see, or her obvious if stifled resentment of the thing he'd almost done. So he'd scrolled through email and looked over notes for an hour and a half before finally admitting to himself that he wasn't really absorbing anything he read, that he would have to repeat all of the work tomorrow. Stopping at Whole Foods—he told himself he could pick up the green olives that Deb liked, maybe some gelato—was just another way to put off the inevitable, to buy a little time once he got home before she started in on him.

But once he parked, he bypassed the entrance to walk around to the back. As serenity practices went, this bench probably wasn't ideal. The strip mall had been built just before the real estate crash, and originally a multiuse luxury apartment building had been slated for the parcel next door: restaurants, a garden center, upscale units. That had all been scrapped, but not before the builders had landscaped the back of the strip mall with trails and retaining walls and plantings meant to overlook the apartment building, the centerpiece of which was to have been a massive water feature. Now the bench overlooked a cleared acre, unnaturally flat and scraped of vegetation, so that only scrub and weeds poked up around the broken concrete and vestigial drainage pipes that had been left behind.

Depressing as hell, which was, maybe, why Ron was drawn to it. Best was at twilight, when the foothills beyond were nearly invisible in the sinking sky. But afternoons like this one were good too. In truth, no one would notice him there except the Mexican gardeners who dutifully mowed the abandoned patch. He stared at the empty lot, at the freeway in the distance with its rushing cars, at the nothing in between. He tried to empty his mind. Sometimes he tried the exercises the therapist had recommended, the ones Deb had begged him to do with her. Mostly, though, he just stared.

The phone rang again. Impatiently, he pulled it from his pocket a second time. Same number. Someone really wanted to get in touch with him. Ron was accustomed to things coming in the mail—no one could stop the freaks from finding out their address, even after he moved. But they usually didn't find his phone number. He supposed he was going to have to get used to this all over again if the appeal really did happen.

Besides, maybe this was just work, since he'd left without tying up a few loose ends. One of the analysts, maybe someone from Glenda's team, needing a last round of approvals before they sent off to production. For a lot of people, July was a slow month—half the support staff seemed to be on vacation—so this could probably wait until he got in.

Whoever it was was leaving a long message. Ron stared at the screen until the ding of the voice mail came through. Then he watched the cars on the freeway and tried to muster the energy to get moving.

It rang again. Same number.

"Aw, *fuck*." Ron's voice was quiet, competing only with a handful of crickets. This was stupid.

He answered. "Yeah?"

"Don't hang up."

A woman's voice, but not one he recognized. "Who is this?"

"Just please don't hang up. All right? Please."

He didn't answer, poised to do exactly that. His finger hovering near the End Call button.

"This is Alana Parker. Maris Vacanti's sister."

"I—I know." Of course he knew who Alana Parker was. When she'd come to court, which admittedly wasn't all that often, she made quite an impression and ended up being photographed a lot, especially when she leaned in to talk to her sister. She had that Caroline Kennedy quality about her, the elegant bearing and the dark glasses and the sense of unapproachability. The photo of the two of them hurrying down the steps, clutching each other, with Jeff trailing in their wake—that was the photo that had been picked up everywhere on the day of sentencing.

Ron and Alana Parker had never spoken before, though.

He could hear her take a deep breath. "You called her. On Monday."

He didn't answer. What was there to say? Already, he could look back on that moment from many angles of regret. He could claim that it hadn't really been him, at least not him in his right mind, and that would be true, in a way.

"I wish you hadn't," Alana said. "She . . . you know she doesn't need that, right?"

"Oh, Jesus," he muttered.

"No, no, wait, that's not what . . . let me just."

The silence between them felt familiar. Ron watched cars, tracking their speeding arcs as they made their way south. The evening was starting to cool, and the air smelled like thyme, the scent of some sort of wild scrub plant. This was far better than air-conditioning, as far as Ron was concerned. Why everyone didn't just sit outside—hell, sleep outside at night in the fresh air, it didn't make sense. Maybe he should go camping again. Maybe he should become a hermit, live in some fishing shack in the Sierra and grow a beard down to his chest.

"I'm calling because I want to ask you to leave her alone."

"Don't worry," Ron said. He rested his forehead on his hand. "I'm not—I won't do anything like that again."

"It's just . . . I don't think she can take it. I know she seems like she's holding it all together. She can do that, she's tough that way."

A memory of Maris, in the bar of that hotel in Sacramento almost two years ago when they'd both chaperoned the school trip, the moment before she'd spotted him. She had a book tucked under her arm, some sort of pastel-covered novel with a picture of a lake on the cover. When her eyes lit on him, finally, she looked amused.

"I always . . ." His voice came out rough, and he cleared his throat before trying again. "I always thought highly of her. Before everything."

"Yes. Well. Jeff left her."

"Aw, *hell*." The news hit him in the pit of his stomach: one more casualty, one more disaster that was, if you followed the long chain of culpability back to the source, his fault. Of course it wasn't a surprise—the statistics were stark. Couples who endured the loss of a child usually lost each other as well, finding no place for another person in their grief—he and Deb had known that practically from the start. After their first counseling session she had held him in the car, so tightly he actually felt the breath leave his lungs, and made him swear that they wouldn't ever leave each other.

"You know, I don't know if it's the worst thing . . . I mean, it's not my place to say. But she was supposed to come down and stay with me at my place. Just while she got back on her feet. And instead she's gone completely off the rails. I talked to her earlier today, Ron. I'm scared for her."

"She's not with you? She's by herself?"

"She told me she was staying at a friend's house in Linden Creek. I don't know what she's trying to do, if she's punishing herself or . . . I really don't know. But I do know that she

140

doesn't need anything else to tip the balance right now. Do you understand what I'm saying?"

Ron tried to remember what he'd read about Alana. It had been his worst penance, during the long months awaiting trial, to comb the media for any news of the Vacantis. And not just them, of course; he had Google alerts set up, and he'd bookmarked Facebook pages and set up Twitter lists, schooled himself in all the social media Karl once scoffed at him for being ignorant of. He allowed himself half an hour in the morning—he adjusted his schedule to get to work even earlier, so there was no one there to see him hunched over his computer—and every morning he forced himself to learn the latest about Karl's grassroots defenders, the protestors, the nuts and the freaks, the accusers and the haters. And most of all, the Vacantis themselves, the ones crushed under the wheels.

Alana worked for a biomed startup, and she had risen pretty high. The article in the *Examiner*, the big one that had been picked up all over the place, called her "her sister's strength," and made much of the fact that there were no other siblings, no parents. It made good press, no doubt, with the moody photos they'd caught of the sisters standing outside the courthouse during the pretrial hearings. Alana was a couple of inches taller, and she favored high-heeled platform sandals with her flowing colorless clothes. She sometimes hid her face behind her hair, which hung around her face in shiny, silvery sheets, so that usually it was Maris that the camera caught, Maris with that eternally stricken expression.

More often than not, Jeff had been relegated to their distant orbit, caught at the edges of photographs. But it was no wonder. Jeff's resting state was a blank expression—had been even before. He was a good-looking man in the blandest possible way, the sort of man who could model a suit for a Macy's ad but fade into a crowd with no effort at all. Ron supposed that Jeff experienced a full gamut of human emotions, but over the course of the months awaiting trial, the days in the courtroom, his expression had barely pressed the parameters that contained it.

"I understand," Ron said, because he knew Alana was waiting for him to say something. And he did, he knew—maybe even better than Alana—what might have made Maris bolt. Some hairline crack had shattered and she'd gone rogue. "She has a lot of friends in Linden Creek, doesn't she? I mean, maybe that's why, maybe she needs—"

"No." Clipped, annoyed. "At least, not right now. She's been a virtual hermit, she's been turning everyone away."

"Well, are you worried that—are you afraid she's thinking of—" He couldn't say it, didn't feel entitled to say it, not after what he'd done.

"No, that's not what this is about. She's not the type to make this about her." Ron flinched: such an obvious jab, but one that he deserved. "She just doesn't need any more on her mind. And there's another thing. She doesn't have any money. Jeff apparently emptied out the accounts, and he's not making enough to swing the mortgage."

"Oh, *God*," Ron muttered, squeezing the skin of his forehead and closing his eyes. Their lawyers had warned him and Deb of the possibility of a civil suit. Maybe now it would come to pass. Ron didn't care—he'd be happy living out his days right here on this bench—but what it would do to

Deb . . . "Alana. Listen. If it's money, there's got to be a way for us to help."

"Fuck you, Ron." It was shocking, coming from her, even if they'd never spoken before this day. She seemed like the last person on earth who would swear. "If that was the issue, *I* have money. Plenty."

"But all I was saying was—"

"If you want to buy off your guilt, you'll have to look somewhere else. That's not what this is about." Her fury made her voice harder, stronger. "I called to tell you to leave her alone, that's all."

"Look, I understand I screwed up," Ron said, and he really did know it, inside. He felt hot at the core, shame and remorse. "And just so you know, I wasn't . . . I wasn't asking her for forgiveness. When I called from the . . . when I called her on Monday."

"*You're* not the one who ought to be asking."

Oh, God, of course he knew that. How many times had he wished he could march across the courtroom and smack his son across the face, jar the words free, pry them out. Anything, just to get Karl to show that he *felt* something.

"Alana." His voice broke, and for a long time, he didn't trust himself to try again. What he wanted to ask her: Was there ever a moment when she'd wondered if Karl might be innocent? Could she now? She hadn't mentioned Mehta; maybe she hadn't made the connection, maybe she never dreamed that the Isherwoods would push for an appeal.

The phone chimed; without looking he knew a text had come from Deb. He'd forgotten to tell her he wasn't coming straight home from the prison. He was predictable enough that she'd probably already guessed he'd been hiding out at work, but now she expected him home.

"Look." Alana sounded calmer. "I shouldn't have said that. I just want my sister to . . . to have a chance, you know? I can take care of her. I can help her. But she has to work through everything she's dealing with right now. And she needs peace for that. She needs to know you're not going to do anything to, you know, revisit what she's been through. Can I promise her that? Can I *really* make that promise to her?"

"You can. I swear it." He was glad she wasn't there to look into his eyes; it was a promise he wasn't sure he would be able to keep. If it was just him, yes—but there was Deb to consider; Deb and her hell-bent determination to open it all up again. "And about the other. I would like to help. Please, if there's a way I can help. I'm . . . I don't know how to say this so it comes out right. But money, that's not . . . it's maybe the one thing we don't have to worry about. Deb and me. And I know she'd feel the same way." A lie, a necessary one. "It's, there's more than enough."

"Thank you." Not quite as hard, now. "I appreciate it. I don't expect she'd ever want that. But if it ever comes up . . . but no, she wouldn't."

"I would like to talk to her—to tell her I'm sorry for the other day. Not now, I know that, but if, you know, if later there seems like a time when it would be okay."

"I'll pass that along. Like you said, if ever it seems like a good time. Right now she's just, I don't think she's all that stable."

"You said you talked to her." His mind cycled through the worst. Some of the parents from the grief group . . . they'd looked like ghosts, their words in a time-lapse mismatch from their faces. Clothes hanging off slumped bodies, eyes purpled with sunken skin. Sometimes they hadn't washed. And others were the opposite—so carefully groomed, so tightly wound, as though the slightest upset would shatter them. "Do you feel like she's, I don't know . . . Headed in the right direction, at least?"

"I don't feel like you deserve to know. I want to hate you," Alana said. "But I don't have the energy. She's all right, Ron. I think."

He could tell she wanted to say more, and he braced himself for it, for whatever hurled epithet she had stored up, whatever emotions she might try to shift onto him. But when she spoke again, her voice was soft and sad.

"She went to the bridge, you know. After you called her. She said she was afraid she'd get pulled over because she was cutting in and out of traffic and driving on the shoulder. By the time she got there you were gone, though. The bridge was backed up, but she drove it both ways and there wasn't anyone there. It *was* the Golden Gate, wasn't it?"

"Yeah—it's the only one you can walk out onto."

"Right. Well, I told her maybe you were faking. Like, just trying to get her sympathy or something. And she told me she knew you wouldn't do that. That if you said you were on the bridge, you meant it. And I asked her how she knew."

That memory again, of Maris in that bar, her upturned face, her expressive eyes. Listening while he poured out his secrets . . . listening while he told her things he had never told another soul and would never tell again. He'd die first. And all the while, her face never changed; it wasn't judgment and it wasn't forgiveness and it wasn't even curiosity. It was just . . . it had felt like acceptance. She had allowed him to confess his sins and not reacted at all.

"She said she just *knew*," Alana said softly. "I wanted to tell her she was being stupid, that no one can know what's in your mind. But, I don't know. Maybe you two understand each other."

Maybe they did.

Alana hung up and Ron texted Deb, promising to be home soon. Then he watched a rabbit lope across the lot to disappear into a shrub. He could hear horns from the freeway. Someone cutting someone else off, everyone in a hurry.

Maris. He'd thought she was exceptional, that heady, wine-fueled night. He'd watched her across the little bar table, over that tiny flickering oil candle and the untouched dish of pistachios, and wondered why everyone didn't see what he saw.

fifteen

"ALL RIGHT," RON SAID, ambushed in his own foyer. His shirt, damp with perspiration from sitting on the bench, had grown clammy in the car's air-conditioning. "All right," he said again, nodding, a pathetic attempt to buy time.

"I'll get you a drink," Deb said brightly. The new attorney watched him sagely, a faint smirk on his bearded, square jaw. He was wearing a sport coat over a cotton shirt unbuttoned just far enough to show a bit of silver chest hair—a look Ron found especially repugnant.

"I'm just going to change," Ron said, his eyes still locked on the lawyer's. His name was Honeycutt, and in an introduction that took less than thirty seconds, his wife had managed to convey that he was very well regarded and they were very lucky to hire him.

Honeycutt nodded coolly and shook the ice in his glass. Ron took the stairs two at a time, fueled by irritation. Deb had blindsided him, but he could see that she'd only been acting on her powerful protective instinct. She wasn't really to blame, any more than you could blame a raccoon for knocking over garbage cans, an eagle for building a nest in the highest aerie it could find.

And besides, he'd done worse to her first. He wouldn't blame her for feeling he owed her.

Back downstairs, in a clean shirt and with a gin and tonic in hand, he discovered that the loathsome Kami was there too. His only consolation was seeing how Honeycutt's mouth twitched when Kami spoke. He too was put off by her murky, nameless motivations. Honeycutt's own goals were crystal clear: publicity, payout. He would look good in the courtroom and he would look good on the evening news, and watching his wife's wide, hopeful eyes, Ron could tell that she thought she'd hit the jackpot.

When he left half an hour later, Honeycutt shook Ron's hand with a bit more force than necessary, and held on to Deb's a little too long. Kami lingered for a few more moments, chatting about nothing, before taking off. Ron rolled his eyes and shut the door, and when he turned to face his wife, Deb was watching him carefully.

"Before you say anything—"

"Deb," he said warningly.

"I haven't signed anything and I haven't given anyone any money."

"Well, that's a relief," Ron said sarcastically, before reconsidering the conversation ahead. "Look, let me just use the john."

He took the time to settle his irritation. He had to do this carefully, or Deb might fly off the handle and decide to do this with or without him. For now, he hoped he still had her natural deference on his side—the old Deb never made a decision, not even something as small as what microwave to buy or which cable service to use, without consulting him.

But she was changing, just as everything was changing. He was not the old Ron, and she was not the old Deb. She was steelier, somehow, and less . . . dependent? Was that the word? She no longer signaled her need for him with the countless gestures he'd taken for granted for so long. She didn't refill his coffee, adjust his tie, ask him if he wanted another pillow when he was reading in bed at night—all the officious little acts that had once annoyed him and that he now missed. Once he'd have laughed at the thought of his wife undertaking some life-changing agenda without his full support.

But so much had happened since then. Now he had to be cautious.

In the kitchen he mixed them each a fresh drink, even though Deb had been drinking bright pink Crystal Light. He took the drinks to the den and sat down in his favorite chair and set her drink on the end table. Curled on the couch, Deb looked relaxed, almost vulnerable.

Ron needed to press every advantage.

"Look," he said carefully, leaning forward. "I'm not going along with this. Karl will never agree."

Deb blinked, and Ron could see a stiffening in her posture. "But—" she said.

"I was just there today. I talked to him. He has no interest—he is absolutely dead set against it, Deb. And he made a good point. The appeal could take, what, two or three years? Longer, if we're unlucky—"

"Mark is *good*," Deb said emphatically. "He's the best there is. He wouldn't take the case if he didn't think—if he didn't expect—"

"This isn't about him, sweetheart." Ron reconsidered; maybe he should have sat next to her on the couch. Been there to provide comfort, put his arm around her and offered his shoulder to cry on. "This isn't even about whether or not our son did it. It's not about guilt or innocence. Honey, you've got to stop looking at it that way."

"I'll *never* stop," she said, untucking her legs from underneath herself and sitting up straight. She clutched wadded tissues in her hand like she was trying to strangle them. "I made a promise to him, to myself, that I would never stop believing in him, stop trying to help him, until the day he walked out of that place."

Ron shut his eyes for a moment, looking for the right words. He opened them and gently tugged at Deb's hands. After a moment she loosened her grip; he uncurled her fingers and the tissues fell to the floor, and he tried to envelop her cold hands in his, but she pulled them back. "I'm going to say something to you, Deb, and it's important. Well, it's important to me, anyway. Do you understand?"

Deb nodded, suspicion clouding her red-rimmed blue eyes.

"All right." Ron made a show of taking a deep breath, girding himself. "I . . . don't know if our son is guilty or innocent. I'm confused. Things I thought I knew . . . I'm not sure about them anymore, at least not like I was before."

He forced himself not to look away. Was this true? The words had come from him, from a place deep inside him where he'd reached for the tools to change his wife's mind, but were they also real? Or only a fabrication meant to serve his needs in the moment?

"When I talked to him today," he continued, and now he

was up there without a net, extemporizing, going with his gut. "He was different. He said I'd never believed him, never given him a chance."

"*I* told you that." Deb followed her sharp retort by picking up the drink he'd made and taking a gulp. "I've always said that."

"Yeah, no, but he was saying . . . always. Before all this happened. Like when he was growing up." Suddenly Ron felt his control of the situation slipping away, the loss of what was known and the suffocating presence of what was not. "That I didn't make him feel like I had faith in him, that I believed in him."

That catch in his voice, the thickening in his throat—where had they come from? He hadn't meant to dwell on this point, only to use it as context for what he meant to say next. To lead Deb gently to the conclusion he needed her to reach. Instead, an image of Karl at eleven came to mind, out of breath and red-faced from running, his thin arm in Ron's grip, the feeling of power as he curled his fingers tighter around his son's bicep. Karl and his friends had been throwing rocks over a creek at the baseball fields on the other side. The other dads could discipline their sons as they saw fit—Ron remembered having this thought, how reasonable it had seemed—but he, Ron, wasn't going to raise some hellion of a kid who couldn't connect actions and consequences. But he wasn't his old man. He wasn't a monster. He made Karl walk out on that field and pick up every last rock, the ones he'd thrown and the ones the others had, and bring them back to the landscaped ridge where they'd found them. Ron waited, stony faced and cold, as the other boys and their parents all went home, as the coach gave him a sidelong glance, hauling the bags to his trunk. *This is a sacrifice for me too*, Ron had reminded himself, watching his son try not to cry, the wind whipping his jacket, as night fell.

"I never hit him," Ron heard himself say, but his voice was so plaintive. "Never. But I might have been too tough on him, in other ways."

"Ron," Deb said impatiently, "I never said that you were a bad dad. *Are* a bad dad."

"Heh." The little laugh that slipped out of him sounded manic, unhinged. He *was* a bad dad. There wasn't a person in the country who would argue in his favor, given the facts.

But he could still try. He thought of Karl, the anguish in those blue eyes that strangers used to remark on—*got his looks from his mom*, that was always Ron's refrain—now set into that puffy, oily face. Wished he could go back to that day on the baseball field. Wished he could go back all the way to the start. To before the start, before Karl was even conceived. Back, back, back—but how does one do that? How do you go back up the family tree, scrambling up the doomed bloodline, and make things right?

He was sweating again, the fresh shirt wilting against his skin. Deb was regarding him with frosty confusion. "Look," he tried again. "All I'm trying to say—Karl was very, very clear with me. If we do this, he's just going to refuse. You know Honeycutt can't do a damn thing for him without permission, don't you?"

Deb scowled, but she didn't say anything.

Ron sighed. "Look, I can, we can try to talk to him again, I guess—"

"I'm going on Sunday."

"I know. So, you can try to talk to him then, maybe you'll have a better shot at him."

"I already tried." She was petulant, like a little girl. That wasn't new, exactly, but in the past such moods could easily be smoothed away by a compliment, some trifling indulgence. Ron doubted that would work now.

"But we can try again, right? There's no deadline on, I mean, I know you said you wanted to capitalize on the news, on Mehta's thing, I get that, but . . ."

He reached for her hands again, rubbed his thumbs over her knuckles. She didn't resist. He was torn between fighting her and pleading with her. He was willing to get on his knees for her, if it would have made a difference. Only, what was he trying to achieve, again?

"Come with me, if you care so much," Deb said abruptly. "On Sunday. I'll get on the system and see if I can add you."

"That's . . . I mean, I guess, maybe."

"We don't have that much time. Honeycutt wants to get started right away."

"Well, he's just going to have to wait a few days."

"Right," Deb said slowly, nodding. "Right."

She was the one who pulled away first. She stood up and took the afghan off the back of the couch. Refolded it and returned it to where she'd found it. It didn't look any different to Ron. She picked up both their glasses and carried them to the kitchen. A moment later, he heard her footfalls on the stairs.

sixteen

THE SIGN WAS EITHER original or someone had paid to make it look that way. Old neon, curving letters: The Coal Mine, with a cart mounded with pink "coal" that flickered off and on.

Maris walked next to Norris, her sandals striking the cracked pavement hard. She was conscious of walking with a man, a tall man who carried himself well. She had been conscious of him in the car as well—when was the last time she'd ridden alone in a car with a man other than Jeff? An entire year, possibly, or even more. Norris's car had been scrupulously clean, with a faint scent of mint, or menthol. Maris herself liked to keep her car neat, and took it—well, used to take it, anyway—to a car wash in San Ramon once or twice a month.

He had made small talk, but she could tell it was an effort. The weather, more stilted compliments on her transformation of the apartment. No questions about her personal life, and no details volunteered about his own, which made Maris think, somewhat wistfully, about her mother, who had an old-fashioned sensibility about prying into things that were none of one's business. A midwestern sense, Maris had come to think of it in the decades since leaving Kansas. She wondered if Norris had grown up in Oakland or come from elsewhere, but it was his very reticence that prevented her from asking him.

"Here we go," he said with what sounded like relief when they reached the bar's open front door. The windows on either side were painted black. People had scratched their initials in the paint, hieroglyphic graffiti, the word *fuck* at least three times. A thick-bodied man sat on a stool just inside the door, his head thrown back, laughing. When he spotted Maris the laugh died on his lips. His gaze traveled leisurely down her shirt, taking in the white shorts, her bare legs. Then he spotted Norris behind her and his eyebrows shot up.

He clattered off the chair and didn't so much hug as slam into Norris from the side, thumping him on the back. Norris endured this with an embarrassed smile.

"Mary," Norris said, wrenching himself free, "this is George. George, this is Mary, the lady who took the apartment."

George offered a little half bow, and Maris couldn't tell if he was teasing her or not. "Hello," she said, more stiffly than she intended. She peered past him into the dim interior, looking for Pet.

"Well, well," he said, more to Norris than to her. "You've certainly moved up to a better class of tenant, my friend."

"She's done a heck of a job on the place. Cleaned it up good."

"So I gathered. What was in those bags, anyway—the guy before you leave his rock collection behind?"

Maris felt herself blushing. She wasn't sure, but she thought he winked at her. Was he flirting? Was that even possible? He was a nice-looking man, his salt-and-pepper beard neatly

155

trimmed, his thick hair a bit on the long side. Strong, masculine features; even teeth and a nice smile. As for herself, Maris knew what she looked like; she looked—cruelly, maybe—like a mom. Mom hips. Mom breasts. Mom haircut. A Target shirt and barely enough makeup to leave the house in.

But still. The attention was nice, even if it made her feel rusty and out of touch. It was the sort of thing she would have once shared with her little network of girlfriends over drinks in one of their kitchens, the impromptu girls' nights that had once been a part of her life. Adrian, Jemma, Heather—the women she'd cut from her life, prying their fingers from her until she could fall freely. Now, only for a second—aware that it wasn't possible, that her long hibernation after Calla's death had caused those friendships to fade to nonexistence—she wished she could joke about all of this over one of Adrian's mojitos.

"Duchess and Tony are here already," George said. "They got the big table in the back and I think Tony might have gone next door for wings already."

He led the way inside, and Norris waited for Maris to go ahead of him. A dozen people stood around the bar, a couple more at one of two round tables, with a pitcher between them. The place smelled of stale beer and creosote, but it was cozy, with plaid curtains hanging in the windows and plants hanging from macramé baskets. Maris wondered how they stayed alive in the darkened room, and decided they must be fake. Along the walls, in between neon beer signs and signed sports jerseys, were a series of amateurish oil paintings. Behind the bar, propped up on shelves crowded with liquor bottles and strung with little white Christmas lights, were framed studio portraits from the seventies: men in thick sideburns and aviator glasses; women with stiff updos and brocade dresses, their lips tinted bright red.

Maris spotted Pet, her back to the door, stacking glasses on a shelf. She was wearing a gray tank top with narrow straps, and Maris could make out more of the tattoo that had been hidden by her shirt before: branches, stark dead ones from the look of it, inked in black with none of the bright colors that had become so popular lately. An odd choice for a tattoo, but then, what did she know?

Maris could feel her heart beating rapidly as she followed George, weaving among the tables, excusing herself as she bumped into a woman splayed tipsily in her chair. It felt like people were staring at her, which of course was an illusion, a trick of the mind. No one was the least bit interested in her. Maris remembered something she had told Calla, long ago, when she was nervous about going to junior prom because at the last minute, fussing with the neckline, she decided her dress was too "gappy." Maris wasn't even sure what that meant—to her, the garnet-colored dress looked lovely, her daughter even more beautiful—but she'd tried every trick she could think of to convince Calla that she looked fine so her daughter could enjoy the evening.

Maris tried to get Pet's attention as they passed the bar. The back room held a pair of pool tables and two long wooden tables. At one, four people sat with a pitcher of beer, taking food out of several large paper sacks. As George led the way, shouting a greeting to someone at the table, Pet glanced over at Maris and then did a double take.

"Mary! You made it!"

Maris flushed with pleasure. It was ridiculous, but she felt a little bit cool—she knew the bartender. She went to stand at the bar, breaking free of the tight orbit of Norris and George for the moment.

Pet leaned across the bar and gave her a squeeze on the arm that approximated a hug. "You survived your first full day on Iris?"

"On . . . what?"

"Iris Street? Oh come on, didn't you know that's the name of our street?" At Maris's blank expression she laughed. "Mary, did you seriously rent a room without knowing the address?"

"I knew it was between thirty-eighth and thirty-ninth." It was absurd, now that she thought about it—but every other move she'd made since graduating from college had involved calls to PG&E, the cable company, visits to the post office to forward mail. She ordered change-of-address cards from the stationer when they moved into the apartment in San Ramon and again when they moved to the house in Linden Creek.

"Well, you survived, like I said. That's the important thing."

"And I finished cleaning. You'll have to come visit again. You can actually see what color the floor is now."

"Then you deserve to get a little hammered. First one's on me. What do you feel like?"

"Um, I don't usually drink mixed drinks," Maris hedged. And never beer. Just wine and the occasional vodka gimlet. But she already felt too stiff, too old. No sense adding to that impression. "But how about a . . ."

She had been about to say "mojito," since she'd been

thinking about Adrian, but who knew, maybe they were already passé here. "Surprise me?"

Pet grinned. "You sure?"

"Uh, sure."

"Okay, I'll bring it to you. Go find the guys, they'll introduce you around." Pet moved off and began pulling bottles. Maris used the time to sneak glances at the other patrons near her. A girl in a strapless top and jeans whose vine tattoos started on the backs of her hands and continued up past her shoulders, grazing her neck. A man with a bushy brown beard that made him look like a Hasidic Jew, laughing at something she was saying. On the other side, two men in their sixties. Escaping their wives, Maris would have assumed, if they were in Linden Creek.

She walked to the back room. George, sitting at one end of the table, was watching her. He gave her a smile that was simply . . . nice. Not lascivious, not assessing. "Hey, Mary, I saved you a seat," he called.

She slid into the chair between George and Norris, hanging her purse on the back, as conversation came to a temporary halt. "This her?" the man on the end said. He was short, stocky, bald, with a bad sunburn and a Minnesota Twins shirt. There were two women at the table too, a pretty blonde with hair almost to the small of her back and a tentative smile that covered braces, and a very thin African American woman with shimmering green eyeliner and a silky sleeveless blouse with a design of a peacock, its colorful feathers fanning across her back.

Norris cleared his throat. "Everyone, this is Mary. Mary, this is George, who you met, and this is Duchess, Bria, and Tony."

There was a chorus of hellos. Duchess offered her hand, and Maris shook it carefully, mostly fingertips. The blonde, Bria, fluttered her fingertips and grinned, reaching for the pitcher. "Do you want some beer?"

"Oh, thank you so much, but Pet's making me something," Mary said. She felt flush with nostalgia and a pleasant, low-level excitement: was this really so different from her grad school days, when she and the other student teachers would meet on Fridays at the Roundup?

"Tony and I work together," Norris said. He had to raise his voice to be heard, which made him seem less formal. He looked more relaxed now, anyway, leaning back in his chair, his beer already half gone. "And if I didn't already mention it, George and I were in the service together. Afghanistan."

"Yeah, and lived together too for a spell, after," George said, leaning in with his elbows on the table. "Worked together, got in trouble together . . ."

"Not much trouble," Norris said, holding his hands in mock defense and laughing. "Least, not that I had anything to do with."

"Here you go," Pet said, putting a glass down in front of her.

"Thank you," Maris said, shaking the drink gently so the ice bobbed against the glass. It was deep amber and smelled of whiskey. "You really must let me take you to lunch now. You've fed me and bought me a drink. What is it?"

"Just try it."

Maris sipped: bitter and tart and deliciously potent, not at all sweet.

"Aw, did you push that shit on her? What did she do to you?" Tony said, smirking.

"It's . . . interesting. But good."

Pet laughed. "It comes with a guarantee—if you don't like it, I'll make you something else."

"Pet's been trying to get people to drink that shit all week," Tony said.

"Hey, come on, it's good. Top-shelf single malt in there," George retorted, but his eyes were on Maris.

"No, it's good, really," she said. "What's in it?"

"Scotch, bitters, Cointreau," Pet said, ticking the ingredients off on her fingers. "Lotus is just unrefined, don't listen to him."

"My name is *George*." He gave Pet a mock glare. "Some folks can't seem to remember."

Maris took advantage of their teasing to look at him a little more closely. In the somewhat better light cast by a faux-Tiffany pendant lamp, she could see that his hair was still mostly dark brown, shot through with silver threads. His face was lined, but in a nice way—the skin of someone who'd spent a lot of time in the sun. She could see a glint of gold in his teeth when he smiled. He wasn't so much overweight as he was solid: big shoulders, thick neck, heavy, muscled forearms. The shirt he wore reminded Maris of the ones her uncle Nate wore decades ago, short-sleeved green plaid, a soft collar, tails untucked from his jeans.

"So, Mary," Duchess said. "Norris tells me you've taken the downstairs apartment?"

"It's just for a couple of weeks," Maris said hastily.

"She's finding herself." Pet said it without irony, then headed back to the bar.

"How do the rest of you know each other?" Maris asked, too curious to resist.

It was Tony who answered, with another chuckle. "That one's mine," he said, hooking a thumb at Bria, "and that one used to be."

Duchess stuck out her tongue at him.

"He's my dad," Bria said, rolling her eyes.

"And I'm the ex-girlfriend." Duchess didn't seem the least embarrassed by that fact.

"And he's the new boyfriend," Tony said, dumping a pile of wings onto a paper plate and nodding in Norris's direction.

Norris looked stricken. Duchess reached across Bria's lap—"Sorry, honey," she said, and slapped Tony's hand. A wing skittered across the table and fell to the floor.

"Hey!" Tony exclaimed.

"You need to apologize to the lady," Norris grumbled.

"Let's eat," Bria said.

Later, after Maris had had a second cocktail and five chicken wings, and washed the orange sauce from her hands, as well as the hem of her shorts, in the bar's diminutive ladies' room, she came back to find that George had moved their chairs slightly away from the others.

"I hope you don't mind," he said sheepishly. "I guess I could try to convince you that I just wanted to show you the art."

He pointed to the wall above him, where a large painting of the *Last Supper* hung under a Budweiser clock.

"That reminds me of paint-by-number kits our neighbor used to do back in Kansas," Maris said, hoping she wasn't slurring her words and trying to hide the illicit thrill it gave her to be talking to a nice-looking man who was apparently interested in her. Or was he? The last hour had been filled

162

with raucous laughter and the five friends—joined occasionally by Pet, when things slowed down behind the bar—talking over each other, competing for her attention.

"That's exactly what it is, doll."

"Really?" Thinking: *do people really still say* doll?—and that she kind of liked it.

"Yup. A few of them were my mom's. I took 'em after she passed. More for . . . I don't know, for the memory of it, if that makes sense, than for the actual paintings. She used to sit at our kitchen table chain smoking and working on her 'pictures,' is what she called them, while me and my brothers raised hell all over the house. Man, she loved those."

"Which were hers?"

George didn't answer for a moment. He picked up his beer, staring at her over the top, then set it down again without taking a sip. "Tell you what," he said. "I'll give you a tour."

She allowed him to help her up, giggling as he picked up her purse and slid it over her arm. She was a little unsteady, but only a little. The bar had emptied out quite a bit. Maris wondered how late it was, as George paused under a small painting of two kittens batting at a bright orange butterfly.

"No," Maris said, widening her eyes. "Really? It's exquisite!"

George laughed, and she congratulated herself on amusing him, and then worried that she'd gone too far. This was what she was like when she drank, and the reason that she rarely did—alcohol made her both more loquacious and, later, mortified when she sobered up.

"Yup. That was one of her earlier works. Over here we've got a triptych, what I like to call the *Three Ladies of Spain*."

And that was, indeed, what hung over the pool tables: two black-haired beauties in swirling flamenco skirts framing a demure young woman peeping over a fan. Maris laughed and sipped her drink, surprised to find it was nearly gone.

Pet had finished up behind the bar and was sitting on a stool, casting them smug glances. George looked at his watch.

"Your ride looks like she's getting impatient. Guess we better wrap up the tour so you can get home at a decent hour, especially since Norris tells me he's putting you to work tomorrow."

"He told you?" Maris was surprised, then wondered why. It wasn't exactly a secret.

"Yeah, and it's about time too. It's a good thing you're doing for him. He's been trying to work up to going through that shit for the last two years."

"You mean . . . because of . . ." The liquor was making it hard for Maris to find the euphemistic phrases she usually employed for delicate subjects. Which was strange, because before George even responded, she knew what he was going to say:

"He was really broken up when his mom died." George put his hand under her elbow and guided Maris toward the bar. Pet was counting out tips, stacking coins and pressing bills flat on the polished wood. "Grief, you know, it can really stay with a person for a long time."

Maris nodded dumbly. Grief. Yes. *Please*, she thought, *please don't let the conversation go that way, not tonight, not just now.* Tomorrow, yes, she would be ready for its inevitable return, she'd be sober and probably regretting not just the drinking but the gaiety, but for now she just wanted a little bit more, please, God, just a little bit more.

"There you are," Pet said. "I was starting to wonder if George clubbed you over the head and dragged you off to his lair."

"I'm wounded," George protested, pretending to stab himself in the heart with an invisible knife. Then, "Do okay tonight?"

"Pretty good. Eighty-eight bucks. Not bad for a Wednesday." She folded the bills and jammed them into one pocket of her cut-off shorts, dropped the coins into the other.

"You doing okay otherwise, though, right?" George persisted. "Working on that chemistry project?"

"Yeah." She grinned and gave him a poke in the shoulder. "Don't worry about me so much. Except it's physics, not chemistry, which I've told you, like, fifty times."

George shrugged.

"I wonder," Maris said, suddenly shy. "Would you tell everyone good-bye, please? I hate to interrupt . . . whatever that is they're doing." A drinking game, she was pretty sure, but one in which Tony and Duchess seemed to be the only participants, and Norris and Bria, their cheering squad.

A look passed between George and Pet. "Sure," George said, while Pet smirked.

"Well, it was very nice to meet you," Maris said, and put out her hand. George took it, and then didn't seem to know what to do with it.

"Aw," Pet said quietly, turning away from them, toward the door.

Duchess came running up in a clattering of high-heeled sandals on the wooden floor. "George! Did you invite her to the barbecue?"

George looked from one woman to the other. "Uh . . ."

"You're impossible! Mary, will you come over for the Fourth? We're barbecuing in the backyard. You can kind of see the fireworks if you get up on the roof. Norris can give you a ride. Or . . ." She looked significantly at George.

"Yes," Maris said, mostly to end the awkward insinuation. "I'd love to."

"Well, good. Pet's got the details. Don't bring a thing, just your pretty self."

She clattered back to the table, where Bria was sweeping the piles of gnawed bones into one of the paper bags. The evening was coming to an end for all of them.

"Like I said—" Pet hooked her arm through Maris's and led her to the door. "Not bad for a Wednesday."

seventeen

IT HAD SOMEHOW BEEN agreed: Pet would drive them home in Norris's car, as Norris—reading between the lines, anyway—would be going home with Duchess. Maris got the idea this wasn't the first time for such an arrangement. She was happy for the ride, since she'd had three of Pet's signature cocktails and each seemed stronger than the last. She wasn't drunk, exactly . . . okay, she was a little drunk.

Maris knew the dangers of alcohol, and they weren't limited to addiction. Drinking could easily loosen the screws of the social structure just a little too much. Those evenings with her friends at Adrian's had been one thing—confessions of crushes, fears about their children, husbands' annoying habits and suspicious late evenings, it was all talk that went nowhere and stayed well within the cozy bounds of friendship. But outside that inner circle, at dinner parties and holiday open houses and summer barbecues, wives drank a bit too much and grew strident, catty, mean. Husbands leaned in close to murmur to women they weren't married to. And those, like Maris, who were cautious—who drank a seltzer between glasses of wine—gathered bits and hoarded them away, ammunition for some future day.

But Maris didn't need that sort of currency anymore. All

the social armor in the world was useless in the face of what she had become. So she drank, and it felt good. It felt right and fine, and George and his friends were funny and kind, and Pet was amusing to watch, and if Maris felt something dangerously close to maternal when she looked over to the bar and saw the girl making conversation and trading barbs and expertly working the taps and bottles . . . well, she had earned it. The past day and a half had been daunting, but she'd come through.

"See you tomorrow!" the other bartender, a young man with reddish stubble and huge round grommeted holes in his ears, called as they left. Maris gave a small wave, searching for George, but he'd disappeared back into the back room. In the street, Pet paused to light a cigarette.

"Which way?"

"Just a block and a half this way." After a moment Maris added, "He keeps that car so nice, I'm surprised he'd let someone else drive it."

"The power of pussy," Pet shrugged, laughing. "We've all been there."

". . . Oh."

"Kidding!" She pretended to slug Maris in the arm. "Sorry, Mary, I shouldn't talk that way around you."

"No, it's okay," Mary said, a laugh bubbling up. It *was* okay. She didn't have to be polite—at least, not the old kind of polite, not here. "Your friends . . . how did they all, you know, get so close?"

"Right, it's like the old TV show, but in Oakland, right?"

Maris couldn't tell if Pet was making fun of her or not. They arrived at the car, and Maris got in the passenger side.

168

"But Norris and George were in the army together," she persisted.

"Air force, actually, is what George told me. Only I don't think they saw any action. I think they were mostly working as mechanics or something. Then they moved back to the Bay Area, only Norris was going through a bad time with his wife—he used to be married—anyway she kicked him out and Norris stayed with George for a while. George had a little construction business and they flipped houses together, or so the story goes, but they also claim they made a fortune and you couldn't prove it to me now. Tall tales get taller as the evening goes on, you know?"

"Mmm."

"Anyway, once the economy tanked, Norris got a job with PG&E. He'd had some training in the service, I don't know, maybe that helped him land the job. George had a few rental properties by then that he couldn't unload, plus the bar, which I don't think he ever meant to actually run, but here we are. He's in four or five nights a week, comes and goes as he pleases, more or less, though he's usually here on the weekends unless an extra one of the part-timers comes in. Norris inherited the house from his mom; she'd been renting out the apartments, but she was old and she couldn't stay on top of it and it had gotten bad, you know? I get the impression they didn't get along, either. Norris can be . . ."

She paused, searching for the right word, then moving on without finishing her thought. "So, he rented me that place while they were fixing up the upstairs for him to live in. George and him, on weekends, they gutted the kitchen and bath, fixed the floors and walls, put in new windows. I guess she hadn't really kept up with repairs and it was floor-to-ceiling full of just crap that had to be cleared out. The plan is, they're going to rehab the downstairs units after they replace the roof and paint the outside, but with rents what they are now, there's no hurry, you know? Not when Norris can get twelve hundred bucks a month for a shithole like yours. Sorry."

"You pay twelve hundred dollars?" Maris gasped, thinking of her first apartment, the musty brown-sided duplex she'd shared with three other girls at St. Mary's. Her share of the rent had been $225.

"Nah . . . Norris cut me a break, I pay nine hundred. He's kind of a softie, plus not a lot of people are dying to live in our neighborhood, you know? Give it a few years, though . . . it'll be fuckin' San Francisco out here."

"Gentrification," Maris said, and Pet snorted.

"Anyway, I got the apartment because after George hired me he called Norris up and put in a good word for me. I was staying on my friend's couch in Hayward at the time, so I was really glad to get it. I've got loans to cover tuition, for now anyway, and I work a few hours a week at the library on campus, and you know, tips . . . I don't exactly report them. So I'm getting by."

Maris marveled at Pet's resourcefulness, her determination. Would Calla have been capable of something like this? Calla had never even had a part-time job, unless you counted her summer camp counselor positions. Maris and Jeff had talked about the allowance they would give her at Santa Barbara; Maris had dreamed of driving down on fall weekends to take Calla shopping for outfits for sorority rush, to brunches at restaurants overlooking the water.

Where was Pet's mother, she wanted to know. How did she feel about Pet working in a bar? How did she feel about her haircut, for that matter, or her tattoo? Her men's clothes and the bar in her ear?

"Do you have friends at Merritt?" she asked.

"Yeah, sure, except it's a commuter school, everybody goes home at the end of the day, so it's not like we hang out or anything. Bria takes a few classes there, but she's switching to a physical therapy program in the fall."

There was an opening for something Maris had wondered about. "She seems nice."

"She's cool."

"And Duchess . . . is that weird? I mean, with Tony and . . ."

Pet laughed. "Come to the barbecue, you'll see. She's the *quiet* one in her family, if you can believe it. Hey, you mind if I stop? I'm out of cigarettes. And before you say it, I know, it's filthy and awful, but I'm down to a few a day. And I'm quitting by Christmas. I promise."

Maris laughed. She was still feeling light, almost weight-less. "Sure."

Pet parked in front of a little stucco-sided grocery store stuck to a street corner like a moth pinned to a board. Neon signs advertised Lotto, beer, Spanish spoken here.

"I'll come in," Maris said impulsively. She'd driven past these places a thousand times—there was one a couple of blocks from Morgandale—but never gone in one.

The place was cramped, stacked floor to ceiling with shelves and refrigerator cases. A bored-looking man stood behind the counter with his finger marking the place in a book with a title in an unfamiliar language. As Pet was paying for her cigarettes, a skinny girl of nine or ten came around the corner, holding a two-liter bottle of 7-Up.

"Miz Vacanti?"

Maris looked more closely. It was a girl from Morgandale. Not one of hers, but one of Lita's friends, from the group that sat together at the after-school program. She was a sassy one, disruptive and loud, a spirited cyclone in the classroom.

But Maris wouldn't have recognized her. Shame wilted her pleasant buzz as she remembered: that she couldn't tell the kids apart most of the time, with their braids and missing teeth and hand-me-downs; that she'd never gone back to explain to Lita why she couldn't tutor anymore.

And then she realized something else. The girl had called her by her name.

Pet was pocketing her change and looking from the girl to Maris in confusion.

"I—I'm sorry, I don't know what you mean," Maris said.

"Miz Vacanti," the girl insisted, poking out one skinny hip and shifting the big bottle of soda in her arms. "From *school*, from last year. It's *me*, Dakota. Where you been at, anyway?"

"I'm sorry, sweetie, I think you have the wrong person," Maris said faintly, backing toward the exit. The clerk was staring at her too. "Thank you," she said to him, feeling ridiculous. Then she made her escape.

"That was strange," she said, not looking at Pet.

"She thought she knew you." Pet unlocked the car and Maris got in gratefully. Away, they needed to get away. Maris wasn't ready for her fragile cover to be broken.

In the car, as she turned the key in the ignition, Pet watched her.

"I don't know, middle-aged white women probably all look alike to her," Maris said. A terrible thing to say.

Pet didn't respond. She drove home fast, catching the lights.

"So let me buy you lunch tomorrow," Maris said when they pulled up in front of the house, but the momentum had drained from the evening. Already she was sobering up, the lovely lush feeling curling at the edges. A faint headache was beginning behind her eyes.

"Maybe. I need to get to the gym. I haven't been for a few days." Pet paused next to the steps leading to her door.

"Well, okay. Whenever you're free, though. You've done so much for me. And you can see the place."

"That really was weird. She totally seemed to know you, Mary."

It wasn't suspicion, exactly, in her voice, but it was more than an invitation to talk. Maris wasn't accustomed to people being so direct. It didn't give you a lot of time to dodge, to finesse your answers.

"She's a kid." She shrugged. "What she was doing out this late—I mean, it's a shame. Okay. Well. Good night, Pet."

She stood for a moment, awkwardly. The closeness, the good light feeling, was gone. She wasn't the hugger some of her friends were—Adrian hugged her babysitter, the gardener—but still, she'd been feeling so *fond*, that was the word. Fond of Pet. But Pet saw through her. Pet saw that she had lied. And to a child too—Dakota had enough to deal with without another adult showing that she couldn't be trusted. Although Maris wasn't anyone to Dakota, just another volunteer at the school where 90 percent of the volunteers were white and only 10 percent of the kids were. If Maris had betrayed anyone, it was Lita, but she couldn't do anything about that right now, either.

Pet turned and went into her house and a light came on, glowing behind the bright-colored drapes. Maris walked around the back of the house. A cat streaked across the graveled drive, under the fence, and disappeared. The motion-sensor light bathed the back porch in sickly yellow light.

Inside, she wished she had an option between the bright light of the kitchen and darkness. She would buy a lamp. A cheap one. Even if she was only here for two weeks, a small lamp that she could take from the sofa to the bedroom, for reading, that would be worth it. Maybe she'd go to Ikea. Or back to Target.

She took off the makeup she'd applied earlier, got into her new nightgown. It smelled like the store; the fabric was crisp. What now? The remnants of the alcohol had left her fuzzy and disoriented. She should sleep, but suddenly she didn't feel like it.

On the bed, she sat with her back against the headboard, her knees pulled to her chest. Through the top of the window, she stared into her neighbor's house. The light was on again. A shadow passed through the room. Man? Woman? Maybe a couple lived there. The man asleep, tired from work; the woman tired too, but folding the laundry, tidying up from dinner. In two weeks, she might never see these people come and go. They probably weren't interested in her, were too busy with their own lives to care who had moved into the house whose back windows faced theirs.

Maris remembered that she should charge her phone, and padded into the kitchen to get it from her purse. There was a text from Alana:

Just thinking about you. Call if you want to talk.

She took the phone back to bed. Sure, she could call Alana. And tell her what? That she'd gone to a bar, flirted with a man, been recognized in a bodega, lied to a child? That she was a Judas, denying the innocent to protect herself?

Loathing crept through the buzz. Funny how that worked— a few drinks made you feel confident on the way up, but on the way down, in the aftermath, they left you pummeled and acutely aware of your every shortcoming, everything you'd done wrong. That alone should be enough to make people keep those next-day promises they always made—I'll stick to wine, I'll quit drinking during the week, I'll never drink around my family—but the lure of the numb was always too great.

Maris's mood was sinking fast. Funny how Alana—never the most self-aware, never that solicitous, even in the terrible days following Calla's death—had made the time to check on her, and Maris kept putting her off. Then there was Jeff, the guilty party, the betrayer; he'd called and called, and when she finally spoke to him it was just to tell her she was on her own, cut loose, broke. He didn't care about her, and hadn't for a lot longer than she'd ever suspected. And look at her— what a joke, she still cared. He still had the power to hurt her.

Why was that? Why couldn't she shake him free, turn her anger into indifference? She clicked through her messages, read through the last dozen from him, going back over a month.

Call if you get a sec.

OK if I stop by—how is 10 Sat (that was the time he came for his contact lens prescription, which she had filed under *V* for vision but he swore he couldn't find, showing up with his hair wet and his jeans pressed, so she knew he'd taken them to the cleaners; he couldn't even manage laundry on his own).

Can u send Dr. Michelson's contact info (the dermatologist, which meant he needed a refill on the Azelex, which meant he was thinking about how he looked, which, you would think maybe he would be courteous enough to shield her from? But no, and he couldn't even bother to Google the doctor, probably couldn't remember where his office was, since Maris was the one who always picked up his prescriptions).

How are you doing?

That one—a week after he moved out. That one infuriated her.

Jeff didn't get to act solicitous. He didn't get to pretend to be generous or caring. Anger welled inside Maris all over again. How could he?

Her thumb brushed against the phone, scrolling back through the messages. Back, and back. Through June, May. The end of April. He'd still been in the house then. Pretending.

Now, of course, she knew that he had been lying all along. And she had fallen for it, over and over. Not because she was stupid. But because she chose ignorance.

April 18, two days before her birthday:

Are you up for Bay Leaf?

As if! As if she could ever go back there again, with its solicitous staff, old school. Linen towels over the arm of the sommelier, an attendant in the bathroom, they used to joke that it was the only place on the West Coast that knew how to make a dinner roll. Every year on her birthday, Jeff would help her into her chair, would order for her. Most years there was a small beribboned box: sapphire studs, a silver bracelet, nothing too grand. They weren't ostentatious; they were proud of that. In the early years, they had a sitter for Calla, Maris came home a little drunk on champagne and kissed her forehead while Jeff took the sitter home.

And he had honestly thought she could go back there again. The rage multiplied, thick like fog rolling over the bay.

Now he'd not only shown his true colors, the snarling lips pulled over his teeth underneath the smile he showed the rest of the world, but he'd managed to bankrupt them. It wasn't enough that he'd lost job after job (okay, that wasn't entirely fair; the economy had taken plenty of husbands down, but in Jeff's case it was multiple times, which seemed just . . . careless), but he'd been dipping into their money, their safety nest egg, without telling her. Stealing, really, from their shared security.

She should get a lawyer. A divorce lawyer, a good one—a *great* one. Line up an offense, build a case so strong he'd never fight his way out of it, make him pay and pay and pay. She knew women who'd done it, been awed by the power of their revenge.

Only, he'd said there wasn't even enough for the mortgage. She might once have doubted him, but not now. He'd been stripped of his defenses too. He'd lost the ability to lie, after his biggest lies had been laid bare. Or maybe he'd just given up, decided it wasn't worth it anymore.

She thought about calling him. Telling him what she thought of him, the words she'd been too circumspect, too proud, to say. Even Alana didn't know everything, not the whole truth. Wasn't this what late nights were for? Late nights and drinking, the genesis of desperate pleas and accusations.

But Maris refused to be *that* cliché.

She thought about flinging the phone across the room. Making it shatter into a thousand little tiny electronic parts. But even that was too good for him.

She plugged the phone into the charger and laid it carefully on the floor along the wall, where she wouldn't step on it if she had to get out of bed in the middle of the night. She lay down and adjusted the pillow, pulled the covers up. Looked up at the window. The little piece of glass on the windowsill sparkled in the light shining down from her neighbor's house.

Maris mentally wished her fellow sleepless night warrior a peaceful vigil.

eighteen

THE DAY BEFORE SHE'D driven to CVS and bought a spiral notebook, two pens, narrow Post-it note strips, zippered plastic bags, packing tape, and Scotch tape, feeling surprisingly giddy with anticipation as she filled her basket.

The key Norris had given her was attached to a yellow measuring tape, a miniature version of the kind carpenters carry. He'd left her a note next to a mug from the Café du Monde: "Mary, please help yourself." The mug was printed with a not-very-good line drawing of the café, which Maris had visited twice: once with her mother and sister after her freshman year of college, and once when Calla was still a toddler. She remembered that Calla had slept, sweaty and pouting, in her stroller while Maris sipped the bitter chicory and Jeff repeated for the second time that he couldn't imagine why people drank coffee at all in New Orleans's climate.

Maris poured a cup and checked the refrigerator for milk. Inside were neatly labeled Tupperware containers in addition to orange juice and eggs and the usual staples: Tomato Sauce, Chicken Parmesan. The handwriting was feminine and looping and Maris thought of Duchess, her long nails, her lip liner slightly darker than her lipstick, the way she'd laughed along with Bria like they shared a private joke.

So she had already assembled a number of clues before she even began to work. She approached the spare bedroom with her coffee cup in hand.

The room was as it had been when she first saw it, other than the missing box spring and mattress. The walls were painted a creamy yellow; new miniblinds were installed in the window. But now that she was looking at it in the daylight, Maris saw that the windowsills and the plastic covering the remaining mattress were dusty; there were dust bunnies skittering along the floor. The rest of the apartment was spotless, so Maris concluded that Norris did not come into this room often.

She pushed the two beds against the wall to give herself more room to work, and then opened her notebook and wrote her first note: *bathroom rug*. She was going to need something to sit on while she sorted, and the rug she'd bought at Target would do the trick.

She lifted the top box from the stack that overflowed the closet and lined the edge of the room: Mom Kitchen. After resorting to peeling the tape with a fingernail, she wrote her second note: *sharp knife*. Then she decided Norris wouldn't mind if she borrowed one, and went through his kitchen drawers until she found a cheap-looking serrated-edge knife that she didn't think he'd miss.

By now it was already nine thirty, and the day was growing hotter. Fan—she'd need to bring up the fan, but she didn't need to write that down because odds were that she'd be desperate enough before long to halt work and go retrieve it.

So far, she was buoyed by the unaccustomed excitement of having a job to do. It had been so long, and the sense of purpose to which she had woken had yet to flag. The items in the first box were wrapped in paper towels, and she took them out carefully and laid them, one by one, in a line on the floor.

Two mismatched porcelain teacups painted with roses, one chipped, one pristine. A metal box containing dozens of handwritten recipes on index cards, some so worn that the pencil was faded nearly completely. A small notebook covered in fake leather, embossed in gold with the words Address Book, and entries made over the course of time, in many colors of pen, some with addresses carefully marked through, new ones written in cramped letters underneath. Half a dozen stainless-steel dessert forks bound with a brittle rubber band that snapped in her hands. A metal trivet shaped like praying hands. Three tea towels, stained and much washed, embroidered in faded thread with daisies. A small wooden rack with grooves to hold souvenir spoons, of which she found three in the bottom of the box: Hawaii, with a little hula dancer; Reno, with a tarnished nugget of "gold"; and Maine, with a lobster. Also a fluted pastry wheel, a plate with a child's handprint, and a cloudy plastic bag containing a hodgepodge of refrigerator magnets.

Maris surveyed the bounty, wondering what she was supposed to do next. She would have to make a pile for things like the recipe cards and address book that Norris might wish to keep, or at least see one last time: memories of his mother's most intimate if ordinary moments. She was suddenly hit with the sort of longing for her own mother that came rarely. By the time of her mother's death, Nadine had converted most of her documents to digital; she'd been a pioneer of the paperless office. She'd never owned a souvenir spoon or a souvenir of any sort at all; she redecorated her rooms on a constant rotation, unsentimentally donating old furniture and accessories to the St. Francis shop.

Maris thought about Calla's room. It was untouched, the door closed on the mild disarray from Calla's last day alive, the bed made haphazardly, two abandoned shirts laid out on the comforter. The corsage from her junior prom was still pinned to the bulletin board. Her books going back to middle school lined the bookshelves. The top of her dresser was home to two American Girl dolls that Calla could never bear to part with, a piggy bank she'd decorated in Girl Scouts, and a ceramic tray into which she tossed her bobby pins and barrettes and hair elastics. The elastics had strands of her golden hair in them.

This, of course, was one of the main reasons Maris had been unable to face the prospect of selling the house, and Jeff knew it, and she'd blamed him for being too weak to name it when he pressured her. But deep down she'd known it wasn't only her who paused outside that door a dozen times a week, who occasionally opened it an inch or two just to stare inside, who caressed the doorjamb because picking up the dolls and holding them to her face would unleash the sort of crying fit that would take a day to recover from.

Maris pressed her lips together and breathed in until her lungs couldn't hold any more. Then she let the air out slowly. She'd been hired to do a job and she would do it; it wasn't Norris's fault that he didn't know what Maris had been through. This was either the worst job for a person in her circumstances or maybe, weirdly, exactly the right one. Who else, she thought as she carefully picked up the recipe box and address book and carried them to the far corner of the room, the start of the for-Norris-to-go-through pile, would understand that every chipped cup, every wrinkled towel, every scrap of paper bore the mark of a moment that would never come again?

By the time the sun had crossed the house's roof and mercifully left the room in shade late that afternoon, Maris had sorted through six of the boxes and organized the remaining eleven. Lining the wall opposite the beds, she'd created several piles, using the boxes she'd emptied to store the sorted objects. In addition to the things she'd set aside for Norris to look at, she had identified several other categories. She had already filled a couple of bulging trash bags with the things that were worthless, like a tarnished can opener and an old-fashioned ashtray with a leaking beanbag bottom. There were also items of no great value that could be donated to charity, and things she thought she might be able to sell. In this latter category were some older Hummel figurines that she thought might be valuable, some collectors' books with old dimes and pennies pushed into the slots, as well as dozens of pieces of costume jewelry that, though only plated and set with faux gems, were in good shape and would be appealing to collectors.

She was saving the paperwork for another day, having decided to pick up some clasp envelopes and file folders to help organize it. Maybe even some of those banker's boxes that held rails from which you could hang folders. She realized that Norris and she hadn't even discussed what he might pay her, and the supplies were a cash outlay Maris hadn't really planned on, but the project had become personal almost before she began. It wasn't just that it was the first useful work Maris had done in over a year; or that she had a heightened sense of the value of the mementos of a loved one who'd passed on. It was also important to Maris, in a way she couldn't have anticipated, that she do a very good—no, a *superb* job of this task. She wanted to excel at something, to exceed someone's expectations. To exceed her own.

It wasn't like any of this wasn't obvious; Maris didn't need Nina to throw around words like compensation and transference to know exactly what she was up to. But she also didn't think Nina could understand how very satisfying the work had been, and how much she had missed that kind of satisfaction.

She was knotting the top of one of the trash bags when she sensed rather than heard the presence of someone else in the room. Turning, she saw Norris standing in the doorway, frowning.

"Oh!" she said. "I didn't hear you come in."

"What's all that?" he asked, pointing in the corner. On the top of the pile of things Maris had set aside for him was a leatherette wedding album that had belonged to a couple named Matthew and Dolly; the black-and-white photographs looked like they were from the fifties, many of them on the steps of a pretty brick church.

"Oh." His tone hadn't been especially encouraging, but Maris went and picked up the album, and presented it to him. He didn't take it from her, just stared at it as though she was offering him something unpleasant.

She held it up, pointing to the couple's photo on the front cover, the woman with a tiny pillbox hat attached to her veil, the man caught in a moment of laugher. "Were these your—"

"You can just throw that out."

"But—" Maris looked into the corner, where all the objects were mounded that she thought might have sentimental value to Norris. "I thought you might want to look through the—"

"Mary, the whole point of you doing this is so I don't *have* to look at it. Any of it." His voice was tight and controlled, his jaw stiff.

"But some of that stuff—"

"Didn't we talk about this? Just—just save paperwork that might be important. If there's something you think you can sell, by all means sell it. If there's anything in that junk you think someone else could use, I don't mind you dropping it off at the Goodwill. And the rest of it, I hired you so I don't have to look at it again. No letters, no photos, none of that—if it's not about money I don't want to keep it. I already went through this stuff with my sister and we each took what we wanted. The rest—well, she hasn't come back for it and so I guess she don't want it and I don't have any use for it, either. Bunch of dusty old pictures . . . everyone in there's dead anyway," he said, jabbing a finger in the direction of the album.

Maris frowned, feeling both embarrassed and deflated. "I'm sorry if I, if I overstepped," she said.

"Yeah, no, it's all right," Norris mumbled, turning to go. "You can— I guess that's enough for one day."

It was her cue to go. Maris quickly replaced the album on the stack, then covered the pile with an old tablecloth she retrieved from the charity pile. She was almost positive the photo album had belonged to Norris's parents. Why wouldn't he want it? What could have happened that was so bad that he didn't even want a keepsake photograph of them?

When Maris had been wandering through the house last week, thinking about the dreaded task of dividing all their possessions, then packing up the house, she had thought dimly about the things that she would end up getting rid of. She would be headed for somewhere much smaller, eventually; a condo or a tiny rental house where she could start over, and even though the words *start over* were as terrifying and foreign to Maris now as they had been the first time Nina had gently uttered them many months ago, she knew that she would take only the most scant collection of belongings with her.

But first on the list would be the photos. All of them, including the ones with Jeff in them—their courtship, the early days of their marriage, the annual portrait with Calla between them, as she grew. She hated Jeff right now, but she didn't plan to always hate him so much. Eventually, she expected to soften in her feelings for him the way Alana had softened toward her own ex. "It's the natural order of things," Alana had explained, when she ran into Creighton at a work function and ended up going out to a boozy dinner with him. "You have to hate them for a while until you manage to forget the worst parts of being together."

And Maris couldn't imagine parting with a single memento of her mother, as there were so few. Her father . . . well, she and Alana were both the product of sperm donors and her mother had a remarkably unsentimental attitude about their identities, which she had never bothered to research. But if Maris had something—a blurry photo, a broken watch, an awl with a wooden handle worn from use (for some reason she pictured her biological father as a gentle man who worked with his hands, while she imagined Alana's donor to be as cool and removed as their mother)—that had belonged to him, she would cherish it.

Norris wanted her gone, so she would go. But tomorrow she was coming back here and digging in further. She would do as Norris asked; she would save for him only the things he wanted saved. But she meant to satisfy her curiosity about his past. It was the first problem in a year that she'd had any enthusiasm about solving.

As she dusted off her hands she noticed one more photo, sitting on the windowsill where she had set it aside. It was an unframed print, a little blurry, and it had fallen out of a much-used cookbook. She picked it up and carried it with her. Norris was standing at the counter, washing tomatoes. His shoulders tightened when she came into the room.

"Norris . . ." Maris said. "I'm sorry if I . . . for not following your instructions better. But I just have to ask. I found this in a cookbook, maybe you didn't know it was in there."

She held up the snapshot: in it, a much younger Norris sat on a couch with a toddler on each knee. The girls, around eighteen months old, were identical, with their hair in matching beribboned nubs; one wore a pink dress, the other lilac. Behind the couch was the torso of a woman with her hands on Norris's shoulders. Her head had been cut off by the photographer.

Norris looked at it stonily. "Didn't we just—"

Maris dropped her hands, pressing the photo against her shorts, covering it with her hand. "All right," she said quietly. "But can you just tell me—are the girls yours?"

"Look." Norris whirled around to face her, the knife clattering to the counter. "Can you do this or not? Because I've been as clear as I can be. This was supposed to make my life *easier,* and you've raised my blood pressure about a thousand percent since I walked in the door tonight. If you can't just— just follow instructions, then let's call this off, okay? I'll pay you for today—"

"No," Maris interrupted. "Please don't, I'm sorry. I won't ask any more questions."

Norris turned back to the counter and picked up the knife, severed a tomato in one decisive stroke. "This was a bad idea, okay? I'll get my sister to do it at Christmas."

"No, I can do it. Please, I won't bother you anymore. I just . . . need the money." Not a lie, not the truth, either.

"Okay, but only if you can stick to your promise. I really don't want to hear about this again until you're all done and you've got that room cleared out. Okay? Think about it and make sure you're up for it, because I don't want to have this talk again."

He kept chopping, and after a moment Maris walked quietly from the room.

By the time night fell, Maris had been sitting at her kitchen table for an hour, her computer in front of her, the remains of a Lean Cuisine pushed across the table. She had decided to start looking for a job in earnest, something in the South Bay, because this little respite of hers would be over in a couple of weeks and then she'd be left with a savaged bank account and time to fill, and it was clear she wasn't about to launch a career as a personal organizer. It wasn't a matter of *if* she would end up at Alana's, but *when*. If the appeal happened—she could hardly even bear to consider the possibility—she'd want to be as far away from Linden Creek as possible. Besides, now that she'd soured her relationship with Norris, he probably couldn't wait to be rid of her.

Maris hadn't looked at her LinkedIn account in over a year. She took her time updating it, drinking iced tea from a bottle and nibbling on chocolate-covered pretzels. By nine, she'd sent a couple of messages and marked a number of jobs that looked promising.

When she'd volunteered at Morgandale, she'd gotten to know a young substitute teacher who augmented her income by finding odd jobs on craigslist. The girl, who was only a few years older than Calla, had done an astonishing variety of things for money.

Twenty-five dollars to visit an elderly woman's home once a month and Windex all the mirrors and pictures.

Twelve dollars an hour for four hours every Thursday afternoon to sit in the living room of a house where an autistic teenager stayed in his room with the door shut.

Two hundred and fifty dollars—only once, because she said it was too creepy—to be photographed in her underwear holding a ceramic object that the photographer had made, which the girl said didn't look like anything at all other than a lump of glazed clay, but that she had the feeling was supposed to be art.

Maris reviewed the jobs she'd flagged. Most of them, she was unqualified for. She could always work as a substitute teacher herself, of course, but that would mean the end of her little ruse, since she'd have to go for her fingerprint test, and her married name would come up in the background check. Which was inevitable, anyway, once she gave in and let Alana help her . . . But for now, the job search was still part of the fantasy, of being someone else, or at least of pretending not to be who she was.

But still . . . if she were to take some little minimum-wage job where they'd just skim her application and check her driver's license, she could keep the ruse going. She imagined herself in a crisp white apron at the Container Store, dusting shelves of merchandise, answering questions and—

No: still reaching too high. Those were the jobs women from places like Linden Creek got when their kids left the nest and they needed a little something to keep themselves busy until their husbands got home from work.

It would have to be a pretty low-level job, something no one else wanted, but that was fine with Maris. How about night clerk in a convenience store? Her boss would be brisk and demanding and dusky-skinned and she would ring up purchases with a brittle smile for those who were out late at night: the drunks and insomniacs and shift workers. Perhaps they would be grateful for the few words of conversation she would offer.

Maris stared at the screen awhile longer. "Prepare invoices quickly, efficiently, and accurately." She hadn't worked in a business office in years; she had mild carpal tunnel if she spent too much time online. Who was she kidding?

The problem was that she had no idea where she could fit in now. She'd been terribly naïve to think it might be here, with these people, in this house echoing with past tenants' memories. No wonder she had seized upon Norris's photos, no wonder she had worked so hard to expunge all the traces of the prior renter. What she was doing was obvious: trying to change the past by sheer force of will, and since it hadn't worked in her own life, she was doing it to strangers'. "Fixing" the apartment, trying to force Norris to reconnect with memories of something good—these were pathetic substitutes for the prayers that had gone unanswered, back before Maris gave up praying and then gave up on God entirely: *please don't let anything bad have happened to her, please help us find her,* and then later, *please don't ever let me forget a single thing about her, please take care of her in Heaven.* Naïve wishes that felt as childish now as her long-ago belief in the tooth fairy.

Friendship, romance, she had seized upon these unlikely alliances with no regard to how fragile they were. She'd lied; she'd pretended to be someone else. Pet and George, Norris and the rest of them, they all thought they knew a woman named Mary, eccentric maybe but brave. The truth was that Maris was ordinary and a coward. This had to end. She had to stop pretending, playacting, and be an adult again.

Maris knew she was on the verge of beating herself up, and working with Nina had at least taught her to steer clear of this hazard, as it could take her down for days. *Pick one positive thing,* Nina had counseled, *and say it out loud, if you need to.*

"This week I . . ." Maris started. In the months following Calla's death it would be things like: *I wrote three thank-you notes* or *I pruned the oleander,* and the exercise felt meaningless. Later, she worked up to *I sat on Calla's bed for a half hour and focused only on good memories* or *I called Adrian and asked about Tristan's class trip to San Diego.*

"This week I cleaned this place," she said out loud. "I got rid of all the disappointment and misery and filth that was here. Now someone else can come here and make it home."

Also, I didn't give up.

Maris closed her laptop and cleared away her dishes. She prepared for bed, slipping on the nightgown and sliding between the sheets that already seemed softer from use.

A series of popping explosions outside made her start, until she remembered it was July 3; people were getting a start on their celebrating with fireworks, the cheap ones, bottle rockets and stink bombs bought out in Livermore.

Another volley, farther away, and then a scream that ended in laughter.

Tomorrow was the barbecue. Should she still go? Could she? George would be there . . . Maris allowed herself to think about him for a moment, his silver-shot beard, his paradoxically formal manners. The way he'd held her elbow as he showed her his "gallery."

Could she ever be with a man like that? Lord knew, he was nothing like Jeff. That had to be half of what attracted her. George wasn't covering up any deep secrets about who he was. He seemed like the type of man who was comfortable in his own skin, and he—

"Oh," Maris breathed, surprised at her body's reaction to the thought of holding him. Putting her arms around his solid chest and belly, feeling the warmth of his face against her forehead. She bet he smelled nothing like Jeff, who often showered twice in a single day, once at the gym and once in the evening, and hated to get dirty, even when he was working around the house. Jeff smelled aseptic, clean to a fault; she imagined that George would be the opposite, a complex tangle of scents he trailed from the places he'd been: tobacco, and cooking, and soap and sweat and motor oil and fresh-cut grass.

Tentatively, she ran her hands down her body, the crisp cotton of the new nightgown abrading her skin pleasantly. She stopped short of slipping her hands under her clothes—it had been so long since she'd experienced any pleasure that way that she doubted her body would even remember how to respond—but it was impossible to resist thinking about being held.

"George," she whispered, and then she closed her eyes and imagined him holding her, wrapping his arms around her while she drifted off to sleep. Protecting her from the pull of sadness, from the eternal grief, and giving her blessed oblivion, if only for a few hours.

nineteen

SATURDAY PASSED SLOWLY. MARIS didn't venture out until she heard Norris leave in his SUV, and then she drove to the Arco for her morning coffee. She wondered where he'd gone: errands, the gym? Whatever uptight emotionally constipated bachelors did on the weekend. She wondered if this was how it was going to be for the rest of her time in this house—avoiding Norris, burdened by guilt and embarrassment over how she'd upset him, sneaking in and out of his apartment to do her work.

She wouldn't be able to avoid him tonight, though. Pet stopped by midmorning to make plans to go to the barbecue together. They would go in Norris's car at six. Maris couldn't bring herself to tell Pet about what had happened; she considered backing out, but that would mean giving a reason and she didn't have any excuses, at least any that she felt like discussing.

A little after five, as Maris was stepping out of the shower, the phone rang. When she saw that it was Jeff, she let it go to voice mail, staring at the screen until it finally beeped—and then played the message back, dripping water on the kitchen floor as she stood with only a towel wrapped around her.

"Hey, Maris. I wish you would pick up. Three things. I talked to a Realtor, he's coming by tomorrow to have a look.

If you want to be there, which, I'm assuming based on our last conversation you don't, but he's coming at eleven. Let me know. Second, I don't know where you are, you have mail at the house, people keep asking me what's going on, I mean, what am I supposed to tell them?" (*How about the truth for once*, Maris thought darkly.) "And third, I'm just wondering if you're going to be at the gala. It's Friday, in case you've forgotten. I would kind of like to know in advance. I mean, I'm going no matter what, and we don't have to make this awkward. You just—I mean, it's—this is going to keep happening, you know, we know all the same people, we won't be able to keep avoiding each other. Okay, well. Haven't heard anything more about the appeal. Anyway, call me."

Maris put the phone down slowly. The gala. Six days from now, the Callendar Performing Arts Center was hosting its biggest fund-raiser of the year and Maris, as a former chair, would be expected to attend. And Jeff was calling her to say *he* was going, to lay the potential awkwardness at her feet as though it was *her* fault? The injustice of it seized up inside her like a jolt of electricity. Four years ago, he'd put on a suit and stayed by her side throughout the evening as she thanked the donors and ran the raffle and choreographed the presentation, and she'd *thanked* him. She'd actually said in her remarks, "and to my husband, Jeff, thanks for taking care of the dishes and the laundry and the carpools," so that she could get her committee work done, and later she and Jemma had laughed about it, because when in the history of time has any man stood up to accept a Super Bowl ring or a Nobel Prize or CEO appointment and thanked his wife for making it possible? And privately—she was too embarrassed to say it aloud to Jemma—she toted up how many times he'd really helped, and come up with a kitchen twice left afoul with the clutter of pizza boxes and laundry left forgotten and mildewed in the washing machine.

Maris deleted the message and left the phone in the kitchen while she went to dress. She might not be going to a gala. But she was damn well going to a barbecue.

Duchess lived half a mile from Morgandale, on the gently sloping hill above MacArthur Boulevard, in a house whose backyard abutted the parking lot of a KFC, so that the smell of the heating coals mingled with the smell of fried chicken to produce what Maris thought was the most tantalizing aroma ever. She realized that she hadn't eaten since her breakfast of a convenience store Danish and an orange, and when one of Duchess's aunts took the plastic wrap off her seven-layer dip, Maris filled a paper plate with tortilla chips and dug in.

She joined Pet at a card table set up in the yard and let herself enjoy simply observing the happy melee. There were two dozen adults and a handful of excited kids running around with plastic pinwheels and sparklers that their mothers wouldn't let them light, not until it got dark. There were beers and sodas in a cooler, and a box of wine set up on a table next to a stack of Dixie cups. There was an elderly man relaxing in a recliner that had been dragged out onto the back deck for the occasion—he nodded and smiled and said nothing at all and Maris decided he would serve as her example. He was excused from conversation, from helping out, due to age, but perhaps Maris could be excused for time served: for all the neighborhood block parties she'd planned and helped at through the years.

On the sly, however, she watched Pet, and thought about Calla. Her daughter, at family events—there had been an annual summer trip to see Jeff's cousins' families at the lake, the Thanksgivings in Orange County—seemed to glow with the delight of being included. It had always given Maris a pang, since she and Alana were the most paltry of families; if it hadn't been for Jeff they wouldn't have had more than a few people around any holiday table. Calla seized upon every tradition with zeal: charades, flag football, soaring shrieking over the lake in the tire swing and dropping into the water at the last minute with a giant splash. Walking into town with her cousin to buy Slurpees; staying up late in the rec room in a sleeping bag with the other kids.

But now, Calla was gone, Jeff was gone. Maris remembered an Easter Sunday nearly a decade ago, when Alana had still been married. Jeff had taken Calla skiing with his brother and his kids, and Maris had showed up at Alana's with a bunch of tulips, and the three of them—Maris, Alana, and her starchy hedge-fund-manager husband—had eaten paillards of lamb and tiny peas to the lugubrious strains of Barber's *Adagio for Strings*. Was that what she had to look forward to? She wondered what Alana was doing tonight and felt guilty for not calling.

When a little plastic boomerang landed at her feet, Maris looked up to find a girl of seven or eight staring at her, her mouth dusted with orange Cheeto crumbs. As Maris smiled and handed the toy back, she was overtaken by one of the bad moments, the ones where Calla's absence felt bigger than her

197

whole body, and her throat closed and her eyes filled instantly with tears. Pet was in animated conversation with a girl who was painting the kids' faces and hands with little flags, and there was a cluster of people standing on the deck blocking the door, and nowhere to go, nowhere to escape—not even a paper napkin to dab her eyes with.

Maris grabbed her purse and started rummaging in it, just for something to do because she already knew she hadn't packed any tissues, but a moment later George was kneeling at her side. She'd seen him come in awhile ago, watched him greet half a dozen people, tried not to be caught looking. But now he placed a hand on her arm and looked at her with concern.

"You okay?"

Maris took a deep breath and let it out. "Um, I don't suppose I could convince you it's just allergies?"

He smiled. "Hey, don't be embarrassed. I was crying just last night, watching *Princess Bride*."

"You were not."

"Well, okay, I wasn't, but I did the first time I saw it."

Maris wiped at her eyes with the heel of her hand and managed a small smile. "You're still lying."

"Yeah, well. I would say, do you want to talk about it, but chicks never want to talk about it when you ask; you all like to spring it on us when we're least expecting it."

Maris blinked, taking in George's soft brown eyes in his deeply tanned and lined face. He'd had a haircut since the other night, and his beard had been carefully trimmed. He was wearing a sea-green shirt and a gold chain with a small gold medallion on it. "That's the most sexist thing I've heard all day," she said.

George squeezed her hand and released it. "Yes, ma'am. It's true. I'm old school, I still think ladies should be ladies and . . . well, I'll shut up before I piss you off any further. Mostly I just wanted to say, I don't know, I'm here if you need me."

It took him more effort to get up than it had to crouch down, his knees popping and his hand holding the edge of the card table for support. *Jeff's in better shape*, Maris thought, *but George—*

The thought was abruptly cut off when the boomerang sailed into her lap for a second time and Duchess's uncle hollered that the hot dogs were ready.

As the sky went purple and the first home fireworks popped elsewhere in the neighborhood, the kids shrieking with laughter and the older women covering the uneaten food and replenishing the drinks, George found Maris again. She'd moved to a perch on a retaining wall at the edge of the yard. Pet and the face-painting girl had gone to get cigarettes and not returned; Norris was helping Duchess in the kitchen. Maris had finished a Sprite and a beer, had touched up her makeup and lamented her out-of-control hair in the bathroom, and was trying to focus on the moment, the way she'd learned in therapy, the soundtrack of her senses overriding her heart's temptation to slide back, back, back to what used to be and what was lost. *The sky is navy blue, she'd been thinking, the girl's shorts are red, I can smell the frosting on that cake, and the cinder block is rough on my thighs.*

George sat down next to her. "Unless you're really committed to watching Duchess's uncle blow his fingers off to entertain the kids, you should come with me."

Maris looked at him, taking in his easy smile with just a hint of uncertainty at the edges. It had taken some courage for him to ask her, she thought.

"I'm ready."

On the sidewalk in front of the house, he took her hand. It was warm, and big, enveloping. They didn't speak as they walked the two blocks to his truck, but when he let go of her hand and opened the passenger door for her, he touched the untamed mass of hair around her face, gave her a shy smile, and said, "Nothing out of line, I promise, Mary."

The way he said her name, she forgot for a moment that it wasn't really hers. How long had it been since Jeff touched her that way . . . that carefully, that tenderly? A lump formed in Maris's throat when she realized that the answer was *never*. Their marriage had been an efficient one from the start, a companionable one for a long time . . . but bloodless. She must have known, back when they were starting out, what she was giving up. She must have chosen to make herself not care, pledged to pretend always that she didn't miss it. Two decades of marriage and Maris had never strayed so far as a cloakroom kiss, until, when Calla got to high school, a few regrettable clandestine encounters once she realized that nothing would ever ignite the spark between her and Jeff. And even those—none longer than a single night, all of them the result of too much wine and sexual convenience—felt more like minor highway collisions than romantic interludes.

And now, when it had been only a matter of weeks since Jeff left . . . now this.

George's truck was an old, boxy GMC, the vinyl seats crackling and cool, the suspension wrecked so that they seemed to hit every pothole as he drove out of the neighborhood, around Lake Merritt strung with twinkling lights, up into streets lined with little bungalows. The nicer part of Oakland, where lawns were mowed and flower beds tended, and drapes hung in windows rather than bedsheets.

The occasional firecracker sounded far away now. Light had disappeared completely from the sky. The dashboard clock read 8:44.

"Is that really the time?" Maris asked.

George gave her a sideways glance. "Um, yeah, more or less . . . is that all right?" he asked, and she realized that he was nervous, as nervous as she was.

"Oh, yes, sure. It's just . . . I guess I didn't realize how late it got, at the barbecue. You know. Time flies."

Neither of them spoke again until he parked at the curb in front of a little square house with shuttered windows and overgrown grass.

"I don't live here," he said, his hand on the gear shift. "I know the guy who owns it, though. He wouldn't mind. Are you . . . can you walk in those shoes?"

Maris lied and said they were comfortable. George held her hand as they went around the side of the house, along a broken asphalt sidewalk, overhung by drooping vines laden with tiny white blooms. The scent was cloying, overripe. Through an open window in the neighboring house, a woman's voice called "Potter? Clara?"

This was the sort of neighborhood Maris and Jeff hadn't been brave enough to move to: pretty old homes being remodeled by young families, private schools, and urban ballot measures. Instead they'd gone for the suburbs, four bedrooms and two and a half baths and a yard, granite countertops and a row of tiny staked crape myrtles. But as she followed George into the moonlit backyard, Maris thought: *Oh, what we missed*. Beyond a wooden fence, a vast dark rolling space unfurled, the Mountainview Cemetery with its marble gravestones and tombs reflecting the moonlight. She'd passed it before, driving home to Linden Creek, but it had never occurred to her to drive through the gates and explore.

"Best view in Oakland," George said. "If you don't mind a little walk."

He ended up carrying her through the thick brush beyond the gate. People weren't supposed to put gates in their fences; there was supposed to be only one way in, the iron gates locked every sundown. But who could resist? A footpath had been worn through the shrubs that clung to the hill above the lawns.

When they'd made it down the uneven slope, George set Maris down gently on a gravel path and dug in his pocket for a flashlight on a keychain. "Here, you take it," he said. "I'm pretty steady on my feet. Low center of gravity." He chuckled, and Maris looped her arm through his. They picked their way along the meandering path until they reached the row of large mausoleums that lined the road near the top of the cemetery.

"Millionaire's Row," George said.

The view was breathtaking: down, down at least a half mile to the entrance gates, over downtown Oakland with the Tribune tower and city hall rising up above the skyline, to the enormous shipping cranes looming over the port. Then the black water, the Bay Bridge lit brightly, the Golden Gate in the distance . . . and San Francisco beyond, a toy town, a sparkly glittering carpet. "This is . . . it's unbelievable."

She didn't feel as apprehensive now; the fresh air, the walking, the feel of George's warm hand around hers had left her pleasantly breathless. They strolled past the mausoleums until George paused in front of a massive white one labeled Ghirardelli.

"The chocolate people?" Maris asked.

"More like the chocolate empire." George laughed as he dusted bits of leaves and bugs off the top step. They sat down, Maris nestled in the crook of his arm. Over their heads, a carved stone angel stood sentry.

A burst of color and light erupted far below, over the water.

"Unbelievable timing," George chuckled. "I wish I could take credit."

They watched the fireworks, holding hands and exclaiming over the most spectacular. Maris was pretty sure George was going to kiss her any second. All evening long, she'd been playing chicken with herself, wondering how far she was going to allow this crazy thing to go. She had lied to George, not only about her name, but—implicitly, anyway—about her circumstances. Where she came from and who she was. What must he think of her—a woman who took a filthy apartment on a whim? Who had no one with whom to spend the holiday weekend other than virtual strangers?

The weight Maris dragged around with her—the *truth*—was so insurmountable, so damning, that it crushed most social opportunities before they could even germinate. Friendships were going to be difficult for the rest of her life; romance, practically unthinkable. Any second chances for a woman like her would have to be shaped and precipitated by what had happened to Calla. Maris might hope to meet someone in a grief group someday, maybe. A widower who had loved his wife so much that he'd allow himself only the facsimile of real love: Maris could imagine herself in that role, a polite alliance whose barriers neither would ever try to cross.

But someone like George—he was the opposite. Full of life. Emotions tumbling from his gestures, his words—he'd expressed more to her in the time they had spent together than Jeff had confided in years. George was Jeff's opposite: profane where Jeff was staid; impulsive where he was meticulous; sensual where he was cold.

And then George did kiss her, his lips soft and full and warm and wet, so unlike the perfunctory kisses Jeff gave her. Had Jeff ever kissed her like this? Had anyone?

George wrapped his arms more tightly around her, gathering her into his lap like she weighed nothing. He kissed the soft skin under her jaw, gently brushing her hair out of the way, twining it around his fingers. "Beautiful," he murmured, and kissed her eyelids.

He pulled away from her so he could look at her face. "Hey," he said. "Hey, what's this?" His fingertip traced across her cheek and only then did Maris realize she was crying. "Are you all right? Did I do something wrong?"

"No, no," Maris said, embarrassed, trying to wipe the tears away on her wrist, to discreetly wriggle out of his grasp so she could collect herself. But he held on.

"Look, Mary, if I . . . offended you in any way, if I—"

"No, no, it's not you," Maris said, trying to smile. The nicest moment she'd had in ages, and she'd spoiled it. "You didn't do anything wrong. I thought—I was hoping you would kiss me."

"Well, then, did I not do it right?" He smiled uncertainly, his brow creasing. "You can give me pointers, I'll take direction—Mary, I really like you. I *really* like you."

Maris made a sound that was half protest and half sob, torn between pushing him away and asking for another chance. How was she supposed to tell him: that her daughter had been murdered, and everything Maris had ever known about herself was shattered? That she wasn't entirely sure she could go on; that she'd landed in Oakland like an exhausted bird alighting on a rock in the waves, too depleted to make it to shore; that she wasn't ever sure she'd even wake up again when she went to bed each night? That she was surprised that heartbreak hadn't already ended her?

"I'm not who you think I am," she blurted, and then she did manage to wrench herself free of his arms.

"You . . . what?"

As she stumbled down the steps, she saw his expression go from confusion to hurt.

"I have a whole other life," she protested when he caught up. "I shouldn't be here. I don't know what I was thinking." She struggled along the path, but one of the painful shoes twisted and she nearly fell, her ankle wrenching.

"Hey. Please." George put his hand on her arm to steady her. "Tell me who you really are then. Or—or don't. I don't—I'll just take you home, okay? You can't walk from here."

"I can call a cab," she said, letting her hair fall forward in her face. "I'll be fine."

"You won't be fine. You can barely walk. At least let me help you get back to the gate."

She accepted his hand reluctantly. He was right; she

205

couldn't even tell which house they'd come from, where the path had brought them through the shrubs. Neither of them spoke as they clambered back up the hill, Maris holding on to his fingers tightly. As soon as they got to the gate—a tin star was nailed to it, gleaming dully—she let go and pushed through by herself.

George drove back down the hill, through the city, back to the house, without saying anything. As soon as he pulled over, she had the passenger door open. "I'm sorry," she said, not looking at him. "So sorry."

"Mary. Whoever you are. Please."

But she slammed the door on his plea, and practically ran down the driveway while his car still idled there. Her feet hurt; she had twin blisters on her heels. She hobbled past Norris's car, the motion-sensor light illuminating the parched lawn, the broken flower pots piled along the shed. She had to pee, badly. There was a light on in Pet's apartment, but she desperately wanted to be alone.

Taped to the glass window of the apartment door was a scrap of paper. Maris had to open the door and turn on the light to see what it said.

Mary: I know who you are. —Pet

twenty

AFTER A RESTLESS NIGHT, Maris awoke to the ting of a text and an accompanying sense of dread. She hadn't given her phone number to anyone she had met since leaving Linden Creek—not George, not Norris, not even Pet. And aside from a couple of "thinking of you" messages from Adrian and Jemma, the only people who texted her these days were people she didn't currently want to hear from.

Sure enough: Jeff, with news that made her sink back into the bed, staring at the little screen.

Thought you should know, Isherwoods' new lawyer talking about appeal in the paper this morning.

They'd known all along that an appeal was a possibility. The media speculation had been strong, following the reading of the verdict, but as the weeks passed, Maris had allowed herself to think it had faded from the realm of possibility or at least of likelihood. The Isherwoods, in the video clips that appeared over and over on the news, had leaned into each other as they left the courtroom that day, looking as broken as she felt. She'd almost been sorry for them. No: she'd been sorry only for Ron, because Deb was a cipher to her. Deb was only the sum of a half dozen meaningless polite encounters, pleasantries exchanged, compliments about each other's children, and shared amusement at their fledgling romance. It all seemed to have taken place years ago. But Ron was a different matter; Ron remained vivid in her mind and in her senses. Ron, even on the worst days, the days she wished the Isherwoods gone from the earth, was real to her.

She forced herself to get up and make the bed. It was almost nine o'clock; she'd tossed and turned for hours before finally, as dawn seeped into her window, falling into a dreamless sleep. She padded to the kitchen and drank tepid water from a glass, standing at the sink, while she thought about what an appeal would mean. Their names in the news again. Calla's picture in the papers. The website— she'd only seen it once; Jeff had asked their lawyer if he could force it to be removed, but it was impossible—proclaiming Karl's innocence. Her dream of disappearing would be shattered; it would be impossible to maintain this fragile distance she'd put between herself and the rubble of her broken life.

She thought of Karl, the last time she'd seen him, the day his sentence was read. He sat impassively staring at the table in front of him. He didn't flinch, didn't cry, didn't even show that he had heard. Shortly after that he was led from the courtroom, and he looked straight ahead, not even acknowledging his parents.

Alana asked her later if she was disappointed that he'd only gotten voluntary manslaughter, with its maximum sentence of eleven years. If she and Jeff would feel better knowing that Karl would never be set free, or at least so far in the future that they could think of him as having paid a crippling price. But Maris didn't see it that way. She—and

Jeff for that matter—had little doubt that Karl was guilty. And if someone had offered her Calla back, she would have gladly traded Karl's life. But she also couldn't bring herself to believe that Karl was inherently evil: he had always struck her as an inherently unhappy boy, one who on the cusp of adulthood was not yet secure in who he was meant to be. It was not the same as forgiving him, and Maris had no desire or intention to forgive, but she also doubted whether his suffering in prison would ever make her feel any better.

And she understood too that if things had been reversed— if it was Calla who had killed someone else's child—she would do everything in her power to try to lessen the price she would pay. She merely wished that this could all play itself out somewhere else, so that she wouldn't have to know about it, wouldn't have to face the public's insatiable hunger for the evidence of her pain all over again.

Maris stared at the stainless-steel sink. She had scoured it with her own hands and it now gleamed dully. On the windowsill were bottles of her favorite Caldrea soap and lotion, and she set down the empty water glass and squirted some lotion on her hands, taking her time, rubbing it into her skin and inhaling the smell.

It was interesting, the return of her ability to appreciate her senses. Or rather: her sensuality had returned. The pleasure of the lotion's tart scent was as unexpected as her body's response to George's touch had been. Or perhaps they were two pieces cut from the same cloth.

A woman, after a year of mourning, emerges into a world that—to her great surprise—has trundled along without her, with all of its noisy, colorful, fecund energy. The world she has thought to be indifferent to her and her loss—it beckons to her now.

A man, holding himself ultimately responsible for his son's crime, puzzles for a year about how to make amends and comes up with no better offering than his own life—a deal no mother, no matter how much she had lost, could possibly take.

One has held her breath and finds she cannot help gasping, in the end, for air. The other flays bits from himself, telling no one, not even acknowledging it in his own mind, until he decides to sacrifice himself and finds that even that can't change the balance.

And outside either orbit . . . this. Maris knew instinctively that Ron was not behind the appeal. It had to be Deb, the architect of this new development, the mother who would leave no stone unturned to save her child.

It had been a mistake to try to make friends, to get to know people. Far better to be a loner, an eccentric, bothering no one, asking only to be left alone. Maris breathed the lotion's scent and wondered if it might still work, if there still might be a way to salvage her refuge a little longer. She had to talk to Pet, and find out what she really knew. Maybe it wasn't what she feared. Or maybe Maris could convince her to keep it to herself . . . she threw on clothes and went around the house to Pet's door and knocked, but she was already gone.

Maris stood on the porch, turning slowly to look out at the diner across the street, the meter maid making her way down the parked cars, the little pile of broken glass that still glittered along the curb. It was naïve to think that Pet wouldn't have figured out the whole truth—that she was Maris Vacanti, mother of the murdered girl, victim of the

Academy Killer. If Maris left now, she could make a clean break. Pet would be left with the memory of a stranger's side trip through her life. Norris might still be angry at her over her handling of his mother's things, but he would get to keep his cash. Hell, he wouldn't have to pay a cleaning service now; he could hardly complain. Maris could just leave the keys on the kitchen table.

A surprising realization: she wasn't ready to leave this place. The last year had scoured from Maris every extraneous trait—generosity and empathy and humor and curiosity and the capacity for love—and now that she was thinking about leaving this humble apartment behind, she realized that she'd stumbled on a place of rest, where she could just . . . be. Where there were no choices, no television channels to flip through, no neatly labeled casseroles in the freezer, no stacks of sweaters in the closet. Where there were no birthdays to keep track of or dinner invitations to return, no neighbors to keep up with or clubs to aspire to join.

She would have to find a way to fill her days. What had she done, back in Linden Creek, for the last year? A lot of sitting and trying not to think . . . a lot of drinking coffee. Cleaning: she'd let the housekeepers go, and still the place had never been so clean. Reading the news, often the same story over and over and over again. Weeding the garden, walking the hills in the dark, before anyone else was awake or after they had gone to bed. Going through her photo albums, over and over, every picture of Calla committed to memory, cherished, longed for.

It had seemed like enough then. Why didn't it anymore? Even today, as she stood here regretting the loss of the refuge she'd never been sure she wanted in the first place, she did not

211

have enough to do to get her to bedtime. She could shower, and read, and shop for groceries, and still, hours would remain. It was ridiculous to think that she could do this, day after day, week after week. The work she was doing for Norris was a distraction, but it would be over soon. Then what?

Maris returned to her overheated, echoing little apartment, knowing that she wouldn't be able to stand the nothing for very long. She could leave here tomorrow and throw herself into what came next. Maybe she'd stop for a fancy lunch in San Jose, somewhere with valet parking, and tomorrow night she'd lie down in the gray-and-ecru guest room in Santa Luisa, breathing the chilled air and listening to Alana's jazz recordings seeping under the door.

Maris stood in the doorway to her tiny bedroom, looking at the narrow bed, the stiff synthetic comforter that refused to lie flat. The Target bags were under the bed where she'd stashed them, and she could fill them up with her folded clothes, the new underwear. She would leave the toiletries, the kitchen staples—Maris didn't feel like explaining any of that to Alana. Let her sister think she'd simply become bored after a few days in the yoga friend's posh house.

Someone knocked at the door.

Pet stood outside, cheeks flushed from the heat, wearing a pink tank top that read Nobody Likes Misogynists and another pair of baggy men's shorts, her backpack over her shoulder. She nodded at Maris as if nothing had happened, and slipped past her into the kitchen, dropping the backpack on the sofa.

"Wow," she said. "I can't get used to it being so clean in here."

"Would you like something cold to drink?" Maris stood awkwardly in the center of the room. "I have seltzer, grapefruit juice, Diet Sprite . . ."

"Diet Sprite, I guess. Hey, look, I'm kind of hiding. Do you mind if I stay here for a few hours?" A self-conscious grin. "It's only until tonight, and then I can get out of your hair."

"Of course," Maris said, both relieved and confused. "What's going on? If you don't mind telling."

"My mom and her asshole boyfriend might be coming by." Pet rolled her eyes, but misery radiated from her tough exterior. "And his fucked-up kid."

"Well . . . that sounds like a story. Do they live near here?"

Pet popped the soda open and ignored the glass Maris set on the table, taking a sip straight from the can. "Brentwood. Not far."

"But you don't want to see them because . . ."

"It's just, you know. A lot of drama." She set down the can carefully. "My mom got a lot of money in the divorce so she doesn't have to work, and she didn't really have much to keep her busy, except for her *politics*—" She made air quotes with her fingers. "She used to take the bus up to Sacramento and demonstrate for marriage equality and shit, but now *that's* over. And then she met John and now they both like to play more-PC-than-thou, because he's an immigration lawyer and he got custody of his kid, who's, like, autistic or something, so it's, like, he thinks he deserves a fucking gold medal. But all that kid did last time they were here was fart and ask me if I have *tits*, over and over." Pet sighed and slid down in her chair. "So I just don't think I have it in me, you know? To put up with that today."

"Where are they now?" Maris asked cautiously.

"Um . . . I'm not really sure. I didn't actually pick up when Mom called, and all she said was she might be coming over. She does that sometimes. They'll just show up on Sundays, because they know I don't have to work, and they expect me to drop everything."

Maris had the feeling there was more to the story, something Pet wasn't telling her. The uneven grin, the pink cheeks, seemed like signs that the girl was trying not to cry. Maris went and retrieved the box of Kleenex from the bathroom. "I'm sorry," she said, setting the box in front of Pet.

"No, no, *I'm* sorry," she said, grabbing a few tissues and swiping savagely at her eyes. "I mean, fuck. It's nothing. I mean, my mom's just being my mom, doing what she always does, and I should be able to . . . to . . . and, I mean, especially." She wadded up the tissues and threw them at the trash can, landing the shot perfectly. "With, you know, *you*. Everything you've been through."

Maris's hands, folded on the table, clutched tighter, but she kept her expression neutral. "Well," she said.

"God, I'm such a dick. I mean about that note, I just wanted you to know I knew, so . . . you know, so it wouldn't be weird. Ha. Right?"

She managed a weak grin through the tears that had finally spilled over.

"Well," Maris said gently, "I'm not really sure how you would have managed that. I mean, it *is* a little . . . weird." A laugh bubbled out, surprising her. Where had that come from?

"I really am sorry, though," Pet said. "Last night, after I got home? I was watching the late news, and they were talking about how there's probably going to be an appeal or whatever, and it clicked—the name, from when I heard that girl say it in the store. And then they showed your picture." She shrugged. "You and your husband, outside the courtroom, from when the guy got sentenced. And, shit. I mean . . . shit."

"Ah." Maris felt curiously numb. She put her fingers to her cheek, to make sure she was still there.

"And look, I'm not trying to make you talk about it or anything. I mean, I guess I should just shut up about it myself. *Shit*."

Maris sighed and reached across the table, covering Pet's hand with her own. "It's not your fault, lord knows. And it was wrong of me to deceive you. It was just one of those things that sort of happened. I didn't plan it . . ."

"No, I totally get how that can happen." Pet squeezed her hand back. "I grew up in a town of seven hundred people, I'm totally used to wishing everyone didn't know everything about me."

"I guess there's no such thing as anonymity anymore, is there? I mean, with social media and everyone you've ever known finding you on Facebook." Not that Maris had looked at her Facebook account for months. "Makes me wish I could just hide here forever, you know?"

"Yeah, that would be tough, but . . . you could hide for a *while*, couldn't you? I mean, not that it matters or anything, but George is, like, totally crazy about you. He texted me twice today asking if I'd talked to you, tried to act like it was because he wanted to return your sweater or some shit. Did you leave it at the party last night?"

Oh . . . right, Maris had brought the cheap acrylic cardigan in case it got cold, and left it in his truck when he drove her home. Last night seemed like it had happened ages ago. "I . . . I must have."

"Well." A small look of triumph on Pet's face. "Don't worry, I won't tell him about, you know, or anything. But, still. Can I ask you something?"

Maris didn't want to say yes, didn't want to risk the thousands of directions curiosity could take. But she owed Pet, didn't she? "Sure, anything."

"Why here? Why did you end up here? I mean, you could have gone anywhere."

"Well . . ." How to answer that question, when Maris wasn't entirely sure herself? "I know the media made it sound like our family was wealthy, Pet—"

"You aren't?"

"No, I mean, we're very *comfortable*, especially compared to lots of people. We have . . . we *had* a nice house."

"Yeah, they showed it on the news."

Maris looked down at her hands. They looked old in the harsh afternoon light—veiny and hairless, like her mother's had been. "I know. They were . . . it was a better story to them if they made it sound like we were all rich. But my husband, my ex, Jeff, he was laid off quite a bit over the last few years. Things were, well, I didn't even know how bad they'd gotten. We're going to have to sell the house. I'm going to have to get a job. Things—things are going to be different for me."

"But there's lots of places you could have gone that aren't . . ." Pet swept her hand around the kitchen: the peeling

216

linoleum, the dented walls, the paint flaking off the window shaft. "Dangerous," she finally settled on.

"You know that little girl we saw the other night? Well, I *did* know her—I'm sorry I lied. Before Calla died, I volunteered down at Morgandale Elementary, in the literacy program. I used to take surface streets, driving through the neighborhoods, wondering what it would be like to live here. Wondering . . . I don't know, I guess how I was born who I was and all these people were born who they were, and none of us having any say in it. I used to see these moms, African American and Mexican and Indian and I don't even know where else they came from, and they'd have babies in strollers, walking to the school to pick up the rest of their kids. Lita—the student I used to work with—she had four siblings and they all lived in a two-bedroom apartment. And there we were, me and Jeff and Calla, in a four-bedroom house."

"Liberal guilt," Pet suggested, not unsympathetically.

"Yes, I suppose, but it was more than that. Oh, I know how this is going to sound, but I was a grade school teacher when I got married, and then when Calla started school I worked as a tutor, doing SAT prep. All these kids, these wealthy kids whose parents had such high hopes for them. Don't get me wrong, I loved them—"

She gasped, the word *loved* tripping something inside her, some delicate thread broken. But she *had* loved them, fiercely, even the sullen ones, the unfocused, the mean girls and the resentful boys. And then, in Oakland, the shy ones and the incorrigible ones and the obstreperous ones.

"I came from an ordinary family," Maris tried again. "I have a sister in Santa Luisa. I never knew my biological father and

217

my mom wasn't exactly warm, but she took good care of us. We had everything we needed. We were . . . close." The word was painful to say, but it was true—the distance between them all now was her fault, all hers. A single word from Maris and Alana would drop everything and come, she had made that clear. "We were ordinary. My only rebellion was that I wanted to be a wife and a mother, which kind of drove my mother crazy, because she was really into her career. But then . . . once I got married and we moved to Linden Creek I kept feeling like something was missing." She grimaced. "I know how this sounds: but I wanted to make a difference. To *someone*."

Because Jeff certainly didn't care, she didn't add. How would things have been different, if only he'd wanted her? If he'd cherished the home she made, the family she tried to create, as much as she had? Would she still have felt that pressing need to see more, do more . . . or would she have been content?

"So," Pet said. "One look at the mean streets of Oakland and you were, like, this is the place for me? Nah, I'm just kidding, I think I kind of get it. I mean, *I'm* here."

"Yes," Maris said, ready to move the conversation away from her. "What *about* that? How did you end up here?"

"You mean instead of staying in the middle of fucking nowhere?" Pet smiled, and Maris blushed. "Aw, you know, the rent's cheap." She was silent for a minute, and her expression darkened again. "Okay, for real. So I dropped out of college the first time, right, and my mom, like, when it happened she told me that if I ever wanted to go back I'd have to pay for it myself. It was, like, her way of controlling me, and when I quit anyway, it was kind of . . . we didn't talk for a while. And now

I think she feels bad about it and I feel kind of stupid because, you know, she was right, I shouldn't have quit. But I keep telling her I have everything I want, I *like* what I do. The bar, and classes. The . . . you know, art. But then, when she and dipshit try to give me money, I have to say no, see? Because if I took it it would be like saying that what I have *isn't* enough. So. Until I figure all that shit out, I'm here."

Maris nodded. "Independence can be . . . well, I guess I'm about to find out what it is. I met my husband while I was getting my teaching certificate. I never really lived on my own, without roommates."

Pet nodded. She finished the soda and crushed the can with her hand. "You know, I have a sister too. Elena, she's a year younger than me. She's working on a senate campaign and taking her LSATs." She scowled. "Dipshit fucking *loves* her."

"Listen," Maris said conspiratorially. She knew this conversation was getting away from her, that lines were blurring that she wasn't ready for. But this was her last night in Oakland, in this borrowed little burrow. Why not share it with Pet, who had been a friend to her? "You're welcome to stay as long as you want. We can order takeout from that Indian place down by the Walgreens. I'll run out and get it and you can stay here, I'll pick up a bottle of wine. Even if your mom and her boyfriend do come by, they'll never know."

Pet laughed. "My partner in crime," she said. "Okay." She held up her hand for a fist bump, something Maris used to do with the kids at Morgandale.

Maris was returning from the restaurant, her car fragrant from the bags of takeout, when she saw George's truck parked in the driveway. Her heart thudded, but she parked under the tree and got out just as he was walking back down the driveway. When he saw her, he gave her an awkward wave.

"Well, hey," he said. "I hear you girls are having Indian food."

"George—about last night. I'm so sorry."

"No, look, don't, I'm the one who should be sorry. Or something. I mean, I'm sure I was wrong. About, whatever. It's just, I was thinking . . . well, can we try that again? No pressure. Just have coffee with me. Or dinner. I mean not now, obviously not now, you've got company and I'm on my way to work. But what about Tuesday night? Are you free?"

Two nights from now, Maris could be at Alana's house, and this might all be in the past. "I don't know," she said, then berated herself. *No*—the answer really should be no. It wasn't right to start something with a man as kind as George under false pretenses. But he hadn't shaved this morning and he looked kind of sexy with his hair wet from the shower, the soft hairs on his arms glinting gold in the sun. And, more important than all of that, he had come for her. She had been kind of awful to him yesterday and still he was here, still he was looking at her hopefully, that sweet half smile on his face.

"Don't say no yet. Okay? Just, have a nice dinner with Pet, relax, do whatever you need to do. I mean, you can let me down the hard way just as easy on Tuesday as today, right?"

He smiled so hopefully that Maris couldn't help laughing. "It's still going to be no," she said.

"I don't hear you," George said. As he passed, he squeezed her arm, letting his fingers trail down to her hand gripping the handles of the plastic take-out sack. His fingertips glanced lightly off her knuckles and even that small, innocent touch sent dizzying sensations through Maris's body.

She hurried to the door, then paused on the stoop, listening to his truck revving and pulling away from the curb, and had to wipe the dopey smile off her face before she let herself in.

They drank the wine and then, as night fell, Pet went to her apartment for a bottle of tequila and a couple of candle stubs and they drank shots by candlelight.

"The thing I don't get," Pet said after a while, rather slurringly, "is how it happened. I mean . . . on TV anyway, everyone always kept saying he was so ordinary. Just an ordinary kid. You know, coaches liked him, teachers liked him, blah blah blah. And that whole breakup violence thing. Oh. Fuck. I'm sorry. I'm doing it again."

"Pet. You've apologized a hundred times. And I've told you I don't mind talking about it." The tequila had left Maris with a pleasant numbness. It wasn't that she didn't mind, but that she didn't mind any more than any other conversation on any other day, and much less than most. She liked having Pet here. She wasn't ready for her to leave. It felt a little like a crutch, but then again, maybe that wasn't such a bad thing.

"Okay. I get it, anyone can lose their shit in the moment. And, I mean. Strangling. It's not like he—um."

Maris knew what Pet was clumsily trying to say. There hadn't been any blood. No broken limbs or savage beatings. Just Karl's hands around Calla's throat, until she stopped breathing. The prosecutor had even outlined exactly how it might have happened, in an effort to spur Karl to talk, citing other cases where killers talked about a momentary loss of

221

control of their own actions, a sense that they were out of their own bodies, watching rather than participating. *Maybe she just wouldn't listen to what you were saying,* the prosecutor had suggested, in his oily, persuasive voice. *Maybe you were just trying to get her attention.*

But later, when he was making his closing remarks, he wasn't so understanding: *Karl Isherwood drove to Byron Ranch with the victim's dead body in the car next to him,* he'd said. *He had twenty minutes at least to think about what he'd done. He put her body in the lake, lifted it with his own hands . . .*

"I'm trying to say, I mean, when I was eighteen, I couldn't have—like, to maintain a lie that long? Without cracking? I mean, fuck, I can't even keep a story straight for two days." She frowned ruefully. "Which is what ended my last relationship, actually."

"I don't know, either," Maris said.

But that wasn't entirely true. And as the evening wound down to its inebriated end, as Pet fell asleep on the sofa and Maris slipped her folded towel under Pet's head for a pillow and lay down with the room spinning a little, she allowed herself to remember another inebriated night, another wandering conversation that might have served as a warning—and for the thousandth time consoled herself that there was no way either of them could ever have known that the tiny seed of rage could explode into an act that could never be undone.

twenty-one

DEB LEFT FOR THE prison at noon on Sunday. She hadn't been able to add Ron to the visitor list after all, and he didn't want to go anyway. She had a three o'clock visiting slot, but she always left extra time for the trip. Ron didn't know what she did with that time—if she sat in her car the way he had, or if she had found a coffee shop somewhere nearby. He could picture her checking her watch, standing up from a café table, throwing away her paper cup, straightening her skirt, reapplying her lipstick. All to prepare to see Karl, to prepare herself for the ways in which he had changed or not changed since the prior week.

He kissed her good-bye and he didn't tell her that Karl had called him that morning. Or rather: that the robo-dial system had called and asked if he would take the call, and that he had hung up. Every call, even as brief as a few minutes, docked his credit card another fifteen or twenty dollars in the ridiculously overpriced prison phone system, but it wasn't the money. He just didn't want to have to admit to his son that he hadn't been able to convince Deb to drop the idea of the appeal.

Ron watched TV for a while but he couldn't pay attention. He got a beer from the fridge and drank it; then he got another one and went outside and stared at the wilting flowers in the flower beds while he drank that one. He drank a third standing in the kitchen and then he went up to Karl's room.

It was Deb who had started calling the guest room "Karl's room" after they moved, though Karl had never set foot in this house, this refuge to which his parents had fled. She'd directed the movers to put all the boxes of Karl's things in the closet—not just his clothes but every book, CD, memento, gaming device; the folded posters from his walls and the lava lamp he'd wanted so badly for his eleventh birthday. Now the room held only his bare furniture. The bed, the desk, the chair, the dresser—all were there, and if by the cruel weight of fate he and Deb were still trapped in this pallid life when Karl was released, he supposed his son would come home and find his room waiting for him. Ron sat in the desk chair and laid his forearms on the cool surface of the desk and pictured how it had looked, before: the huge monitor set up on a stack of old textbooks, the *South Park* bobbleheads and the beer stein from Ron's own fraternity days that Karl used as a pencil jar.

After a while he opened the empty drawers one by one. It wasn't the first time he had done this. He inhaled the air trapped in them, touched his fingertips to their surfaces. Looking for proof that Karl had once inhabited this space. He slid his hands along the seams and, jammed toward the back, stuck into the narrow gap of the seam, he found a photograph. What was left of a photograph, anyway: most of it was sliced into narrow ribbons, so that only by carefully laying it out flat could Ron see that it was a picture of the two of them from a school dance back in January, Karl's arm slung around Calla's shoulders. Karl had made a dozen cuts, slicing through their clothes, their arms.

Only the heads had been cut all the way off. There was no sign of the missing part of the photograph.

He sat there, heart thudding, for a few moments, thinking. "Nobody could have seen this coming," the refrain had gone. It was what he and Deb told each other, what their pastor had said—even the prosecutor had suggested that breakup violence could strike anyone, even "nice" kids, kids like Karl.

But what of that night when Karl put his fist through the wall? The fury that Ron had seen—had *recognized*—in his son's eyes?

Of course Karl had done it. The sharp edges of the cut-up photograph poked into the soft flesh of Ron's palm as he crumpled the thing. How could he have been lulled into doubt? He got up from the chair and stalked down the hall to Deb's office. She had never wavered in her stated faith in Karl, but she had shown her cracks too, the way she wouldn't look at him when she left for the prison. And what of the box? The carved wooden box that she obsessed over, that had become her touchstone after Karl was taken from them. How many nights had Ron come upon her in her office, hastily closing the lid and locking it with that key, that key that was nowhere to be found, not in her jewelry box or desk drawers, because he had looked, oh yes, he had looked. Ron was not above doing his own investigation. He deserved answers too.

Standing in the door of the little office he saw the box in its place on the shelf. Tacked to the fabric bulletin board were cards and pages torn from magazines, stickers and pressed flowers. *God Alone Knows His Plan*, read a postcard that he hadn't noticed before, rendered in watercolor with a lavender ribbon pinned to it.

He got the box from the shelf. It wasn't heavy. Felt around the clasp, the lock, the hinges. The metal parts were old, purely decorative. Ron took a letter opener from the ceramic jar on Deb's desk and jimmied it into the crack along the back. The old brass hinges bent under the pressure and then one of them popped. Ron was beyond caring about the evidence he left: he shoved the letter opener's blade along the split and attacked the other hinge until the burnished metal fell away and then he pried the box open, the clasp bending until he could shake the contents loose.

As soon as they fell to the surface of the desk he knew what they were and how mistaken he had been to think the box might have held clues. It was only the letters from the early days of Ron and Deb's courtship—before cell phones, before texting. They were written in his careful, self-conscious hand on lined paper. She'd even saved a few of the envelopes. There was the address of that tiny apartment she'd shared with her cousin . . . a drawing of a sheep, despite it all Ron was mortified to remember how he'd written "I love 'ewe,'" covering up his desperation to tell her and tell her and tell her, to make her understand how much he loved her so she'd be his, always.

He searched through the pile, wincing at the earnestness of his words, his sentiments laid so much more bare in hindsight, the need he thought he'd masked fairly bleeding from the page. Deb had known and she had loved him back anyway, had believed in her ability to be what he needed, the vessel for his brokenness to rest, salve for the hurt and protection against the rage. Deb was clear-eyed with her love: she didn't miss his flaws, but saw the way that she would mold her love around them, to make him better.

The front door opened downstairs. The sound of Deb's shoes on the floor in the foyer, her purse being set on the little table. Coming up the stairs. He could have shoved the letters back into the box, the box back onto the shelf. He could at least have gotten up from the desk, slipped out of the room, bought himself some time. Instead he just sat there.

A moment later she was standing in the doorway. She looked at the ruined box, the letters spread out on the desk. She pressed her lips together and then she spoke and her voice wasn't angry, only tired. "What did you think you'd find?"

"You know something," Ron said. "I know you know something about what happened and you aren't telling me, and I understand why and I'm even—I'm impressed, you know, when I look at it critically. I mean, all this time. Under the pressure, the questioning . . . but still."

She moved into the room, standing inches from him, the soft pressed fabric of her skirt up against the corner of the desk. "I've only ever cared about two things," she finally said. "You and him."

Ron nodded. He knew that. He'd always known it. "But he still won't go along with it, will he? The appeal?"

Deb didn't say anything for a while. She picked up one of the letters, scanned it briefly, then folded it and laid it in the bottom of the box. "Not yet," she said softly. "But I'm not giving up. I'll never give up."

Anger simmered somewhere in Ron, in the forbidden place where he'd learned to lock his fury. "So you get to decide?"

he asked quietly, but coiled in his voice was the potential for everything he had worked so hard to keep buried. "Just you? It's both of our lives, you know. All three of us. What makes it okay for you to drag us all through this again?"

"You could leave," Deb said after a chilling pause. Her voice didn't even waver. "If you don't—if you can't do this, I wouldn't blame you. I won't fight you."

"You would—" Ron struggled to find the words. He pushed back with the chair and it spun lazily on its axis. "You would throw away everything, our marriage, just to pursue this thing? If I refuse to get on board?"

"Oh, Ron," Deb said, and she slumped onto the end of the chaise, her shoulders rounded. Her makeup was smudged and her hair had lost its glossy finish in the heat. "What have I got left anyway? You hardly even come home from work at night. You made us move here—I don't know anyone here. I mean, people in this stupid development don't even come out of their houses. They get in their cars and put up the garage doors just long enough to make a getaway."

"I did that for us," he said woodenly.

"No. You did it for *you*. Do you know how hard it was for me to pack up his room? You took away the home he should have been able to come home to."

"Deb, that's *years* away, he won't even be—"

"That's the *point*," she snapped. "Goddamn you, Ron. Will you for *once* in your *life* just listen to me? It doesn't have to be years!"

A dozen arguments went through Ron's mind and he let them all go by. Because it wasn't about any of it: the length of the appeal, his son's reluctance, the inexorable turning of the wheels of justice—truth itself, and what it meant to any of them.

What was left when everything fell away was his rage.

"You've never cared what I wanted," he said, using the last of his will to keep from bursting from the chair, from picking up the fussy little lamp and hurling it to the floor, kicking the flimsy desk, grabbing his wife's hair and pulling her off that stupid chaise. Cracking his hand across her slack and exhausted face. The urge had not been this strong in a long while, but when it came back, it always came back like this: overpowering, enormous, devastating.

He stood up and backed away from her. He would go for a run, he would run until he couldn't breathe, until he collapsed on the dead weeds on the fire road.

"That is not true," Deb said in a voice so quiet and resigned that he had to strain to hear it. "I've *only* ever cared about you. I've been waiting, ever since I met you, for you to be ready to trust me."

"How can you think that?" he said, because what else was there? "I love you."

"Just not enough."

"Enough?"

"You don't *talk* to me." She pushed herself into the corner of the chaise, huddling there. "You don't tell me what you're really thinking. You hide yourself. You hide your pain."

"I don't . . . I don't do that." Even as he protested, Ron knew how ridiculous it was: of course he hid his pain. Of course he locked himself down. It was his duty. What he had to trade, in order to deserve a family, a woman of his own.

"All those years and I would have listened. All those times

I went to see him with you, that I had to watch the way he talked to you, I would have done anything for you."

"Who?" Ron was genuinely mystified, but he also, on some level, recognized the shape of what was coming toward him. It was terrifying.

"Who do you think? *Magnus.* Your father. The way you grew up. The things you endured. I could have made it better. I would have been there for you. If you had just let me in, if you had just let me . . ."

"I don't . . ." He faltered, his body sagged against the wall.

But it was true. He had never let Deb see who he really was, at the core. He'd made that promise to himself on the day he asked her to marry him, and he'd never faltered. He'd never told the truth to anyone at all.

Until that September night a year and a half ago in that hotel in Sacramento, when he'd carelessly spilled his secrets like ball bearings across his father's shop floor.

twenty-two

September, twenty-two months ago

IRONICALLY, IT WOULD NEVER have happened without Deb's intervention. She came home from a planning committee meeting for the Los Angeles trip and told him she'd signed him up to chaperone. The committee was desperate—the kind of parents who could afford the Gale Academy were not the kind who could—or would—easily give up a three-day weekend. Once in Burbank, a good seven-hour drive, the parents were off the hook; the teachers would take it from there, shuttling the kids from the Museum of Tolerance to the Korean Cultural Center to the Nibei Foundation, a senior trip designed to make them more thoughtful, more broad-minded. Or maybe to make a deposit in the bank of their own liberal guilt so they'd eventually turn into generous alumni. It was just the drive down on a Friday, and back on a Sunday, but Deb had already committed to help out with a fund-raiser her friend was running.

And with Ron having a lighter workload since selling the company, Deb had thought—he didn't mind, did he? Take a bunch of kids in the Explorer, maybe visit his aunt in Thousand Oaks, it had been such a long time, and they shouldn't really take her health for granted . . .

And Ron didn't mind, really, though his aunt Regina hadn't known him the last time he'd seen her and he saw no reason to put himself through that. Instead, he'd focus on his relationship with his son. He'd begun what he privately thought of as his "Cat's Cradle" initiative, pursuing Karl for any spare moments of togetherness, even though Karl wanted nothing more than to get out of the house and off with his friends. And since the carpools were arranged with rigid fairness, a lottery system meant to stave off cliquishness and preserve Gale's we're-a-village patina—that meant, possibly, time in the car to talk. Put Karl up front in the passenger seat, let the rest of the kids sit in back. The car was a powerful incubator of conversation at this age.

It had worked modestly well, at least on the drive down. By Sunday, Karl's romance with Calla had begun, and on the way back the two of them defied the carpool assignment and managed to switch with some kid so that Calla wound up in the Explorer. The two of them rode all the way in back in the third seat, oblivious to everyone around them, leaving Ron with the burden of talking to some kid he'd never met before for hours. But on the way down, Karl and he managed to talk about any number of things, the conversation moving easily from one topic to the next, interrupted by long comfortable silences when Karl stabbed at his phone or turned up the sound for songs he liked.

But the most unexpected part of the trip turned out to be the first night, once the kids and teachers had been dropped off at UCLA for some evening colloquium, and the five parents drove back to the La Quinta out by the Burbank airport. One of the moms, a brassy woman whose son acted in theater productions in San Francisco, had suggested the five of them meet for dinner at the Elephant Bar a block away, in the parking lot of a mall. Ron had begged off, claiming a need to make some calls for work, but not before he glimpsed Maris Vacanti watching him with an amused expression. So he wasn't entirely surprised, an hour later when he was hiding out in the bar at the Hilton across the street, eating a rib-eye at the bar and watching ESPN on the TV mounted from the ceiling, when Maris came walking in.

Of course they ate together, being complicit in this misdemeanor, their shared escape from the other parents. "I don't know why we can't just let the kids go to Universal Studios," Maris confessed, ordering a second glass of wine and poking at a salad. "Would it kill them to spend one weekend without someone trying to make them feel guilty just for existing? Though I guess that's why we pay the big bucks for Gale."

And Ron, fueled by Jameson, had entertained her with stories of the basketball team bus trips from his own high school days. Even when Ron ordered another drink, the two of them having repaired to upholstered chairs in the lounge after dinner, he was merely happy to have some company to wile away this evening in an ugly-ass part of town. It didn't occur to him until the waitress had brought another round and most of the other guests had cleared out that he might have wandered into some other territory.

Maris had been telling a story about Jeff, her husband, who had insisted on dragging his French horn from high school on every move they had made since getting married— even though she'd never heard him play it.

Suddenly, her eyes shone with tears. Ron, who hadn't been paying strictest attention, one eye on the game, was alarmed. More so when Maris leaned closer, her soft sweater gaping open to reveal the edge of her black bra. He hadn't seen this coming. Ron was that most rare of suburban species, a relatively happily married man.

If there had been signs of some attraction between them, the few times they'd met, Ron had missed them. As she kept talking, Ron wondered if she was just tipsy and desperate for someone, anyone, to talk to. *Jeff was too busy, Jeff looked right through her, Jeff didn't ever share what was on his mind anymore, blah blah blah.* Intrigued, and maybe testing to see how far Maris would take the flirtation, Ron responded by telling Maris about a period in his own marriage when he and Deb had been uncharacteristically distant with each other, making up a few supporting details.

Ron had only cheated on Deb once, and that had been in the early years of their marriage—his last few unsown wild oats, pure and simple. That urge was put to rest in the guilt-ridden days that followed. And he hadn't been tempted, at least not to the point of acting on any attractions, since then. He loved Deb, and their sex life was good, they still had fun together. He would have called her his best friend, if asked.

But Maris was so different from Deb as to seem exotic, at least by Linden Creek standards. She was opinionated and, if not outspoken, at least unafraid to say what she thought when asked. She had interests beyond their sheltered little suburb. She had a compact, trim attractiveness that was heightened by her ready laugh and somewhat sarcastic wit. She dressed simply but seductively, favoring spare dresses that showed her well-shaped arms and calves. Ron had, as it happened, once masturbated to a fantasy that featured her in a tennis skirt she was wearing when he saw her at the bagel place.

So when Maris paid such close attention when he spoke, her eyes wide and attentive as she sipped her glass of wine, concurring that yes, it was so hard in the early days with a baby, when everyone was sleep deprived and intimacy was the last thing on anyone's mind, it almost seemed like they were having two conversations at once, one finding common ground and one moving inexorably closer to something exciting and intimate. Which was why, perhaps, Ron didn't censor himself carefully.

"He was just such a tough baby," Ron recounted. "Two months of nonstop crying. Nothing worked. Deb and I were just both so tired. I think it was during that time we decided we were only going to have one—and then we both felt so defeated that one seven-pound baby had ground us down so easily. And as for adult conversation, well, you can probably guess that went out the window."

But that wasn't the whole story. This was the point, in the occasional recounting of Karl's childhood, when Ron usually gave a self-deprecating laugh and segued into his kindergarten escapades. Karl, in kindergarten, showed an early aptitude for things mechanical and proved it by disassembling everything he could get his hands on: a pencil sharpener, the stacked bookcases, plush toys with internal speakers, a child lock on a small refrigerator. These were the sort of "safe" anecdotes suitable for dinner parties and other gatherings, getting the point across that one's child was exceptional without actually claiming superior aptitude. Deb, who was better at this sort of thing than Ron, would gracefully take his handoff and run with it, freeing him to recede back to silence, until the couples gradually separated into groups: women in the kitchen, men by the wet bar or the television.

This, however, wasn't that kind of occasion. As they talked, Ron had the sense that they were coconspirators, refugees from the vapidity of the other parents—who were no doubt now finishing their onion flowers and umbrella drinks and headed back to watch the late show in their rooms.

And the conversation deepened.

Maris circled around some revelation about her marriage, and though it was clear to Ron that she wouldn't reveal the details, no matter how much she drank, she was in the mood to test and examine its secret depths. She too seemed to be feeling the odd freedom of their circumstances: this dim hotel bar, this aimless evening. Her murky hints and intimations lifted a corner on the curtain of her life and Ron was eager for the view.

"He's not the person I thought I married," she finally summarized, a bit slurringly, after a series of vague hints and parries.

Ron, who'd never formed much of an opinion of Jeff—he was away a lot, working in other cities, the kind of smugly successful guy who was a dime a dozen in Linden Creek—felt paradoxically moved to defend him.

"None of us are, though," he interjected. "It's impossible to reveal your whole true self to someone you love, if you want to keep that love alive."

Where had that come from? Slightly embarrassed, Ron looked down into his whiskey, shaking the ice against the glass; the bartender had poured the last couple a little stiffer after Ron had slapped a ten down on the tray for a tip.

"Oh, I don't know." Maris frowned. "Some people can. Some can't. I mean, I'm pretty much the same as who I was before I got married. I didn't hold anything back. I mean I know people change, and I've changed some, I guess. But the core—that's still the same."

"But there must be things, you know, things that happened or that you did, that you didn't tell Jeff about. That you didn't tell anyone. I mean, come on, we all have that, parts of ourselves that we grew out of or, I don't know, mastered."

Maris gazed at him thoughtfully over the rim of her glass. "But that's just what I'm talking about, with Jeff. I feel like there are . . . parts of him, that he, that maybe he covered up or disguised or whatever. That he *kept* from me."

"But, Maris." Maybe, if he hadn't been drinking, if the chemistry between them hadn't seemed so strong, he would have simply changed the subject. But here was the perfect opportunity to explore something unsettled within him— with this woman who had grown not only more attractive to him but far more interesting, with her melancholy and her self-deprecation, the sense she gave him that she not only wanted to hear but wouldn't judge him for anything he said.

And it was suddenly very tempting to talk. There were things, deeply hidden things, that Ron had wearied of keeping buried. He didn't need a confessional, that wasn't it exactly; the burden he carried wasn't something he thought he could divest himself of by telling. It was the hiding that galled him, the fact that having made the decision long ago to keep a part of himself in shadow, he'd unwittingly committed himself to a lifetime of careful masking. Which could be pretty fucking exhausting, really.

"Say Jeff had some things in his past that he wasn't proud of. Not telling you—in a way, that's a high-order compliment. Or, no, that's not exactly what I mean."

"It's the whole gender thing," Maris said. "The strong-and-silent stereotype, is that what you're getting at?"

"Well—yeah. But I mean, with these things, it's always possible to look at them a few ways. Dr. Phil and his whole crew want men to vomit up all kinds of revelations all the time. It's like an epidemic."

"The emasculation of the American man."

"You laugh, but there's something to it. A man wants to be strong for his family, his wife . . . the people who look up to him."

"Okay, Lone Ranger," Maris said. That smile, both elliptical and encouraging. "So what are you covering up?"

Looking back on it much later, Ron would identify this moment as a turning point, a sea change launched by one crossed line. What he would never understand was why it felt so right to say what he did next. Of course he had fantasized about telling someone, some fair and gentle confessor who would remind him that he was still a good man. Someone who would still respect him, after. But why this woman, why this night, this bar, when he was far from home and so much time had gone by, so much water under the bridge? When the statute of limitations even for one's own inner voices, the harshest critics of all, should surely have run out?

And besides: there was something overtly sexual about her

invitation. She wanted his story . . . but her encouragement was shaded with the promise of more. It was something far different from the pleasant guilty rush that came from imagining one of the women at work—Renee Baker, most often, from HR—with her skirt hiked up in his office.

It was the being seen. Being *understood*.

"Well." More rattling of the ice in his glass. "Before I was married—hell, before I turned eighteen—I got into some trouble. Sealed juvie record kind of trouble. And I've never told anyone since. Not even Deb."

One finely shaped eyebrow went up. "What happened?"

"I . . . beat up a guy. It wasn't just me, there were four of us. It was after a football game. State championship, us against De LaSalle. They were full of themselves even back then, came down in a rented bus like they thought they were rock stars. Only after the game, these two jokers stuck around. They wanted trouble. Came looking for us; we were leaving a party they must have heard about. They had bats, they started on the car, smashed a couple of windows. Later they said that was all they were going to do. But one of them took a swing at one of my friends."

Ron had managed to put this episode in the past for the most part, but there was still the dull vague pall that fell over him every fall, when the kids put the hand-painted banners up around school, the home games and snack shack and all of that. Gale's team was mediocre, but Ron had still been relieved when Karl picked water polo over football. Having to sit in the stands, that would have been tough.

"So there was a fight?" Maris asked. Her lips were stained red from the wine, even after she licked them.

"Well . . . okay, yeah, I guess. The truth is, though, I went kind of nuts. I took a swing at the guy and I just got lucky, no other explanation, he dropped his bat. My friends took the other guy down. But I just kept going." He swallowed, tiny beads of perspiration popping out on his forehead. "I got him on the ground. He was big, solid, not too fast and kind of drunk, but I just couldn't seem to make anything connect, you know? I mean he was *meaty*, I kept hitting him but it felt like it wasn't really hurting him."

Until he really hurt him.

Ron gulped his drink before continuing. "He was on his back on the sidewalk. His legs were kind of flopped over in the street. And I . . . I—I broke his shin. Both bones."

"Oh my God." She winced, and Ron had to look away. "How?"

"Uh, well, I pretty much put all my weight on his leg." Jumped on it, a fact that even his friends seemed shocked by. The sound, the cracking of bone and the screaming that followed, instantly killed whatever rage had built up inside him. "I knew right away it was the worst mistake of my life up until then. I stayed with him while the other guy went to call the ambulance. My friends took off but I . . . I stayed."

"Wow." Maris sounded more awed than horrified. "I can't really even imagine. Was that the end? Or did it happen again?"

"It . . ." Was he really going to do this? It was tempting, because Maris hadn't recoiled from him. It felt like absolution and it felt like something more. Maybe he was conflating the two; maybe, when sober, he would realize that he'd mistaken a hard-on for an opportunity to unburden himself. "There was one other really bad time. I mean, I had the temper, I guess you'd call it, all through my younger days, but I mostly managed to stay on top of it."

His better sense took hold as he teetered on the brink of telling: about the fury that would surge for no good reason; how a bad day, a snub or slight or provocation, could seem like the world turning on him, and how tempted he was to respond with violence. But Maris's sweater had dipped again, showing the creamy expanse of her neck, her fine collarbone, the black lace of her bra. The wine was gone; so was his drink.

Ron dug in his wallet for a few bills and tossed them onto the table, never breaking Maris's gaze. "My whole point is that we all have these things inside us, things we'd erase if we could," he said carefully, as he slid his hand across the table and laced his fingers with hers. She didn't pull away, and the corners of her mouth twitched. "But we're all at the mercy of our emotions, wouldn't you agree? Of our hearts? Even if it's just in the moment?"

Maris slid her chair back and stood. She picked up her purse and smoothed her skirt.

"I'm in room 330," she said. "Give me five minutes, in case the lemmings are still out of their cages."

twenty-three

MONDAY MORNING MARIS WOKE with a pounding headache
and a horrible taste in her mouth. She brushed her teeth,
and then brushed them again. She was showered and up to
Norris's apartment by ten o'clock, but fifteen minutes into
trying to work she realized it was hopeless: every time she
leaned over a box, she felt nauseous. After writing Norris a
note saying she didn't feel well but that she'd be back to work
on the sorting tomorrow, she took the coffee he had left for
her and went back downstairs.

She could spend the day working on her job search, revis-
ing her résumé and emailing it to Alana to look over before
she started submitting it in earnest.

She stared at the job listings in the South Bay for a while
before she finally got up the nerve to type *Oakland* into the
search box. Just for fun. Just to see.

Tuesday, she felt much better. While Norris was at work, she
managed to go through the remaining boxes of the papers
and organize them by type: several refinancings, years' worth
of tax records, the titles to two old cars, medical records,
insurance claims. And more unusual things: a set of blue-
prints for a one-story house labeled Cottage II, a receipt for

cremation from Caring Pet Cemetery, a police report for a fender bender. She put them all in labeled folders and packed them into bankers' boxes where Norris could deal with them when and if he was ready.

There was still quite a bit to do, but Maris wanted to knock off a little early. She'd bought a new razor, shaving cream, tweezers—she still wasn't sure what she was expecting from her date with George, but she had decided to take a little extra time getting ready.

It was when she was moving a box of linens that she made an unexpected discovery. On top of the first was a quilt whose blocks were each embroidered with a woman's name, the sort of friendship quilt that Maris's friends' mothers back in Kansas owned, gifts from weddings or keepsakes from a place left behind. Maris suspected that it had belonged to Norris's mother, and she carefully unfolded it to see if she recognized any of the names from the paperwork.

After examining it, she folded it back up and was about to replace it when she noticed that in the box below the quilt was a large clasp envelope stuffed with papers that she had missed. She took it out and discovered that underneath it were baby clothes. Maris took them out and laid them on the bed: pinafores, bonnets, footie sleepers, ruffled diaper covers, all soft from washing—two of everything. She glanced at the two pretty painted headboards, one missing its mattress, and shook the papers carefully from the envelope.

A small plastic album fell out. Maris flipped through: there were photos of twin baby girls from birth through age two or three. If they weren't identical they were close, and in several of the photographs, one or both of them were being held by Norris.

She set the album aside and went quickly through the papers. There were more photographs, mostly school pictures once the girls got to be five or six years old. In the most recent, the girls were eleven or so, their hair fastidiously styled, braces on their teeth. Their names were Kayla and Keyna, and they were pretty, with their father's wide-set eyes and strong chin.

There were a handful of letters, painstakingly written in a childish hand: *Dear Daddy Thank You for the Presints*. A torn envelope with a return address in Bakersfield. And a handwritten ledger on a piece of lined paper, dated 2004, in which the months were listed down the page, next to figures ranging from $450 to, in December, $1,125.

Norris had had two daughters, and it seemed that he'd been careless enough to lose them.

Glancing at the clock, Maris refolded the quilt and laid it on top of the contents of the last box. She was cutting it close if she wanted to take her time getting ready. Besides, she needed time to think.

George arrived at six and announced that he had cooked, and Maris pretended to change her mind and join him only because he promised homemade pasta. He lived in a duplex near the Berkeley border; his neighbors' yard was full of Big Wheels and Little Tikes basketball hoops, and while he worked in the kitchen Maris could hear a baby crying through the walls, a television blaring PBS. George was unfazed, soon setting a plate in front of Maris with enough spaghetti carbonara to feed her for a week.

There was a candle in a Chianti bottle and Neil Young playing softly, a moment when George asked nervously if the food was all right, a joke that Maris had told before but, miraculously, managed to deliver just right for once. And then, before she'd made a dent in the enormous mountain of pasta, they were suddenly rushing upstairs to George's bedroom, their arms around each other, and when Maris saw how carefully he had made the bed, turning down the covers and putting a flower in a water glass on the bedside table, it broke her heart a little. But then he kissed her and she was in another place, and happy, oh so happy to be there.

Afterward, they sat in his bed drinking the rest of the wine from tumblers.

"I haven't done that in a while," Maris admitted.

"Could've fooled me."

Maris blushed; George stroked her foot, which he had taken into his lap.

"You're sweet," she said. "I mean, really sweet."

He looked up at her with mock suspicion. "Is that a euphemism for I need to spank your ass next time?"

Maris laughed, a full-belly laugh that felt as rusty and welcome as the shivering orgasm half an hour earlier. She knew she had to make a decision—put a stop to this, or come clean about who she was. Things had gone too far for her not to be honest with George. But the moment wasn't right. Didn't she deserve to enjoy one evening of simple pleasure, of uncomplicated joy? Besides, she had some sleuthing to do.

"Can I ask you something?"

"Um, sure."

"Does Norris have daughters?" She briefly explained what she'd found.

"He doesn't talk about that much," George said when she'd finished. "That all happened pretty quick after we got back from the Gulf. We fell out of touch for a while and I don't know, I mean, you see it with some guys, it's like they want to do it all right away, everything they figure they almost missed. We had some close calls over there—I'll tell you about it sometime. But yeah, those girls were born in ninety-two, they'd be grown now I guess, and Renatta left Norris in ninety-three. Reason I remember is we started our business in ninety-four. He used to talk about them all the time, but he's a hardheaded man, used to be anyway. He and Renatta never did get along, and when she moved the girls to Bakersfield he threatened to take her to court, but in the end he just stopped sending her money.

"I know he always regretted that, felt like shit about it. By the time they were in grade school he was sending what he could, but things never got right with Renatta and he felt like she poisoned the girls to him. A couple of years ago when he got the house, he tried hard to reconnect, thought they might like to come visit from time to time; he used to talk about them going to college here. But you know, girls at that age . . . well, I don't know, I never had kids."

Maris tensed, because here is where it would come: the natural question of whether she'd ever had them, ever wanted them. So far she'd escaped with only oblique references to an ex, to the past. She burrowed against him, hiding her face against his chest, and felt his arms circle her protectively. His breath was warm on her neck, and even that—his face touching her skin—was more intimacy than Jeff had given her in so long.

"My mystery girl," George said, as if reading her mind. "So now that you've slept with me, do I get your phone number? Or is that like a five-date rule with you?"

twenty-four

ON WEDNESDAY MORNING, RON stopped at Noah's and picked up breakfast on the way to work like he usually did. Then, he went the wrong way on 580, realizing his decision was made only when he passed the windmills outside Livermore.

The bagel sandwich went untouched on the passenger seat of the car. Half an hour later, Ron couldn't stand the smell anymore and pulled over at the next exit and threw the paper sack away in the parking lot of a Walmart.

The drive to Fresno would take almost three hours. The return would be a little longer, even going against the traffic. That left only an hour or so, but Ron wouldn't need more: over the course of the last couple of years his father's mild dementia had become much worse.

As he drove, the sun beating through the windshield relentlessly and burning into his eyes even as the air conditioner left him uncomfortably chilly, Ron cycled through an endless loop of recriminations. Karl. Magnus. Himself. Mostly himself. Deb's face, as she told him he could leave her. *You hide yourself. You hide your pain.* What had she really been saying? Was she giving him an ultimatum? Get behind her plans for the appeal, or leave—as simple as that?

After years of trying to convince himself he had been a good husband, he had decided, overnight, that he had not been. He had been unfaithful twice, the first time meaningless, the second, anything but. The night Maris and he had spent together had not been merely the boozy flare of some misplaced emotion. He had felt more in those hours with her than he had in an accumulation of years with Deb—but it wasn't love. No. They didn't love each other and they could never have loved each other. Each was the repository for some desperate need of the other. Maris had been almost savage that night; he'd ended up with scratches that he'd had to make up a story—taking a fall while out running in the hills—to cover up. And he had woken in the chilled, antiseptic hotel room at five in the morning, hung over, with Maris's head on his chest and her hair tickling his nostrils, and instantly been far more sorry that he'd confided in her than that he had fucked her. If he could take only one thing back, it would have been that.

They'd avoided each other after that when possible. Their children's romance seemed, to Ron, like a clumsy attempt at irony from some peevish Fate. When the two couples saw each other at school events, Deb and Jeff didn't seem to notice that Ron and Maris barely interacted. When Calla broke it off with Karl, Ron's relief that the thing was finished eclipsed his concerns about what he perceived to be his son's overreaction.

Never, in all the months that followed, had he and Maris spoken again, until that day on the bridge. Ron had, for a while, attempted to convince himself that she had forgotten about the whole thing. He'd let himself out of her room without waking her; she had been drunker than he. After Calla died, each of them was so consumed with their own despair that it couldn't have mattered anyway. But Ron remembered just enough of his high school Shakespeare to have a sense that deeds like theirs weren't fully settled until they'd lost everything—not just their children, God help them, but their identities, their very lives, and everyone they loved.

Ron, realizing he was crying, smacked the steering wheel and pressed the gas a little harder. The thing, the thing. Yes, he had invited this disaster down: first by passing on his blood legacy of violence, and then by tempting fate by bedding Maris. He might as well have put a gun in Karl's hands. Except for one thing, one stubborn mitigating factor that, no matter how many times Ron tried to force the equation to a resolution, left him just shy of culpable: he was not the progenitor, he was not even the patient zero of the legacy into whose path poor Calla had stumbled. He was victim as well as villain.

Penance was not Ron's natural gift. He'd spent a lifetime parceling out mildly good deeds as a defense against the sins he feared his unchecked self would commit. And it had seemed to work. His wife was happy with the bland tokens of his affections, doled liberally but with little effort; his employees basked in the glow of the shared accolades they didn't realize meant nothing to Ron. Even when he'd become sloppy, he kept succeeding. The happy fool, the guy who got credit for showing up. The last Father's Day card that Ron had received, almost a year to the day before life as they knew it ended, had been emblazoned with the words "To the Best Father in the World." A card, a sentiment, purchased by his wife and signed by his son.

"The best fucking father in the world," he muttered, aware that if the highway patrol was out, his desperate errand was going to be brought to an abrupt end, or at least an expensive interruption. Ron was not a habitual speeder: behind the wheel, as in most things, he was deceptively moderate. But here, now, take note, he thought: the true nature of the man is revealed. Eighty-five, eighty-seven . . . he was flirting with ninety miles per hour and even that wouldn't be enough. Not enough to satisfy the hunger that had waited so long inside him for release.

(God, why hadn't he just jumped? The thing on the bridge, that had been stupid, self-indulgent, dramatic, even histrionic. But only because he hadn't followed through. If he'd pulled it off, wouldn't that have been a measure of penance, the real kind?)

Ron, heading hell-bent toward a score that he was too late to settle, had never loathed himself more. Magnus, sly upper-hand hoarder that he was, had managed to exit quietly from the world before Ron could finally exact his due, or even confront him with an honest examination of the facts.

Before it happened, before his son crushed the life from another human being, Ron had last visited his father over the holidays and convinced himself he'd forgiven Magnus. Ordinarily he tried to go every few months, but the Christmas visit had been unsettling: Magnus had called him by his brother's name twice; he'd seemed to forget that Ron and Deb were there. He'd bellowed an unintelligible string of curses at some imaginary slight committed by another patient, and at one point had stood and stalked down the hallway, his pants sagging off his bony hips, clutching the handrail with his gnarled hand. When Ron had sought out another patient, an old man he thought was his father's friend, the man had turned away in his wheelchair, shaking his head, eyes downcast. "A shame," he muttered. "A shame."

Another son would have been mobilized to act, maybe, though he and his brothers had researched care facilities with a zeal they all agreed Magnus didn't deserve four years ago when it was clear he could no longer live alone. There were a few strained phone calls with Neal, the brother Ron got along with best, but Neal was in Michigan and every phone conversation ended with him asking, "Well, do you want me to come out there and help?"—something they both knew was pointless and made no sense. What were they going to do, exactly? Their father had dementia. But he was a cruel bastard, and what Ron suspected that Neal was asking, really, was what did they owe the man who had raised them.

Maybe the answer to the question was his failure to act itself, the span of time that became longer and longer, with no visit and no call.

Last year, last terrible June, when Karl was arrested, Neal had offered to come out to California. So, to be fair, had Keith. But Keith had been laid off again, and Neal and Jess were having problems of their own, some drama with their daughter, which Ron barely paid attention to, and besides, he didn't want them there. He'd only wanted Deb. And now, a year had gone by and he'd dutifully gone to see Magnus earlier in the year when Neal finally came out with the daughter in question. The four of them—Ron and Deb, Neal and Ashley—had driven down to Fresno only to find Magnus snoring in his bed with a crust of something yellow around his mouth. They'd taken turns shouting at him—"It's me, Dad." How often did the staff hear variations on that theme echoing exasperatingly up and down the halls? They pushed his geri chair into the garden where they sat until he started to complain about the heat. Ron had noticed the look of revulsion on Ashley's face with something like satisfaction.

What would Ron find today? What state would his father be in?

Around and around his thoughts swirled. Finally he reached Fresno, found his way by memory through the strip-mall-choked outskirts to the facility, a palm-tree-lined turd of a building. The receptionist was unfamiliar; the faces of the patients all looked the same. He might have recognized some of them, but perhaps not. There, the screamer—that one, at least, Ron remembered because the bent old man screamed obscenities all day long until his voice was hoarse.

"Don't mind him," the receptionist said calmly. "You here for?"

"Isherwood," Ron said, his voice cracking. He hadn't spoken a word since saying good-bye to Deb this morning; she'd been poring over her iPad and barely lifted her gaze, even though he broke his habit of years and didn't kiss her good-bye. "Magnus Isherwood."

"Mmm-hmm," the receptionist, who on second thought was perhaps a nurse, given that she was wearing scrubs. They all wore scrubs; it was impossible to tell them apart. Nurses, nurses' aides, and jobs even more menial than that, the luckless women and occasional man who'd been charged with bathing Magnus and wiping the shit from his ass and dressing him and strapping him into the geri chair when he grew too restless; who tried to return the possessions that the patients stole from each other's rooms on their eternal wanderings; who asked in loud voices who the darling children were on the laps of all the slack-mouthed, clueless patients in the photographs their loved ones left behind in frames bought cheap at Marshall's because everyone knew things went missing.

Saints, all of them, Ron thought, every one a better man or woman than he.

"You know where you're going, sir?"

"Room 219?" Ron asked, just in case they'd moved his father in the months since he'd been there, in case some new precipitous decline had consigned him to a different wing or corridor or cagelike common room. And was that a note of censure in her voice? Surely Ron wasn't the worst; surely there were other family members, sons and daughters and spouses, who never came at all. Besides. *Isherwood*. Didn't she *know*?

"That's right," she said, handing over the plastic guest pass. Ron looped its cord over his head and thanked her.

The smell, the familiar sounds of moaning, the staff nodding to him as they passed pushing carts of supplies, medicine, bottles, and trays: it was all the same as before. Ron avoided everyone's eyes, patient and staff alike.

His father's door was cracked a few inches. Ron pushed it open, cautiously. The faint smell of shit mixed with disinfectant assaulted him. A single light was on, in the bathroom, and the drapes were pulled shut, but his father was in his chair facing the window nonetheless. Some orderly's idea of humor? Or, more likely, simply the most expedient course for workers with too many charges on their hands, too few hours in the day to care for them.

His father's hair had grown too long, the silvery-gray strands clumping gummily together down to his neck, his pink scalp showing through. A shirt that Ron didn't recognize, wooly plaid in shades of gray, sat slackly on his bony shoulders. A blanket had been placed on his lap, fuzzy green cheap-looking acrylic. His father was worrying the blanket with his hands, folding and rubbing the fabric in his restless fingers. Ron had seen him do it before. It was common among Alzheimer's patients, apparently. Some do-gooder group made the blankets as a charitable project and sent them over. From this angle, seeing only his father's arm jerking and moving, it was possible to imagine that the old man was masturbating, a thought that curdled any remaining sense of filial trepidation that Ron had brought with him like the rime at the bottom of a bucket.

"Dad."

The hand kept scrabbling at the blanket, but his father's head tilted to the right. He made a sound, a sibilant word like *since*.

Ron stepped forward, propelled by so many emotions it was impossible to know what he was hoping for from this deplorable errand. He put his hands on the handles of the chair and turned it, slowly, so that his father was facing the upholstered armchair in the corner of the room. He pushed open the drapes, blinking in the sun, and sat down in the chair. His father's knees were only a couple of feet from his own. The geri chair—a contraption that was like an ugly vinyl-upholstered rolling armchair, except for the straps and armrests to which trays or patients' arms could be fastened—had been outfitted with a plastic cover that presumably could be washed or disposed of. Someday—someday soon—his father would no longer occupy this holding cell; he'd be churned into the earth (Magnus had insisted for decades that he wanted to be cremated) and some other withered, doomed old person would inhabit this room, this chair.

"God, Dad."

Magnus made several more attempts to speak, spittle spraying from his mouth. His hand rose from the blanket and pointed; Ron shrunk involuntarily from the trembling finger.

You're pathetic, Ron wanted to say. Had practiced saying, even, at odd moments during the past year. *You're nothing now but a stinking sack of shit. You can't hurt me. I could hurt* you. *I could crush you with one hand.*

All of these things were true, and yet somewhere—dormant in his bowels, the rusted detritus of his childhood—the fear was still there. The anticipation of the sucker punch, the slap to the face, the cruel twist of the wrist. Or worse: the invective, the insults, the denouncing. Magnus, in his prime, could look at you and know what your eleven- or thirteen- or fifteen-year-old self feared the most, what secret shame you carried. He could cut you down with a few casual words. "Out of your league, boy, and always will be," he'd once said when they ran into Miss Tate—assistant middle school principal given to transparent blouses over tight camisoles—in town. How had he known, the ache in Ron's balls when she passed too close with her cloying perfume? Or, when Ron had been awarded (and no one was more surprised than he) the French Award at the end of eighth grade, Magnus had raised his eyebrow at the certificate and said "French is a faggot's language—that ought to serve you well."

"Tay—tay—tay—" his father stammered, leaning against his straps.

"I haven't been here in a while," Ron said. "I'm here because—"

"You're the one," his father said, his voice suddenly, unexpectedly, clear. He pointed the same trembling finger at Ron, the gnarled yellow nail untrimmed and ragged.

Ron was taken aback. Clarity wasn't what he had anticipated.

"I'm—what, Dad?"

His father arched an eyebrow at him and his eyes shone with mischief, or triumph, or amused contempt—it was impossible to say. But for a few seconds he seemed both present and lucid, and that pointing finger—the same one that had underscored Ron's many failures, during any number of fights before Ron finally learned not to engage—seemed to pin him to the spot.

His father chuckled, and the finger wagged twice before a fit of coughing overtook him. Magnus hacked and coughed, and a gobbet of yellow sputum flew out of his mouth and hung from a thread of drool, quivering inches below his chin.

"*What?*" Ron demanded. "No, you bastard, don't do this. Don't you go off and hide now. I came here to *talk* to you and I'm damn well going to talk."

He'd dragged his chair closer, leaning forward and speaking in an ever more agitated voice. The rage was there, the urge to strike out, to crush and punish. Ron was sure he'd never hated his father more than in that moment, but already Magnus's mind had splintered once again into confused and unsalvageable shards.

"Is everything all right?"

The voice from the doorway stopped him cold. Ron realized he was leaning forward in the chair, and he made a conscious effort to sit back, averting his eyes so he didn't have to look at his father's slack face. He took a breath to steady himself and forced a smile onto his face before turning to face the person who had spoken.

A woman wearing duck-patterned scrubs, her hair pulled into a gray-blond ponytail and reading glasses dangling around her neck from a chain, was watching him with concern.

"Oh, I'm fine," Ron said, the familiar pall of guilt and shame washing over him. "We're fine."

"I just thought I heard voices . . ."

Raised voices, was what she meant. Here he was, a grown man, in the prime of his life, yelling at a frail, elderly man. From her perspective . . . hell, from any sane person's perspective, what Ron was doing was uncalled for, even abusive. Of course, she hadn't been forced to grow up with him, hadn't lived under his roof and under his iron fist.

"I wasn't sure if he heard me," Ron said stonily. The lie was obvious, but what was she going to do about it?

"I know it can be hard," the woman said. She took a couple of steps into the room and folded her arms over her chest. "Hello, Magnus. How nice that you have a visitor today."

Magnus rolled his head at her, his features twisting into the same sly smirk. He lifted his finger and pointed again, but without the same insistence as he had a moment ago. Or was Ron imagining that?

Was he really going to drive himself crazy here, ascribing complex thoughts and emotions—psychic powers and prophecy, even—to a man whose brain no longer connected thoughts or processed memories?

"My . . . my. My show."

"Your show? You want to watch your show on television, is that it?" The woman seemed unflappable. Dangling below the glasses on a lanyard was her staff ID. It showed her looking prettier, carefully made up. "But you have a visitor right now, Magnus. Is this your son?"

Magnus's smile didn't so much slip as simply drain away, and he twisted in his chair to stare at the window. He made a quiet humming sound and went back to twisting and folding the blanket in his lap.

"I'm his son," Ron admitted bitterly. "Ron Isherwood."

"Oh, of course. You were here before. Around New Year's? With your family?"

"My brother. And his daughter. Yes."

"Well, I'll leave you to your visit then. Just . . . if you need anything, come and get me, all right?" She hesitated in the doorway. "You know, I do remember your father talking about you. When he was more verbal. You have a couple of brothers and sisters, right?"

"Just brothers, two of them. I'm the oldest."

"Right. And you're his favorite."

"Me?" Ron couldn't contain the bitter bark of laughter that escaped his lips. "Keith, probably. The youngest."

"No, he always talked about you. Ron. He was very clear about that." She gave him a smile. "He said he always knew you were special. You went to Sacramento State, right?"

"Uh . . . right."

"And you had your own company. Quite the success,

according to your father. You would think his friends would have gotten tired of hearing about it, the way Magnus went on—didn't you, Magnus?" The old man didn't appear to hear her. "But that's the good thing about a dementia ward—you can tell the same stories over and over again, and no one minds."

"Well, thanks, yeah, I guess that's true," Ron said, turning away from her, willing her gone.

His father continued to stare out the window. For a while the two of them sat in silence. The shouted obscenities came faintly down the hall. A burst of music came on somewhere and was quickly turned down.

"Dad." Ron kept his voice low now, though he felt it more strongly than ever, the urge to communicate with his father, to reach him somehow. "Why would you say that? You were . . . you were a terrible father. A terrible parent. All you did was try to cut me down, to remind me I was worthless."

Magnus folded and rubbed the fabric. A bit of spittle bubbled on his lips and then formed a dribble down his chin. It was tempting, watching him, to imagine all kinds of thoughts going through his head. But that wasn't possible, was it? There was nothing in there. Gone were the memories of the past, the people Magnus had known, his deeds and misdeeds.

At some point, had he known his mind was slipping away? Had his father ever had a moment of clarity amid the confusion, when the disease had eaten away his denial, but illuminated what remained?

Magnus had told a stranger (well, to be fair, the woman was hardly a stranger to Magnus; she'd spent far more time with him than his own family, particularly Ron, who lived in the same state) that he was proud of his son, something Ron was absolutely certain Magnus had never said when he was well. Not to him, to his mother, to Magnus's friends. So the disease had taken the meanness—that was one possible interpretation, anyway. Could it be that the pride, and perhaps even love, had existed all along? That it was the cruel put-downs, the insults and snubs, that had been lies?

"*Dad.*" Ron said it again, more urgently. He leaned forward and closed his hand on his father's thin, bony wrist. Magnus stared at Ron's hand with consternation, his frantic worrying of the fabric temporarily interrupted. "I'm what you made me. You don't get to . . . to act like none of it happened. Like you were father of the year, like you . . ."

He was trying to have a conversation with a mute, with a mind as blank as a block of wood. It was pointless. Ron squeezed his father's wrist; he could feel the bones beneath the skin. They felt as fragile as chicken bones, the skin papery and greasy.

He squeezed harder. And harder still. Magnus murmured and sagged in the chair, but he didn't try to tug back his hand. Ron continued to squeeze. Enough to hurt . . . if he kept it up, if he used two hands, he was sure he could break his father's wrist. It wouldn't even be a down payment on vengeance for the thousand taunts and injuries Magnus had visited on him, but it would be the first time Ron had ever stood up to him.

Instead, Ron dropped his father's arm, and the old man went immediately back to worrying his blanket. Ron shook his head—in disgust at himself, at the pointlessness of this whole exercise.

261

What had he thought he would find—answers? Absolution? Someone else to blame?

"You never even had to know," he said softly, as he stood up. Maybe that was the only conclusion to be drawn here. By the time Karl had gone to jail, Magnus—who still remembered Ron from time to time—had lost all memories of his sons' spouses and children. "You lucky bastard."

Ron left the room, not looking back. Maybe that was the only conclusion that he'd ever be able to draw: it wasn't poison that seeped down the family tree, generation after generation, only misfortune. Some were lucky and some were cursed.

He saw the nurse or therapist or whatever she was, in the activities room, kneeling next to an elderly woman who held a large yellow plastic ring in her gnarled hands.

The woman looked up. "It was so nice to see you again, Mr. Isherwood. Your father certainly enjoys your visits."

twenty-five

BY THURSDAY AFTERNOON, MARIS was nearly finished with the sorting and organizing of Norris's guest room. It had taken all day yesterday and most of today, but the trash had been hauled to the Dumpster, the giveaway pile boxed and delivered to Goodwill.

She'd found a coin dealer in San Leandro who'd bought the whole lot for three hundred dollars, which she'd left in an envelope on Norris's kitchen counter. She boxed up the mementos of Norris's daughters, labeled it Keyna & Kayla, and left the box between the twin beds where he was sure to see it. The banker's boxes containing his mother's papers were neatly labeled and stacked in the closet. Her last errand was a trip to the Home Consignment Center to drop off the Hummels and the jewelry, and by three she was heading back to the house with a receipt in her purse.

George had called three times—twice yesterday and once today. Each time she let it go to voice mail, then obsessively replayed the message. This last one sounded wounded, and Maris didn't blame him. The night that they'd spent together had been so much fun, right until the moment when he'd delivered her home at 6 a.m. yesterday, on his way to check on his rental properties in East Oakland.

He made the first call from a doughnut shop near the Coliseum. "I've got to bring you here, Mary, this is seriously the best Boston cream doughnut you'll ever eat."

The second, late in the afternoon, was adorably self-conscious: "Just driving by your exit, thinking of you. Well, obviously, I haven't stopped thinking of you all day. And I thought if you picked up—but you're probably busy. So just ignore this. Unless you want to call me back or something."

She'd been tempted. What would it hurt to spend one more night with him as Mary? The problem was that it was getting increasingly difficult to keep her identities straight. With Norris she didn't mind being vague, letting him fill in the gaps with his imagination. But George didn't seem to be holding anything back, and when she was with him, she felt more like herself—her *real* self—than she had in ages.

He deserved to know.

She spent most of the time driving around doing errands, trying to figure out the right way to tell him. She was worried he might feel used or tricked when he found out, or put off by the sheer weight of her past—and despite her promise to herself that it was nothing but a fling, it felt like something far more significant.

Her plan was to call him tonight, when he was at work and she would get his voice mail. Maybe she'd write it down first, just to make sure it came out right. Something like *Hey, I was hoping we could get together and talk. I really haven't told you much about myself, and there are a few things from my past that I didn't feel comfortable* . . . No, no. That made it sound like she was on the run from something. She was starting to wish she'd blurted it all out over dinner at his place, but one thing had led to another, and . . .

That was another thing: her libido seemed to have been kick-started right into high gear. Which wasn't really convenient. In the days ahead, she would need to gird herself for the media circus, look for a job, and figure out what she was going to do about Jeff and the house. Not to mention coming clean to Alana and figuring out where she was going to live. Liaisons with a sweet, gruff carpenter/bartender didn't really fit into the picture.

First things first. Deliver Norris's receipt, plan out her phone call, heat up a Lean Cuisine, then maybe go browse the bookstore she'd seen on College Avenue until it got late enough that she was sure George would be too busy to pick up the phone.

When she parked in front of the house, there was a woman sitting on the top step. She had graying hair down to her waist, an embroidered peasant blouse over jeans, dirty sneakers. She was stabbing furiously at her phone, but when Maris got out of her car and started walking toward the house she jumped up.

"Have you seen Pet?"

Maris paused uncertainly. "Are you her mother?" There was a resemblance there, in the squarish forehead, the narrow nostrils, the Cupid's-bow upper lip, but the woman was nothing like what Maris had expected. She was restless and indifferently kept, her clothes wrinkled and something—a twig, a bit of lint—in her hair.

The woman narrowed her eyes, regarding Maris suspiciously. "Yeah. Who are you?"

265

"I rent the apartment in back. Mar . . . Mary Parker."

"I'm Liz Urbanik. Do you know where Pet *is*? I've been sitting here for over an hour."

"Was she expecting you?"

"Well," Liz said, and scratched her elbow. She looked anxious and unhappy, her mouth twisted into a frown, her shoulders slumped. "I mean, I've been trying to call her all day."

"She's probably at class," Maris said, wondering if Pet was hiding again, and where she'd gone to avoid her mother. "And she's working tonight."

"Fuck. Fuck!"

Maris took a step back in alarm. There was something obviously wrong. "Are you . . . is everything all right?"

"*No*, everything is not all right. My boyfriend—it's a domestic abuse situation. I can't be there right now."

"What?" Maris said stupidly. Did Pet know? Was it even true? "Do you want me to call the police? Social services?"

"Oh, God no, not until I have somewhere to go. I mean, he's totally un*stable*. I just need, what I need is to maybe spend a night or two here. Give things time to settle down while I figure this out."

Maris wasn't about to let on that she'd talked to Pet about her mother, that she'd already heard of the boyfriend, the disabled son. Something about the woman made Maris deeply uneasy; she wondered if Liz was on drugs.

Maybe she could pretend she'd forgotten something, leave and go to the bookstore. Except then, whenever Pet *did* show up, she would know: that Maris had abandoned her to her mother, had left her waiting on the porch. For a moment she wondered if maybe Pet didn't know that her mother was in trouble, and then the pieces fell into place:

Of course Pet knew. This probably wasn't the first time her mother had done this. Who knew if the abuse claim was true? If Pet said there was a boyfriend, then Maris believed her; there was no reason for Pet to lie about that. If she said he was a psychologist, then he was probably that as well. But clearly there was a lot more going on than just a couple of people cohabiting. Pet hadn't wanted Maris to know the rest, that was all. And maybe part of the reason she'd hidden out in Maris's place was to prevent Maris from having to see.

Maris felt a surge of hot shame that she had been about to run off and leave Pet to deal with her mother alone. Pet had cared enough for Maris to try to shield her from the mess of her own family. At the same time, she'd accepted Maris's own story without a glimmer of judgment.

"Listen," Maris said, clutching her purse a little tighter, "why don't you come and wait for Pet in my apartment."

At four o'clock, after Liz had drunk the last Diet Sprite and fallen asleep on the couch, Maris heard Norris come home. She gave him a couple of minutes and then let herself quietly out of her apartment and went around the building and rang his bell.

He met her at the bottom of the stairs, looking surprisingly happy to see her. "Hey, Mary, I just got home, but I see you finished up in there. Way to go."

"Oh, thanks," Mary said. "I've got some paperwork for you, I'll go get it. But the thing is that Pet's mom showed up a little while ago and she seemed . . . well, kind of unstable. She's at my place, asleep and I wasn't sure what to do."

"Oh, Lord, here we go again," Norris said. "Tell you what, come on up. If she's out, she's likely to be out for a while. We can keep an eye out for Pet. She'll probably be home before she has to go to work. If she's not back soon I'll call her, but I prefer to tell her in person. I kind of hate to do anything without checking with her first."

"Do . . . like what would we do?"

"Call the cops," Norris said without hesitation. "This is the third time that woman's done this. Last time she showed up after midnight and started banging on the windows."

Maris's heart sank; this wasn't going to be easy, then. "She said . . . there was domestic violence."

"Hah," Norris said morosely. "Maybe those two fools will just kill each other, that would solve a few problems. Just kidding. Liz was actually clean for a while last spring, and Pet got her hopes all up again. That's what I hate the most."

"Oh," Maris said in a small voice. She was such an easy mark. "What . . . is she on?"

"What isn't she on? Heroin, mostly likely; that's what got her last time. I don't even want her in my house, you know? But man, poor Pet. Look, come on up. Best you be up here when Pet comes."

Maris didn't know what else to do but follow him. He opened a bottle of seltzer water and poured them each a glass without asking, and they carried their drinks to the living room. Maris took the sofa and Norris settled into a big wing chair. She took a sip, the bubbles going into her nose. Unexpectedly, tears came to her eyes. Norris looked at her in alarm.

"Hey . . . hey, Mary, you okay?"

"Yes, I feel stupid, I just—" She wiped at her eyes in frustration. "God, I've become such a *crier*. I never used to be like this." It was true once. "Anyway, I don't know why I'm . . . just a lot going on."

For a moment neither of them spoke. "Well, now," Norris said carefully. "Seems maybe you've seen quite a few changes in your life recently."

"Oh." Maris blinked, nodding. "Yes. That's true."

"New place to live, new work, new man . . ." He peeked up cautiously from under his eyelashes. "Not that I'm prying," he added primly. "But George, well, he's quality."

If things were different, Maris might have been amused and touched by this comment. Men were just so *bad* at showing their emotions. Except, come to think of it, for George, who in the short span of their relationship didn't appear to have any trouble saying exactly what he was feeling.

But this line of talk was going to lead places she didn't want to go. "Not that you're prying," she said, trying for a lighthearted smile.

"No." He returned the smile. He was trying, and Maris was touched. Again she was struck by how virtual strangers had come to mean so much to her in such a short time. "Look. I owe you an apology, Mary. I came down hard on you last week. When you got into Mother's things. I know you were just trying to help. I didn't . . . well, there's parts of the past I'd just as soon like to keep buried. You see what I'm saying?"

"Like Keyna and Kayla?"

Maris wasn't sure why she'd said it. Why she was bringing

up the girls when he was trying to be conciliatory, provoking him when he'd been kind. Especially because she herself was hiding behind a fake identity; she had no right to expect anyone else to do better in the self-examination department.

Except . . . Norris had been given a chance to be a father and squandered it. Oh, Maris was sure there were mitigating circumstances, that others were just as much to blame as he, that youth and impetuousness hadn't helped. But she would never again get to be a mother, and that knowledge burned in a way that she had not allowed it to burn for a long time.

Norris scratched his neck and looked at her with resignation. "That box of theirs was up in there?"

"Uh-huh."

"Damn. You didn't throw it out, did you?"

"Of course not!" Maris didn't tell him that she'd left it practically on display. "They're beautiful girls."

Norris nodded. He looked out the window, his face tight and gloomy. "They're turning twenty-four this year."

"Are they still in Bakersfield? It was on the return address of one of the letters," Maris added hastily.

"Yes . . . Keyna's studying to be a medical assistant. Kayla's got a little one of her own."

"You're in touch with them?"

His scowl deepened. "Wouldn't call it that, exactly. I just . . . their mother sends me a note now and then. Once I caught up on back support, anyway."

"When . . ."

"Was the last time I saw them? You sound just like Duchess." But he didn't sound angry so much as frustrated. "You women, you know you're all the same."

270

They both heard the footsteps on the porch below, both jumped up from their seats.

"Pet," Norris said, instantly concerned.

But when they got downstairs, it was Liz who was standing on the front porch, trying to peer into Pet's window. She looked at Maris with no trace of recognition.

"Liz," Norris boomed disapprovingly. "What are you doing coming around here again?"

"To see my daughter," Liz said haughtily. Her face bore the imprint of the scratchy couch cushion. "Not that it's any of your business."

"Well, now, you made it my business, didn't you? Last time you were here, when you tried to break that window?"

"Fuck off," Liz said, and started pounding on the door.

"She isn't here," Maris said, but as she looked past Liz into the street, she saw a figure walking toward them, her backpack slung over her shoulder, still half a block away.

She caught Norris's eye and pointed, mouthing "I'll go." Norris nodded fractionally and took Liz's arm, giving Maris a chance to escape unseen. She hurried down the street as the sound of Liz's voice escalated, shouting curses at Norris.

Pet was standing uncertainly next to a parked van, half hiding. "That's her, isn't it," she said softly when Maris got to her. "My mom."

"Um, yes," Maris said carefully.

"Oh."

There was so much resignation and shame in that one syllable that it was worse than the anger that Maris had been anticipating.

"She . . . uh, well, she relapses. Obviously."

"Pet—"

"Look, I'm sorry I didn't tell you. Or warn you or whatever. I was just hoping . . ."

"Pet, please, you don't have anything to apologize for. I mean, we already determined that I'm the asshole here, lying to everyone." The word *asshole* felt foreign to say, but not in a bad way. She put her hands gently on Pet's shoulders. "What can I do?"

"Well . . ."

"Norris seems to know what he's doing."

"Yes, he took care of it last time. Which is probably why she's giving him shit. He'll call the cops and maybe they'll get her into treatment like they're supposed to this time. Of course, she'll probably just turn around and leave the minute the hold is over."

She sounded so miserable, so helpless, that Maris wished she could just take Pet with her, make her see that none of this was her fault. That she didn't have to apologize for her mother's behavior. There were other parts of the story that didn't match up. Like the money, for instance . . . Liz didn't look like a woman with resources to spare. No wonder Pet was working two jobs and living in a place like this.

"Oh, sweetie," she said softly, pulling Pet into a hug. "You've got a tough road, don't you?"

"Look who's talking," Pet said through her tears.

They decided that Pet would go across the street to the diner to wait, doubling back and approaching from the other side of the street so she was out of Liz's view. Maris went to consult with Norris, who had already called the cops while Liz hunkered down on the top step, rocking with her knees

272

pulled to her chest. When Maris saw the cop car coming down the street, its lights flashing, she waited until Liz was distracted by the officers before heading over to the diner.

If the woman behind the counter recognized Maris, she didn't let on. Pet was sitting in one of the cheap plastic chairs with her earbuds in, her eyes closed, and the unopened copy of *East of Eden* in her lap.

"Bacon egg sandwich," Maris said. "Make it two."

She sat down across from Pet and gently tugged at the cord coming from her ear. Pet sat up and gave a weak smile, pulling off the earbuds.

"I know how this is going to sound," Maris said. "And you can ignore me if you want. But it's going to be fine. I mean, I really believe that."

"Then you're not as smart as you look," Pet said. Then: "Fuck, I'm sorry."

The sandwiches came. Maris unwrapped hers and contemplated it. "I wonder how many calories are in this thing?"

Pet just shrugged. Maris folded the waxed paper back over it. "Well, you're a grown-up," she said. "So I'm not going to tell you that you ought to eat something. Or ask you when you last ate."

Pet glanced up at her and flashed a smirk. "Actually, you just did. You just asked. By saying you weren't going to."

"Um, yeah, obviously. It's a mom thing."

Their eyes met while Maris realized what she had said. The first time she'd laid claim to that territory in such a long time. But she didn't look away. Not this time.

"I had a Clif Bar before class," Pet said in a small voice. "And a Rockstar."

"Oh, Pet. Listen. You want to stay with me?" And there went her getaway; there went her easy out. The fantasy she nurtured of running away again, leaving the mess she'd made behind her.

"Thanks, but she's in for seventy-two hours no matter what, unless they don't take her. But when she's like this, it's a pretty easy call. They'll get her calmed down in the hospital and then John will come for her and he'll be extra careful with her for a while, and as long as she takes her meds . . . Anyway, the next two nights are like a vacation, because I don't have to worry about her while she's in the hospital."

"Oh." Maris had a thought . . . an audacious thought that seemed like a potentially bad one the more she considered it. So she decided to just blurt it out. "You don't work tomorrow night, right?"

"Not on Fridays . . ."

"How would you like to go to a thing with me?"

"A thing?"

Maris grinned, not even sure why. It wasn't like either one of them had much to be happy about. "A gala. A fancy fucking gala."

"Did you really just say fuck, Mary?"

"Do you have anything decent to wear?"

274

twenty-six

AN HOUR OUTSIDE OF Fresno, Ron pulled the car over to the side of the road, got out, and vomited on the hard-packed ground. A large, ragged black bird landed not far away and hopped around, squawking angrily. The stench was instant and awful. Ron backed away from it, pulling his phone from his pocket. He squinted at the browser window, barely able to make out the number without his reading glasses, and dialed.

Six rings before anyone picked up.

"Hey, can you tell me if I can get on the visiting schedule today?"

"Walk-in only, sir."

"I can walk in?"

"If there's an opening."

"How do I find out if there's an opening?"

"Just show up."

"Well, can you tell me how likely—you know what, forget it," Ron said.

It was sort of on the way home and it wasn't like the world would stop turning if he didn't ever show up at work today. Besides, waiting in the lobby of a correctional facility didn't sound any less appealing than any of his other options.

Back in the car he floored it, digging in the console for

gum. Maybe he'd get pulled over, maybe he wouldn't. At least if he did, it would take the matter of what was next out of his hands, even if just for a moment.

No one else was trying for the walk-in appointment, as it turned out. But when Karl was brought out, he looked even unhappier to see Ron than he had the last time.

"What's that smell?" Karl said, after they'd taken their seats.

"It's . . . never mind."

"Mom's attorney is apparently coming to see me," he said angrily. As if Ron had anything to do with it. As if Ron had any control over anything.

"He's not Mom's attorney. He's your attorney."

"Not if I say no."

"Karl," Ron said heavily. "Why didn't you just say no already, then?"

"Why are you here?" Karl retorted.

Ron sat with his second thoughts, his self-recrimination. Two tables away, a woman in an impossibly short skirt struggled to keep a squirming baby on her lap.

"I asked you to do one thing for me," Karl finally said, deflated. "Just keep Mom under control."

"Oh, sorry," Ron said sarcastically. "I wasn't aware I owed you."

"Dad!"

His voice was so anguished that Ron looked up in alarm. Karl's eyes were bright with emotion. "You act like I've been shit all my life. But I wasn't. I wasn't. You've never—not even before, I could never do anything right for you. You've always hated me. Why are you even here?"

"Wait, I never—"

"Every day in that courtroom? You never even looked at me. You looked at every damn thing in that room, but you couldn't stand to look at me."

"I *love* you," Ron whispered, the air stagnant in his lungs. What had happened here?

"*Now?* Now you say it?" Karl stood up but immediately sat down, before the guard could even react. "You never told me that," he said miserably.

But Ron had. When Karl was a baby, he'd said it all the time when it was just the two of them, when there was no one else around. He whispered it at night and murmured it into Karl's soft scalp when he was in the Snugli. When had he stopped saying it out loud? When had he locked the words away?

When Karl was old enough to understand? When he was old enough to say the words himself?

"I know I was . . . tough on you," he tried. "Karl. I know that. I just wanted . . . I wanted you to be strong. I wanted you to be able to be proud of yourself. To know you could take care of yourself. It was, it was—" It was the only thing he'd been able to hold on to when he was growing up, he wanted to say, but didn't know how to explain it. That every time he survived one of Magnus's bouts of anger, every jab or slap, he'd consoled himself with the knowledge that he'd endured. That he'd been strong. Staying silent and getting back up every time he was knocked down, that had come to symbolize survival for Ron.

Keith had been the soft one. He was the one who still hurt, who had been in and out of therapy and addiction treatment for years. Keith was divorced and lived in a shitty apartment that smelled like burning chemicals and always ended up getting laid off for no good reason. Ron hadn't wanted that for Karl. Keith was proof that if you let your guard down, life chewed you up and spit you out.

So instead he'd taught Karl to turn everything inward. Where it had festered and simmered until the day it spilled over in one disastrous torrent.

"Oh, God," he said. "I did this to you. I'm why you're here."

"That's . . . Dad. *Dad.*"

Karl's anger turned to alarm so fast that for a moment Ron could almost imagine he was like before, a teenager mortified by his parents' very existence. He coughed several times, trying to mask his crying, trying to pull himself together. But when would he get a chance to tell Karl again? Would he be able to express his remorse any better in five years, or seven? Would he ever be able to make it right?

"Karl," he said, clearing his throat. "I'm sorry. I haven't stopped trying to talk to your mom. I'll see what I can do, if you really don't see the value in trying to appeal. And meanwhile, maybe you and I could, I could come more often and we could, I could write, too—"

"Dad. I—I did it."

Ron stopped midsentence. "What? What did you say?"

"You heard me, Dad. I *did* it." Karl's eyes sought his. "Look, tell Mom if she keeps up with the appeal, I'm going to say it. Like to the reporters. To everyone."

"You . . . Karl, are you just saying this to try to—"

"I *did* it, Dad. I killed Calla. I didn't mean to, you have to believe that. I never meant it, even after it was . . . after, even when I was driving her, I still couldn't believe it, I kept

278

thinking, I mean, right up to when I got to the lake. And after. The next day? I mean, I couldn't believe it was me. Sometimes . . ."

His skin had gone ghostly pale; his eyes hollow. His hands, clasped on the table in front of him, gripped so tightly the knuckles were white. "Sometimes I still can't believe it," he whispered.

"Karl." Ron felt light-headed. Now, more than any time in his life, he wished he could touch his son. The table between them could have been a continent. "Karl, am I the only person you've told this to?"

Karl stared at him bleakly and then shook his head, very slowly.

"Who do you think helped me wash the car?"

twenty-seven

HALFWAY HOME, RON STOPPED at a gas station and bought a toothbrush and a travel-sized toothpaste. After brushing his teeth in the station's restroom, he splashed water on his face and slicked his hair back. He used a damp paper towel to blot out a spot of vomit that had gotten on his shirt.

Then he was back in the car, where he would have driven even faster than he'd been driving all day except that he hit traffic starting in Tracy and didn't get home until nearly eight o'clock.

Deb met him at the door, frantic. "Where have you been? Oh my God, where have you *been*? I've called you half a dozen times!"

He hadn't wanted to talk to her until he got home. Had been counting on being able to look her in the eye when he told her that he knew.

But he hadn't expected her to throw her arms around him, sobbing.

"What the *fuck* is wrong with you?" he muttered, prying her arms off him, shoving her away.

She staggered back, confusion and hurt in her eyes. "Larry Loughlin called. They needed some file you were supposed to send out. They said you weren't picking up. And then I called

Anita and she said you never came in this morning. I called the cops, they've put an alert out to the bridge patrol, Ron. I thought . . ."

She thought I'd really done it this time, Ron thought with amazement. But how was that possible? Deb knew him better than he knew himself.

"Oh—I have to call them. To tell them you're home. I told them the minute I heard . . ." She was practically running for the kitchen. Ron stood in the foyer listening while she talked to one person and then another, repeating over and over again that her husband was fine, that he was home. And apologizing, and thanking. Finally she came back, stopping in the hall, and they stared at each other over a gulf of travertine tile and processed air.

"We need to talk," Ron said.

She didn't deny any of it.

"You took an Ambien that night," she said haltingly. "I saw the bottle on the counter."

She'd waited up for Karl, alarmed when he wasn't home by 1 a.m., frantic by 1:30. She was getting ready to try to wake Ron when she heard the back door open. She'd only waited that long because she knew how the Ambien knocked him out.

She'd gone downstairs to find her son standing there like a zombie, his shoes muddy, dirt tracked onto the hardwood floors.

"He told me right away," she said. "He kept saying she was dead. Over and over. *Calla's dead.* At first I thought there had been an accident, that he was in shock. We walked out to the car together and I thought for sure it would be all smashed

281

up. I wasn't thinking straight because why would they let him drive home, if—and that was sort of sinking in. He said it one more time, Calla's dead, and I made him come sit next to me on the chaise by the pool and I took both his hands and I said, 'You're telling me Calla's dead?' And he said yes and I said, 'How did it happen?' And he looked at me and he said, 'Mama, I think I did it.' Not Mom. *Mama*. Just like when he was five. He told me he thought he'd accidentally choked her and I said where *is* she and he said in the lake and then we were both crying, Ron, we were both crying so hard and holding each other. And it took the longest time for me to understand that he had *put* her there, that no one else knew. That . . . there was still a chance to keep it from ruining his life."

"Oh, Deb," Ron said. They were sitting on the couch in the family room, their knees touching, and the rage that had fueled him all the way home was gone, just like that it was all gone. He tried to put himself into Deb's shoes, tried to imagine what it was like to carry that weight, to know something unknowable, to endure it, alone.

"We washed the car in the dark. It wasn't dirty, there weren't any marks on it that I could see, but I just wanted to be sure. When we were done the sprinklers were coming on and I knew no one would be able to tell we'd washed it. I pulled it into the garage and then I checked the inside, but there wasn't . . . there wasn't anything, Ron. It wasn't like you'd think. It wasn't like you'd expect."

The investigators had found several of Calla's long blond hairs in the passenger seat, but that had been easily explained. As recently as a few weeks before her death, Calla had been in the car with Karl.

"I told Karl he had to get some sleep. I gave him one of your Ambiens. I knew you wouldn't notice one missing, and he always slept so late on Sundays anyway, I knew you wouldn't think anything of it. I put him to bed just like he was a little boy—" Her voice cracked, just a little, and she put her hand to her throat until she could continue. "And I told him he had to forget it, he had to tell himself that he hadn't been there. That it would never work unless we both decided together to just—to change the past. That we could do it, together."

Ron thought about that Monday, when he'd picked Karl up at school. How his son, his six-foot-one grown son, had sagged against him in the car, and how he'd held him. That would have been a time to tell him he loved him. That would have been a good time.

"I was so angry when he told me today."

"You should be angry. At me." When he didn't look at her, she took his chin in her hand and forced him to look at her. "At *me*, Ron, do you hear? Not at Karl."

After a long moment, he nodded. "But you'll drop the appeal thing," he said quietly, just to be sure.

She let her hand fall to her lap. "Yes."

He gathered her into his arms, and she lay there motionless for a moment, before her shoulders started shaking. He held her tighter. "Deb," he murmured against her neck. "I need to tell you something. Something that happened to me, a long time ago."

Ron had never told anyone the greatest failing of his life—it was his alone. Between him and God.

God, whose judgment he'd carried with him for so long; whose opprobrium was a weight on his shoulders that was sometimes unbearable. It had been almost two decades. Wasn't that long enough? Hadn't his good behavior entitled him to some release, some relief?

"One night, when Karl was only eighteen months old," he started, and then he faltered. Was it really possible? To unhitch the stone he'd been dragging for so long? Deb squeezed his hand, and he closed his eyes for a moment before going on.

"You'd been sick, you had the flu. Do you remember that? You'd taken some nighttime cold medicine and I said I'd get up with Karl. It was back when he hardly ever slept all the way through, and I had a feeling this wasn't going to be one of those nights. I'd been working on a presentation and I hadn't had much sleep the night before. So yeah, I was wound tight. He was up screaming at eleven, then again at two, and he wouldn't take a bottle and he wouldn't go back to sleep. He just wouldn't sleep."

Ron closed his eyes, remembering. The sensations came back to him. The thrumming of his nerve endings, the tightness of his breath, the near-manic skittering of his heartbeat. Muttering *please, please, come on buddy, you know you're tired, just fucking please please go to sleep . . .*

"I did everything I knew to do. Remember how it used to calm him down if I held him on his stomach like an airplane, and walked him . . . I walked up and down the stairs to the basement a dozen times. I was halfway up the stairs when he twisted around in my arms, screaming his head off—I almost dropped him. I was so scared, you know?" There were no rails on those stairs, and the basement floor was concrete.

And Karl didn't care, he just kept fighting and *screaming.* "I went down the stairs to where we had that old couch in the basement, and suddenly *I* was yelling at *him.* I put him down on the couch, but I still had his arms in my hands, and I was telling him to shut up to please just shut the fuck up, shaking him, and it . . ."

He swallowed, remembering: how good it had felt to finally let the fury out, to shake those tiny, treacherous arms, to yell into that screwed-up face with its squinting eyes and its wide-open mouth, how as Karl kept screaming, he'd squeezed harder and harder and—

"And there was this sound, this horrible sound, and I could feel his arm snap. I mean, not in half, like a bone, but like a pop, and I knew I'd done something. Dislocated the shoulder, at the very least, and just like that all the anger was gone and I was myself again, I was kneeling on our basement floor with our baby, and his screaming was different now and I knew he was hurt."

"Oh my God," Deb said, her hand to her mouth. "You did that? *You* broke his arm?"

Ron nodded miserably, afraid to look at her.

"You told me it was an accident." She pulled her other hand free from his. "Why didn't you tell me what really happened?"

"It didn't really sink in at first, what I'd done, I went right into problem-solving mode. I wrapped that old quilt we used to keep down there around him, I guess I thought maybe it would keep the arm still. I got my keys and put him on the front seat. I didn't even put him in the car seat, which shows you that I wasn't thinking clearly. I kept one hand on him so he wouldn't roll off the seat and I drove to Mercy General. And the crazy thing was, by the time we got there he was asleep. And I started to wonder if I was crazy, if I'd *imagined* hurting him, but I took him in and we got seen right away, it was a slow night. I told the admitting nurse that Karl wiggled out of my arms. I kept mostly to the truth, I said he'd fallen onto the couch but that his arm twisted at a bad angle.

"Once they took him in the back I started to think more clearly again. I called the house, but you didn't pick up—those nighttime cold meds had knocked you out. By now it was around four thirty, and this doctor, or intern or whatever, came to talk to me. I told you about that, remember?"

"How they were trying to see if you hurt him . . ." Her voice was faint, her posture stiff.

"Deb, this isn't easy," Ron said, but it sounded defensive to his ears and he tried again. "I'm not trying to hurt you. I'll stop if you want. You have every right to be angry with me. But I just—if we're going to be honest with each other now—"

"No, tell me. All of it."

He tried to gauge her reaction, how repugnant she found him, how much damage he was doing to her trust, but she seemed to have withdrawn inside herself, pressing into the far corner of the couch. "It's just . . . I mean, you know they have to do it, right? Make sure you didn't hurt your kid on purpose? And I was thinking, how the fuck am I going to get through this, should I just admit it straight up? I mean, I can't be the first person who ever did something like this, but then again they were cracking down back then, remember all those shaken-baby cases in the news? And what if I'm the guy they decide to make an example of? And you—I know how this is going to sound, but it's the truth. I swear to you, Deb, I couldn't bear that you would think—that you would know that I'd *hurt* our baby."

He was shaking now, sweat under his arms. He glanced up at Deb: now he just wanted this over; the telling exhausted him.

"Anyway, he did ask a few things, but it was like a checklist, like something they'd made him memorize, you know? I could tell right away he didn't think I did anything to hurt Karl. So I answered his questions and then all I had to do was wait and they brought him out with his arm in that tiny cast, and I signed all the papers and headed back to the house. Drove about twenty miles an hour the whole way; Karl was asleep in his baby seat. By the time you got up I had a pot of coffee made and the whole story, you know, I'd practiced it, like what a dumb-ass I was and how clumsy, and like that, and—well, you remember, right?"

"Yes. I . . . I remember how sweet you were about it. You kept telling me how sorry you were. You didn't let me help at all that morning, you stayed home from work and took care of both of us that day."

He had been afraid of more than just her censure: he'd been afraid she'd leave him, if she knew. Never let him see their son, around whom he couldn't be trusted. Never forgive him for letting his temper get the better of him.

"I was just so . . . I couldn't believe I'd done it," he said, his voice finally breaking. "That I'd lost control."

"Like your dad. You were afraid you were becoming your dad."

Her voice was gentle, but the words felt like a slap. They were the truth, the dread that he had been carrying around with him since that day. Before that, it was possible for Ron to believe that the incidents of violence that littered his past were isolated, that they were part of an unhappy and frustrated youth that was now behind him. When he became a father, he had looked into his infant son's face and vowed to never do anything to hurt a single hair on his tiny, perfect head.

And then he'd done this unconscionable thing and it was like Magnus had reached through time and forced his hand. Thinking of his father, it wasn't the old man's slack and drooling face that came to mind, but a younger, meaner, craftier version, the one who'd terrorized Ron for so long.

"I never wanted to be him," he gasped. "You have to believe that."

"I know," Deb said quietly. "It makes sense now, the way you were that day. That you were beating yourself up. Do you remember, after it happened, how careful you were around him? I didn't understand it then, how overnight you seemed to turn into such a worrywart. You treated him like he was made of glass."

"I don't remember that," Ron said. What he did remember was that when both Karl and Deb were finally both asleep that morning, he'd lain awake, despite his exhaustion, wondering how he could ever make it up to either of them. But he had also had a rogue impulse, quickly squashed, to simply abandon them. If there had been a way he could have left, and kept going . . . maybe not forever, but just to get away from what he had done. From the evidence of his guilt.

288

Instead he had stayed. He had looked at that cast every day until it finally came off, and every day he castigated himself all over again. "I was . . ." Ron said, but his voice cracked with emotion and he had to collect himself before he could continue. Deb slipped her hand lightly into his. "I was so afraid of what I'd do to him the next time."

"But there never was a next time," Deb said.

He looked into her eyes, longing to believe he could deserve the comfort she was offering. "How can you be sure? For all you know . . . my father never did anything to us when my mom was around. What if I only hurt him when you weren't there to see?"

But she was already shaking her head. "I know you want to take the blame for this," she said, her voice trembling with emotion. "And I won't lie, there were times I tried to make it your fault. You weren't a perfect father. I wasn't a perfect mother. But we were *good*. Sweetheart, we did our best. You didn't abuse our son. Whatever he did, that's his responsibility. You have to believe that."

"I want to. God, I want to. I mean . . . sometimes I feel like I could bear it all—like I could be there for him the way you always are, maybe even forgive him. If I could just believe I didn't make him that way."

"You didn't. I swear it to you."

Age had mellowed Ron. He'd be forty-nine this year, and the passing decades had diluted the rage. He still felt it sometimes, swimming eel-like deep inside him, looking for an opportunity to escape. But most of the time Ron was able to push it back down. He hadn't had an outburst—no yelling, kicked door, even a moment of road rage—in years.

But it was Deb's belief in him that gave him real hope.

"I'm so tired," she said now, scooting back next to him on the couch. He opened his arm to her and she curled against him, her hand on his chest and her breath warm against his neck. It had been a long time since they'd sat together like this, a long time since he'd let his mind empty and just held his wife. Her breathing grew even and deep, and in a while she was asleep in his arms. Ron would get up and they would go up to bed, together—soon. For now, he was content to simply hold her.

"You're safe with me," he whispered.

twenty-eight

NORRIS STOPPED BY WITH an update after the ambulance left. By then, Maris and Pet had snuck back to her apartment, going around the block to avoid the scene out front.

"All clear," he said.

"I'm just so sorry this is happening," Maris said yet again.

Pet just shrugged. "That's her third 5150," she said. "I know the drill."

Norris looked around the room before he left. "You know . . . maybe you should think about staying, Mary," he said. "Maybe we could work something out with the rent."

When he was gone, Pet and Maris both burst out laughing.

"Oh my God, you're one of his charity cases now," Pet said.

"Only because I'm good with a bottle of Windex," Maris said, but she was secretly pleased.

Pet got up and stretched, popping her shoulders one at a time. "I guess I better go get ready for work before fate has a chance to send any more drama my way. You want me to say hi to George for you? Or maybe send him home early if it's slow?"

Maris could feel her face flaming, but she attempted to sound nonchalant. "I'm going to bed early myself. I'm beat."

"Yeah, doing the sunrise walk of shame can really take it out of you."

"Oh, God . . . did you see me come home yesterday?"

"Ha! Lucky guess. I mean, I knew something was up, because I was getting ready to go for a run and I looked out and saw George pulling out of the driveway. When I saw you were still wearing what you had on the night before, it wasn't that much of a stretch."

Maris covered her face with her hands. "Ugh, I wish I knew what I was doing."

"Have you told him? You know . . ."

"That I've been lying about my identity? That I used to be a pampered housewife with a stick up my butt? Not exactly," Maris said.

"But you like him, right?"

Maris didn't want to tell Pet how close she'd come to simply running away. Not just from the possibility of being found out, either, but from the very real risk that she was starting to care about Pet and George and even Norris.

"I guess he's okay," she said, yawning. "But you'll notice that when I needed a date to make my ex-husband sit up and take notice tomorrow night, he wasn't first on my list."

Pet beamed. "Well then, I guess you'd better get that beauty sleep," she said. "Let's do this right."

At five fifteen the next evening, Maris knocked on Pet's door, wearing an outfit she had bought hours earlier at a consignment shop on Piedmont Avenue. It was a bit dramatic for both the season and the event, but Maris had loved the metallic embroidery and passementerie on the gray silk jacket, the precise tailoring of the sheath underneath. She clutched the mother-of-pearl-handled evening bag she'd bought for twenty dollars and waited.

Pet opened the door with a flourish: she'd made an effort too. She was wearing a retro patchwork moto jacket over a white men's undershirt and a pair of black leggings tucked into green suede boots.

"You look fantastic," Maris said.

"I wasn't sure what the dress code was."

"For stalking my ex? Hmmm, I think you've hit the nail on the head."

In the car, sitting in traffic approaching the tunnel, Pet dug into her messenger bag and took out a square foil package. "Okay, before you say no, hear me out," she said. "You only need a little bit of this. It's really strong."

Maris glanced at the package, and laughed. "You're offering me a pot brownie?"

"Well, a pot cookie, anyway. But it's legal, I've got a card."

"Pet, that's a very generous offer, and I'm touched, but I think I need to do this, um, straight."

"Okay." Pet tucked a piece the size of a marble into her mouth and tossed the rest back into her bag. "It's here if you change your mind."

When they arrived at the performing arts center, Pet looked around at the landscaped parking lot, the white-shirted caterers moving among the guests gathered on the stone terrace.

"So, it looks like a nice event," she said cautiously.

"Indeed."

"And do we have, like, a plan or something?"

293

"Now that you mention it . . . not really. The thing is, I used to be on the board of this thing. I know half the people here. We get invited every year. You'd think Jeff would realize that the tasteful thing to do would be to simply send a check, but . . ."

"But you're both broke," Pet pointed out.

"True. So maybe don't bid up anything in the silent auction, come to think of it."

"Well, for what it's worth, I think it's brave of you. You got to get back in there, you know? Show people that you're better off without him."

"I *am* better off without him."

"So what are they raising money for, anyway?"

"All of this. They finished building this place in 2012, late and overbudget, and they've struggled ever since." A problem that, come to think of it, would no longer be Maris's concern if she really did leave Linden Creek for good.

"Well . . . do you want to sit here for another hour or two talking yourself into getting out of the car, or do think we can go now?"

Maris sighed. "Look, I want you to know how glad I am that you're here. I really, really don't want to have to face him alone."

"My pleasure," Pet said, and Maris opened the car door.

Maris spotted Jeff while she and Pet were at the bar getting a drink. He was in a group of people that included the woman who'd replaced Maris as chairman.

"Please, tell me that woman in the blue dress looks fat," she said, grabbing their plastic cups of wine and ducking behind a decorative column.

"Okay, she looks . . . actually, Maris, to be honest, she looks fine. What do you have against her?"

"Well, first of all, that's my ex in the houndstooth sport coat, standing next to her."

"Ah. He looks . . . harmless. He's actually kind of attractive, in a low-budget, hot-for-teacher porn kind of way."

"Hmm. It's just . . . he's talking to *my* friends. I guess this is how it starts. You know, after a divorce. The scramble for the people you knew before. Everyone running for the lifeboats."

"Were you really close to her?"

Maris wrinkled her nose. "No . . . she has this really annoying habit of looking over your shoulder to see if she can spot anyone more important than you."

"Then what do you care?"

"I guess I don't. It's just, I don't know, I haven't been that good about staying in touch with people in the first place. And I guess . . . I don't know, I worry that they'll all end up picking him."

"And you'll be stuck with just me and George and Norris?" Pet stuck her tongue out at Maris. "Yeah, I can see why you'd be worried."

"That's not what I meant!" Had Maris really been thinking of leaving Oakland without even saying good-bye to Pet? Standing here in her thrift store jacket, drinking sour white wine, Maris couldn't imagine getting through this evening with anyone else.

"Hey," Pet said, "I think he saw you. Just, you know, in case you were about to try to blend in with the potted plants or something."

"Oh no." Maris set her wine down on the nearest cocktail table and wiped her hands on her napkin. "I'm not ready. This was a mistake."

"Calm down. He's bringing a friend. A wingman. He's probably just as nervous as you."

Maris stood her ground, working a stiff smile onto her face and pretending to not notice Jeff approaching.

"Maris!"

She looked up in fake surprise. There he was, wearing that damn houndstooth jacket, the one Maris had bought him when he got his current job. She'd picked three shirts and three ties to go with it; Jeff wasn't wearing any of them. He put his hand on her arm and kissed her cheek before she could put up her hands to deflect him. She wished she could wipe away the feel of his lips on her skin, the quick glancing blow of his embrace. Instead, she just smiled harder.

"What a nice surprise. I thought you said you weren't going to be able to make it," he said. There was something strained about his voice—too cheerful, too effusive. A distinction you'd have to know him to notice.

"Well, it turned out that the evening was free after all. Jeff, I'd like you to meet my friend Petra."

Jeff glanced at Pet in surprise. What did he think, Maris thought indignantly, that she would come to this alone?

"Nice to meet you," Pet said sweetly. "Maris tells me such nice things about you."

"Really?" Jeff's chuckle was even more awkward. "That's so great. Where did you two meet?"

Pet turned to the man who'd followed Jeff and now stood in his wake uncertainly, ignoring Jeff's question. "Hi," she said, putting out her hand, so that the man had to step forward to shake it.

"I'm Jared, nice to meet you." He turned to Maris. When he took her hand, his skin was ice cold. "Nice to meet you, Maris."

Oh, thought Maris. *This is it.* The moment she'd dreaded from the moment she knew that her marriage was over. "What a pleasure."

"Alana tells me you're house-sitting," Jeff said after an awkward beat had passed.

"You talked to Alana?"

"She was looking for you," he said, a little defensively. "She said you haven't been answering your texts." If he meant it to be a barb, he hid it well.

"We have plans to meet for lunch tomorrow, actually."

"Oh. Well. That's good."

"It was so good to see you, but I promised Joanne I'd talk to her about the program committee," Maris said. "Pet's interested in volunteering."

"Oh, of course, of course. We can catch up later."

"Sure. Sounds good."

When they were safely out of earshot, Pet grabbed Maris's arm.

"Is there something you want to tell me?"

"What?" Maris said, as innocently as she could.

"For starters, how about the fact that your ex already has a *boyfriend*?"

Maris sighed, and downed the rest of her wine. "Pet. Is it really that obvious?"

"Well, Jeff, maybe not completely. Although I don't think it would have taken me twenty years to catch on. No offense.

But Jared? Oh fucking yeah. And the way he was hovering there? Like begging for someone to notice him, but at the same time he wants to kill Jeff for ignoring him? I mean, that's total second-wife behavior. I should know, my dad's on his third."

"*Second wife*." Maris felt a little faint as she said the words.

"Oh shit, sorry, was that insensitive?"

"Well, maybe a—"

"Shut up, Mary, I was kidding. Seriously, how long have you known? And why didn't you tell me?"

"Not long, is the answer to your first question. I had my suspicions, but I think the first time I ever let myself know, like *really* know, was actually at Calla's funeral. There were some friends there I didn't know, and Jeff kept . . . he disappeared from the receiving line for twenty minutes to talk to them. I mean, there were, I guess you'd call them clues. Or hints. Going back to the beginning, especially if I knew then what I know now."

"And the reason you didn't tell me . . ."

Maris looked around the room. "Do you think there's a bar with a shorter line?"

"Don't avoid the question."

"I'm not, I just—look, Pet, I just, I didn't want to offend you."

Pet stared at her with her eyebrow raised, amused. "Uhh . . . let me understand. You were worried that I, your apparently only lesbian friend, from what I've gathered from our conversations, would be offended to be introduced to a gay man?"

298

"Oh my God, no," Maris said. "And you're not, by the way. At all. I know *plenty* of lesbians. It's just, I don't know, I mean I never *really* asked you if you're gay—"

"I am," Pet said serenely. "If you really want to take all the mystery out of it."

"—and I didn't want to be all like, so I have this *gay* ex, because then I thought you would think I was just pointing out the gay part because I thought *you* were gay."

"Which I am."

"Right, but—"

"And which, if I wasn't, but somehow you got the impression I *was*, why would I be offended?"

"Oh, I know, that's not what I meant, either, but—"

"Relax, Mary."

Maris stopped stammering. "Um, so, thank you. Okay. You're the first person who officially knows."

"Oh, I don't think I'm the first," Pet said. "Others appear to have blazed the trail. Did he see men a lot while you were still married?"

"I don't think so. I mean, how would I know, right? But even though he's been a dick and even though I kind of wish he'd just die and leave me the insurance money, I have to say that I don't think he knew himself, until pretty recently."

"I find that hard to believe."

"Listen, Pet, back in our day we didn't pop out of the womb with our politics perfectly formed," Maris protested. "A lot of us didn't really know what to think until your generation came along and figured it out for us."

Pet raised an eyebrow. "Well, what do you know? You actually are capable of humor. Congratulations, Mary."

"It's Maris, when I'm in Linden Creek. And what are you saying, I'm not funny?"

"You're plenty funny enough. And you know what? 'Maris' doesn't even sound right out here in the suburbs."

"How about we find that bar now?" Maris asked, secretly pleased. "This one's on me."

"The *last* one was on you."

"Yeah, but I invited you. Hey, how long does that cookie take to work, anyway?"

"You're still nervous?"

"Nah, I just thought it might make these people more interesting."

"There you go again. You *slay* me. What's gotten into you, Mary?"

"I don't know . . . you know what, I shouldn't have said that. I had good friends here. Really nice people." And they had been. They'd tried to support her, to be there for her, in all the ways they could think of.

It wasn't their fault that Maris had gotten more solace from the daughter of a junkie and a child-support dodger and a man who looked like a lumberjack and kissed like a . . . like a very, very good kisser.

"I'm sure they are." Pet put a hand on her arm. "Seriously, Mar, if you want I'll help you make a quick getaway. But you can do this. It's . . . I mean, if you think about it, it's not all that weird."

Maris gaped. "What about this scenario can you possibly say is not weird?"

"Well, I mean, you guys were together, you broke up, you both moved on. Same old story, tale as old as time."

300

"Wait, wait, wait. I didn't move on. I didn't go anywhere. I just stayed in my house, being . . . married. *I* didn't leave."

Pet's eyes narrowed. "How can you say that? I mean, sure, he went first, but you have to admit you had your eye on the exits. Just because you weren't admitting it to yourself—I mean, come on, the first chance you got, you went way off the grid."

"So you're trying to say it's just as much my fault—"

"Hey." Pet elbowed her way to the front of the bar line, and grabbed two glasses. She put one into Maris's hands. "There's no fault, okay? That's not why you're here. That's not why *I'm* here, anyway. Now look like you're having fun and smile your ass off and be charming. Okay?"

"Okay," Maris agreed.

On the way home, Pet fell asleep, snoring softly, but she woke up when Maris had to swerve to get out of the way of a car changing lanes at the 580 split.

"So. You okay?" Pet asked.

"I'm fine."

"It wasn't that bad, right?"

Maris smiled in the darkened car. "It wasn't terrible." After a few minutes she added, "Jared seemed okay."

"You still hate Jeff?"

"Well, yeah, for some things, anyway. But maybe not, you know, like, forever."

"Okay. Good." Pet yawned and turned her face against the window. "Wake me up when we're home."

twenty-nine

MARIS HAD BOUGHT ALANA a gift when she was out shopping on Piedmont: a T-shirt with the phrase I Hella ♥ Oakland over an outline of the famous shipping cranes. It had seemed funny in the store, but as she slipped the tissue-wrapped package into her purse, she wasn't so sure. She'd just wait and see how the lunch went. She had some making up to do—and she still hadn't decided what to tell Alana about her future plans.

When she came out to the drive, she saw Norris kneeling next to the mailbox, pulling weeds around the post.

"Oh, hey," he said, standing. "I just wanted to tell you again. Thank you, for, you know, taking care of everything. I've got your cash upstairs, give me a minute and I'll go get it."

"No, just hang on to it." Maris sucked in her breath. Was she really doing this? "I was thinking you could apply it to my rent. If you don't mind."

"Seriously?"

"Yes. I think. I mean, I've invested a lot of Comet in this place."

"Well. That would be nice. Real nice. Me and my ladies, that'll keep Duchess on her toes. And maybe get George over to visit a little more often. Speak of the devil."

Maris followed his gaze; rolling slowly past the house was George's familiar tan-and-brown truck.

If she made a dash for it—

If only she'd thought this through before committing to staying—

Or maybe he'd get the hint and find some other, more appropriate woman—

"Hey, real quick, speaking of Duchess," Norris said in a low voice, ducking in close. "She and I had a talk. She thinks—I mean, *I* think—I'm going to take a little time off in August and go see my girls."

"Really? Oh, I'm so happy to hear that."

"Yeah, I figure if I just show up, they can't exactly refuse to see me."

"Norris. You're doing the right thing. Really, I'm so proud of you."

"Okay, all right, okay," he said, tugging her hand off his arm. "Your date's here, though, so you might ought to go tend to him."

"I'm not her date," George said. He was hesitating on the drive, a large black plastic case in one hand. He was wearing a silky blue shirt and Maris caught a faint whiff of aftershave. The scent, etched forever on her memory, instantly turned her insides to jelly. "I'm just returning your drill."

"*My* drill?" Norris demanded, laughing. "The one you borrowed two years ago? The one you're always saying you can't find? That you accused me of forgetting who I lent it to?"

"I don't know what you're talking about," George said, his cheeks flushing pink.

"You two can stand out here and jaw all day," Norris said, taking the case and heading up the porch steps. "I've got important things to do."

Once he disappeared inside, George cleared his throat. Maris was afraid he was going to turn around and leave.

"I owe you an apology," she blurted. "It's kind of a long story." She stared at the pearl buttons of his shirt, unable to look into those amber-brown eyes, afraid she'd lose her place, her momentum. "Two things. First, my name isn't really Mary. But I'm thinking of changing it. And second, if you're not busy right now, how would you like to meet my sister?"

thirty

Two months later

RON WAS UP EARLY, as he was every Saturday these days. He'd found a new rhythm for the weekends, now that he was going to the prison on Sundays with Deb. At first it was a patch for his nerves, a way to steady himself, to remind himself that he could get through the visit. Now that all these weeks had gone by, it was taking on the pleasant feel of ritual.

First he took a long run out past the townhouses they were putting up down Black Canyon Road, past the old pear orchard and around back by the middle school. By then, the farmer's market was getting under way, and he bought two large cinnamon scones and a bag of ground coffee from the redheaded grandmother who came down from Petaluma to sell her baked goods. Once home, he brewed the coffee and set the scones on plates. For the last two weeks, he'd snipped roses from the garden and put them in a vase on the table. All week long he'd had his eye on a few fat pink buds on the bush by the garage; today they should just be starting to open. He'd picked up a couple of books for Karl; he had no idea if his son would read or even appreciate them, but the guy at the store had taken some time with him and showed him what they were doing with graphic novels these days. Deb said that

Karl was drawing, and if his son hadn't gotten around to showing him his work yet—if the boy still wouldn't look him in the eye—so what? It wasn't like either of them was going anywhere anytime soon.

Ron dressed in his shorts and T-shirt, took one last look at his wife sleeping with her hand curled up under her chin, and headed downstairs. He opened the front door and nearly tripped over a woman sitting on his front step.

Then he saw who it was, and swallowed hard.

"Jesus," Ron muttered.

Maris jumped up, patting the dust from her shorts, and turned to face him. "Ron, I'm so sorry, I didn't—"

She'd thought about this moment so many times. Seeing him again, after—after they'd each gone back to the lives that had been left to them like fast-food wrappers stuck to the bottom of a trash can. The ones left behind, abandoned, condemned to a life that wasn't really living.

And maybe that's what she would have found if she'd come here six months ago. Or even three.

But the man who'd emerged from this pleasant fortress didn't look all that destroyed.

"I was just going for a run." He gestured—at the street, the hill, anything.

"I know I shouldn't just show up like this. With no warning. I just thought, I wasn't sure you'd—I wanted to see you in person."

"Well." Ron put a hand to his face, rubbed at his eyes. The skin there seemed slacker than it had during the trial. Or before, that one time Maris had been with Ron when he'd seemed truly unguarded. "After what I pulled—the bridge thing. I mean, I don't even know where to start, to apologize."

"No, look, that's not why I'm here." She looked down the street, at the cul de sac where someone had left orange traffic cones out so their kids could play safely. "Um, do you mind if we walk?"

"No. Sure." They fell in step, along the sidewalk to where the trail joined up with the street. Ron was in good shape; he barely seemed to mind the incline that left her breathing hard.

When they had climbed halfway up the hill on the trail, their shoes stirring up little clouds of dirt, Maris stopped.

"This is far enough. I don't have a lot to say, I just didn't . . . I don't know, I still feel so exposed, you know?"

"Yeah," he said, and Maris knew he understood completely. Maybe everyone who'd ever been at the center of a news story or a scandal felt the same way: as though around every corner, in every crowd, someone waited to expose them, to broadcast their most private pain.

"Look. I've had an interesting few months. Jeff and I are splitting up, for one thing."

"I . . . I heard." He shrugged awkwardly. "I guess I'm not really surprised."

"Oh, God—you knew he was gay too?"

"What? No, I only meant—"

"No, it's okay." Maris sighed. "It's just if one more person tells me that they always suspected . . . He *is* gay, I guess I should start with that. He's moved in with his boyfriend. *Boyfriend*, it just still sounds funny to me, you know?"

"Uh, I can imagine."

"I mean, it's okay. Really. It was hard at first, because *I*

307

didn't suspect. I mean, deep down, yeah, I guess I'd wondered, but . . . let's just say I never dreamed the day would come when I was invited to sign the documents for the sale of my former house at my ex-husband's apartment, while his lover served me coffee using my own wedding china." She laughed. "That's actually pretty good. I should write about that."

"Write? Like for publication?"

"No, no, not yet anyway." Maris hadn't really meant to bring it up. Even if it felt good, revealing this little glimpse into the life she was leading now. "Although I'm thinking of submitting something if I can get it polished the way I wanted. I'm taking a class . . . but it's only my first one, I'm just starting."

"You went back to school?"

"Just a class at the community college. For now. I'm working, though. In Oakland. I'm an assistant produce manager at Village Hall—do you know it?"

"That fancy market by the BART station?"

"My boss would die if she could hear you. They prefer to think of themselves as a 'collection of boutique offerings.'"

"Wow, that's quite a mouthful," Ron said. He seemed to have relaxed. "Do they make you answer the phone that way?"

"Ha, probably. I don't use a phone, though. All of the assistant managers use tablets. It's very hipster, practically everyone has tattoos and rides their bike to work . . . I'm like the mother hen."

The word *mother* hung between them; Maris felt her face freeze, her heart's rhythm staggered.

"I do love it, though," she went on. She could do this. She'd already proved to herself that she was braver than she'd ever imagined, when she and Alana finally went through Calla's things, getting ready to sell the house. It hadn't been easy, but she'd done it. She'd survived. "I'm living in an apartment for the first time since I was getting my teaching certificate. I can eat popcorn for dinner if I want. I'm thinking of getting a cat. A shelter cat."

"That's great, Maris," Ron said, seeming sincere.

"Ron, how are you guys doing?" she asked. It was the question she'd come here to find the answer to, the key to the serenity she'd been toying with giving in to. "Really?"

Ron frowned and stared at the ground. He pushed his toe over a bent weed, crushing its fragile blossoms. "Well, it's not something I ever expected to have to do. Rebuild a relationship with my son before he's even old enough to drink. Ask him for another chance when he was the one who blew up our lives."

"I . . . can only imagine."

"I know. I know, Maris. That's why . . . I don't even know how to talk to you about this. They say Karl could still be out in five years. He'll be barely twenty-five." He paused, giving Maris a chance to react.

Maris didn't need anyone to tell her the numbers. Numbers didn't mean anything anymore, when it came to Calla. Her daughter was with her in the morning, when she stepped out of her apartment as the sun was just beginning to rise up above the distant hills. She was with her during the hectic days at work, as Maris arranged shelves and helped customers and ended the day with a pleasant ache in her calves. She'd kept only a few of her daughter's things, and even those were still in their boxes in Norris's shed, wrapped lovingly in tissue

309

and waiting for the day when Maris was ready to hold them in her hands. But the things didn't matter, anyway.

"I don't know what will happen," Ron said. He cleared his throat. "I don't know . . . anything."

"But that's why I'm here," Maris said. She took a moment to center herself, to draw her mind to the place where she taught herself to linger. "Look, I don't have any big plan or goal. I'm not trying to forgive you or even Karl. I just . . . somehow, this summer, I started living again. I can't explain it. I could point to pieces, I could say that this thing or that thing made it easier. I mean, I've been dating someone, which I can't even believe . . . I'm going to start volunteering again in the fall. My sister and I are talking about going to Mexico for the holidays. What I'm trying to say is, there are good parts of my life now, things to look forward to, but that isn't what made the difference."

Very gently, she placed her hand flat against his chest, over his heart.

"Before Calla died, I didn't know who I was. I guess that sounds like hyperbole, but I mean it literally. I didn't know how I had gotten to be me—forty-nine years old, married to a man who barely spoke to me, with a C-section scar and lactose intolerance and my dead mother's rosary in my jewelry box, staring down the next half of my life with no idea what to do with it. One of the last times Calla and I talked—I mean, *really* talked, one of those nights we stayed up for hours when I went in her room to say good night—I told her to never let a chance go by without thinking long and hard about taking it. She was having second thoughts about Santa Barbara—you know, typical fears for a sheltered only child, thinking she'd rather stay close to home. But the thing was, and I didn't even realize it then, I wasn't talking about her.

"I was talking about *me*. It was kind of my own pep talk to me. To be braver, to stop settling for good enough."

She lowered her hand, warm from his skin through his shirt.

"And then, you know, for a while there I was just lost. I guess I don't need to tell you. I thought I hated Karl, I thought I hated you and Deb . . . Jeff, my sister, everyone. I just wanted the whole world to shut down and disappear. And then Jeff told me he was gay, that he'd been miserable for years, trying to keep it all going. He'd had an affair a couple of years ago and called it off when it got serious. Decided to recommit himself to me, to Calla. And then she died . . . and he said he just couldn't do it anymore. That there wasn't any more reason to lie. And at first I couldn't imagine anything more cruel. Because it made it sound like I was *nothing*, you know?"

"Oh, Maris," Ron murmured.

"No, no, it's okay." Maris didn't have it in her to be anyone's victim anymore. "I was really angry, and to be honest, even *that* was better than feeling nothing. Feeling numb. So I . . . that was when I moved out. Things were a little crazy for a while. And you calling, that was confusing, you know, that day . . . on the bridge. But after a while I started to understand. Jeff and I, we didn't have enough between us to survive. We were never like you and Deb, even in the beginning. And so he found something he *could* hold on to. And I finally did too. I mean, not one specific thing but . . . well, after a while, all the pieces began to feel like they might actually add up to a *life*. A real one, with ups and downs and good days and bad ones, and friends and . . . and just being *surprised* again. You know that feeling? When you think you've seen it all and done it all, everything you could possibly get any joy out of, and then suddenly there's something new.

"I don't know, I'm probably not even making sense. So I'll just wrap up. I came here because I feel like we were friends once, that we understood each other, and I tell you, that doesn't happen to me very often. And I don't want to be your friend. I don't. I kind of hope I don't ever see you again after today. But I wanted to tell you to *live*. Don't hold back for me, or Jeff, or Karl, or even Calla. Just don't. I'm not asking you to start a foundation or, you know, think deep thoughts or go to Nepal or anything like that. Just . . ."

She wiped the tears impatiently from her eyes, and turned away. She walked back down the hill, her shoulders square, her head high, leaving him behind. When she got to the street she turned around. Ron was watching her from high up on the hill. "Just live!" she shouted, and then she ran back toward the life she had now.

Acknowledgments

Extraordinary circumstances demanded extra measures of compassion and faith this time around, and I can't adequately express my gratitude to those who somehow both kept me close and gave me room. Barbara and Abby—I've rewritten this sentence a dozen times, and I still can't find the words to thank you. Dana, you may have thought I didn't notice all the times you covered for me, but I did. I won't forget. Stephanie and Marla, thank you for keeping all the balls in the air.

My patient friends—especially Rachael, Julie, and Roseann—you sustained me. You forgave my extended trip into the cave, and I was so glad you were there when I came out again. To my family, thank you for sharing my burden, forgiving my many faults, and being there when you were needed. Love abides. My children: you are everything, always.

A letter from the publisher

We hope you enjoyed this book. We are an independent
publisher dedicated to discovering brilliant books,
new authors and great storytelling. Please join us at
www.headofzeus.com and become part of our
community of book-lovers.

We will keep you up to date with our latest books, author
blogs, special previews, tempting offers, chances to win
signed editions and much more.

If you have any questions, feedback or just want to say hi,
please drop us a line on hello@headofzeus.com

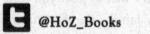
@HoZ_Books

HeadofZeusBooks

www.headofzeus.com

HEAD of ZEUS

The story starts here